Who wan...

"We need to start ..." said Dr. McQueen.

Betsy stared at h... I've been poisoned'...

"I don't know who Godwin is," said Dr. McQueen, "but if he was the one who insisted your food be tested, you need to thank him. One sample contained arsenic, and that urine sample was also positive."

Betsy rolled over gingerly and tried to relax. But alarm over possible side effects took most of her attention. And there were two other thoughts rabbiting through her mind.

Who wanted to kill her?
And why?

Praise for Monica Ferris's other Needlecraft Mysteries, Crewel World and Framed in Lace:

"A wonderful amateur sleuth tale . . . Hobbyists and amateur sleuth lovers will enjoy the novel due to the deep, believable characters that provide local color to an interesting story line." —Harriet Klausner

"Abounds with tidbits of information about knitting, needlepoint and the art of creating needlework . . . [A] very entertaining book with a good dose of suspense." —*Affaire de Coeur*

"Filled with great small town characters . . . A great time!" —*Rendezvous*

"Fans of Margaret Yorke will relate to Betsy's growth and eventual maturity . . . You need not be a needlecrafter to enjoy this delightful series debut." —*Mystery Time*

"*Crewel World* does a good job of informing as well as entertaining." —*Williamson County Sun* (Texas)

A STITCH IN TIME

Monica Ferris

BERKLEY PRIME CRIME, NEW YORK

A STITCH IN TIME

A Berkley Prime Crime Book / published by arrangement with the author

PRINTING HISTORY
Berkley Prime Crime edition / July 2000

All rights reserved.
Copyright © 2000 by Monica Ferris.
This book may not be reproduced in whole or in part, by mimeograph or any other means, without permission. For information address: The Berkley Publishing Group, a division of Penguin Putnam Inc., 375 Hudson Street, New York, New York 10014.

The Penguin Putnam Inc. World Wide Web site address is http://www.penguinputnam.com

ISBN: 0-425-17511-1

Berkley Prime Crime Books are published by The Berkley Publishing Group, a division of Penguin Putnam Inc., 375 Hudson Street, New York, New York 10014. The name BERKLEY PRIME CRIME and the BERKLEY PRIME CRIME design are trademarks belonging to Penguin Putnam Inc.

PRINTED IN THE UNITED STATES OF AMERICA

10 9 8 7 6 5 4 3 2 1

Acknowledgments

I can't imagine doing this series without the help of both friends and willing strangers. Luci Zahray, toxicologist and poison guru, terrified me with how easy it is to poison someone. Chad Eschweiler knows about bankruptcy estate sales. The people of the real Excelsior, Minnesota, remain sanguine about my use of their beautiful town as my setting—and I want to add that all of these crimes and their perpetrators are entirely fictional. The members of rctn, the internet newsgroup, are a godsend to people as ignorant as Betsy Devonshire—and me.

On the actual writing end, I sincerely thank my official editor, Gail Fortune, and my unofficial editor and dear friend, Ellen Kuhfeld.

1

John Rettger regarded the bustle and noise in his church hall with pleasure, hope, and concern. He was short, with mild blue eyes and ears that stood out beneath a circle of white, fluffy hair. He sat on a hard wooden chair, his offer to help gently but firmly refused, partly because he was the loved and respected rector of Trinity Episcopal Church, and partly because he was clumsy.

Renovation would begin after the Christmas holidays. A columbarium would be added, something that had been talked about since before he became rector over ten years ago. The library would be expanded, the administrative offices reworked and redecorated, and the long hall between the old chapel and the new church upstairs would have a magnificent hammer-beam roof and a tile floor installed.

But first, the church hall would be gutted and redone. The haphazard collection of small rooms that over the years had halved its size would be removed, and a modern kitchen installed. The antique and dangerous wiring would be replaced, the plumbing updated, the walls and ceiling repaired and repainted, the floor refinished, and new furniture brought in. The only thing unchanged would be the big, functional fireplace.

He turned from the volunteers for a moment to look at the fireplace. It had a native pink limestone surround deeply carved with apple trees—the Wealthy apple was first grown in Excelsior. Beside it was a magnificent fir tree eight feet tall, the annual gift of a Christmas tree farmer. Still on it were a few construction-paper ornaments, made by poor families in the area. Parishioners had been selecting one or two during Advent to buy something suitable for the person described on the ornament. They'd wrap their gift and bring it to Trinity by the last Sunday in Advent, which, this being Thursday, was three days off. The gifts would be delivered Christmas eve.

As Father John watched, three men came to tilt the tree, then lift and carry it up to the big hall outside the nave of the church. The instant they touched it, it shed needles as an alarmed cat sheds fur. He smiled to himself: fir tree, furry cat.

Before the renovation began in earnest, all the movables in the church hall had to be taken away. The valuable things had already been removed, and the volunteers who ran the thrift shop had emptied their area. But there were long tables (some with legs that used to fold, the rest with legs missing), a pair of grubby wing chairs, two very shabby couches, an army of bent folding chairs, assorted broken hand tools, old Sunday school texts, a half dozen dim and ugly landscape paintings in cracked frames, an enormous collection of *House and Garden* magazines, a shoe box full of broken mouse traps, on and on—things needing hauling to recycling centers or a landfill.

As the rooms had taken haphazard bites of the church

hall, odd little corners had developed. Some were turned into closets or storerooms that were later closed off. The very farthest had a floor that had never been finished.

Phil Galvin, a retired railroad engineer, came from that newly reopened room. In his arms was what Father John first took to be a piece of carpet or a small rug. The smell of mildew was strong.

"What have you got there?" asked Father John, his nose wrinkling.

Phil was short and gray, but his manner was brisk and his voice loud and a little harsh, as if he had spent his life shouting orders in all weather. "I dunno. But it's probably been back in there a hundred years."

Phil looked around and saw an elderly card table still standing. He unrolled his find across it. The rug was about four feet wide and long enough to hang off both sides of the table. It reflected its wadded-up past in uneven creases. "Well, looky here! It's a tapestry! And hand stitched, too. Betcha it was done by the women of the parish."

Father John came closer. "Why, it's the Good Shepherd," he said. The tapestry depicted the Savior in a white tunic with a dark orange mantle draped over it. He was carrying a lamb on one forearm and held a shepherd's crook in the other hand. A bright metallic double halo surrounded his dark head and beard, and six grayish-white sheep huddled close to his knees, their black legs making a complicated crosshatch over the bottom of the tapestry. The design seemed unsophisticated, the figures without shading or perspective, and the background a lightly mottled tan. But every line of it was drawn boldly, by a real artist. Something about the sheep said they felt safe, and by his expression, Christ was pleased to have found the lost lamb.

"Nice, ain't it!" barked Phil. "I was wrong, it's not old, that design's too modern."

It was nice, very nice. But it was also dirty and odorous with mildew. The stitching appeared to have worn away in several places. A long strand of tan yarn hung off one edge.

Phil, his head turned sideways as he studied it, said suddenly, "Say, I bet this is Lucy Abrams's work!" He explained, "She was Father Keane Abrams's wife. Father Keane was your predecessor. She liked big needlework projects and designed some of her own."

"Ah," nodded Father John. He had never met his predecessor's wife. She had died of a heart attack the same day her husband suffered a severe and unexpected stroke. By the time Father John was called to be rector, months later, he had been greeted by an interim priest. Now, eleven years later, Father Keane still lived, but he lay helpless in a nursing home, beyond any ability to understand what had happened to him.

"Say, Mrs. Fairland!" yelled Phil suddenly. Father John jumped, then realized the man was summoning her, and he turned to look.

Patricia Fairland was a member of the vestry, a beautiful, talented, and intelligent person, one of those upper-middle-class women who intimidated Father John effortlessly. But apparently not Phil, by the way he'd shouted and was now gesturing impatiently at her.

She was in khaki slacks and a cotton sweater and had wrapped her hair in a complicated way with a silk head scarf. Though she had been working hard for hours, she looked fresh. She came toward them with an inquiring look, pulling off cotton work gloves.

"What's up, Phil?" she asked. "Oooh, where did you find this?"

"Back room," said Phil, pointing. "What do you think?"

"Attractive," she said. "I don't remember ever seeing it before. Moths have been at it, though. And uh-oh, it reeks of mildew. If I get a vote, mine is for tossing it."

"I think this was designed and stitched by Lucy Abrams."

"You do?" Patricia looked at it with more interest, though she didn't come any closer. "Why do you think that?"

"Well, I know she was working on a big project just before she died. She and Donna Claypool and Marge—oh, what was her name, I can't remember—and maybe some other ladies. I never saw it, and I thought she hadn't finished it. But here this is, and it's like some other designs she made. I'd look close for her initials, but it stinks pretty bad."

"Her initials?" said Father John.

"She liked to put her name or her initials or her husband or daughter's name somewhere in her work. One time she did it by crossing blades of grass so they spelled out *Lucy*. You'd never notice it unless someone told you it was there."

"That's right, I'd forgotten about that." Patricia started to come closer, then waved a hand in front of her nose and sneezed twice before she could step back out of range. "Allergic to mildew," she said thickly. "Whew!"

Phil asked her, "Still think we should toss it?"

She hesitated, then asked back, "How sure are you this is Lucy Abrams's work?"

"I'm not sure about anything except death and taxes. We can ask her daughter to confirm it, but I'll bet you a dollar she'll say it is. You sound like you're changin' your mind."

"Well, you know the parish thought the world of the Reverend and Mrs. Abrams. And mildew's not hard to get out. From here it looks like it's done in continental or basket weave, so it should be easy enough to repair. And it is a very nice piece. So yes, I am changing my vote—on a contingency. If it is her work, we should try to restore it. And if we succeed, I think it should go in the columbarium. Or better, the new library." She brightened. *"Which* we should rename in honor of Father Keane."

"Say, that's an idea!" said Phil. "I'll help you with the repairs, if I may."

"I was counting on you to volunteer."

Phil saw the look Father John was giving him and said, "I'm a pretty good needleworker, took it up when I retired."

Patricia said, "He designs and stitches steam engine needlepoint canvases. He has them all over his living room. Extremely nice work."

"Thank you, Patricia," said Phil with a little bow. "Coming from you, that's a real compliment." Phil had very old-fashioned manners.

"How much will this cost?" asked Father John. He had been increasingly alarmed at the ever-rising estimates of this renovation—the hammer-beam roof being a particularly costly item—and the reluctance of his parishioners to be as generous with donations as they were with ideas.

Patricia gave him a quelling look. "I'm sure this won't cost Trinity a cent, Father," she said. "Once people find out what it is and what our plans are for it, they'll be more than willing to contribute to restoring this marvelous find."

Father John had heard that tone of voice before. It meant that will he, nil he, this tapestry was going to get cleaned and repaired in time to hang in the Reverend Keane Abrams Library.

When Betsy came down to Crewel World on Friday morning, she saw out the big front window that it was snowing, huge flakes like the ending of a Christmas movie. Betsy sighed. It had seemed so beautiful a few weeks ago—and it was no less beautiful now. But also, she was now resentfully aware, snow had to be shoveled. Shoveling was not pretty.

Even the Christmas lights around the window didn't jingle her pleasure circuits. White Christmases should be a novelty to Betsy, who had spent many years in California. But they were no novelty in Minnesota, which often saw white Thanksgivings—they had, this year. This was the sixth snowfall since mid-November. Hardly any had melted between the last three storms, so it was really piling up. Betsy was already tired of snow.

She went to unlock the front door and let Godwin, her one full-time employee, in. He stood a moment on the plastic mat, dusting his shoulders and stamping his feet. He was young, blond, good-looking, an expert at all kinds of needlework, and Betsy's most valuable asset. She was ashamed she couldn't pay him what he was worth.

He hung his beautiful navy blue wool coat up in back, and they began the opening-up routine, turning on lights and putting the start-up cash in the register. Betsy stooped to turn on the radio hidden on a shelf half behind three counted cross stitch books. A local station was playing all Christmas music all the time, and Betsy kept the radio tuned to that, though at this point she was more than weary of singing heraldic angels and Rudolph's cruel companions.

Godwin got out the feather duster and began dusting.

She looked around. "A-rew?" came a cat's polite inquiry.

"I see you, Sophie." The big white cat with the tan and gray patches had come downstairs with Betsy and made herself comfortable on "her" chair, the one with the blue gray cushion. The sweet-mannered animal was as much a part of Crewel World as the Madeira silks or the eighteen-count needlepoint canvases.

"Rrrr?" trilled Sophie hopefully.

"No snacks," said Betsy, and the cat sighed and put her head down to wait for a more malleable visitor.

Betsy went to the back room to put on the ugly but warm coat she'd found at a secondhand store and went out to clear the sidewalk in front of her shop.

When she came back in, breathless, falling snow had already laid a thin white cover upon her work. She went to plug in the teakettle and put the shovel away. Godwin had finished dusting and was restocking the yarn bins.

The shop door opened—*bing!* went an electronic bell—and George Hollytree came in, feebly stamping snow off his galoshes. Betsy hurried to take his attaché case and help him with his heavy tweed overcoat. "Hello, Betsy," he piped in an old man's voice.

Mr. Hollytree was eighty-nine. His small, rheumy eyes were set in a pale face as rumpled and folded as an unmade bed. His hands were roped with blue veins and his fingers were gnarled, the fingernails thick and yellow. He was, God help her, Betsy's accountant.

But for all his years, he looked Betsy up and down with an appreciative smile. Betsy was plump by today's standards, but the old man would have described her as voluptuous. More, her complexion was fresh, her clear blue eyes were friendly and intelligent. Her cropped hair had some natural curl to it, and she had recently converted its gray streaks to blond with a home coloring kit. And she was nearly forty years younger than he was, a mere child.

Mr. Hollytree walked stiff-kneed to the library table in the middle of the shop. He sat on the chair at the head of the table and opened his attaché case and brought out a very up-to-date calculator, the kind with several memories and the ability to print a tape.

"You are doing quite well keeping up with transactions," he piped, speaking slowly around ill-fitting false teeth. From a pocket in the lid of the case, he extracted a file folder with Crewel World in thick black letters on its tab. Betsy noted two other file folders in the pocket as she walked behind him, and wondered who else was keeping this man from a happy retirement in a warm climate. She sat down at his right, prepared to listen.

Mr. Hollytree had turned up a couple of weeks after her sister Margot's death. He'd explained that Margot kept computer records of sales and purchases related to the shop, and he turned them into tax records and an account of profit and loss. Frail as he appeared, he seemed to know his business. And Betsy, helplessly ignorant, had reached for his expertise like a drowning sailor grabbing at a broken spar. She had followed his instructions, and the second time he appeared, she had a computer disc ready for him. He had insisted on explaining the charts he made of her data, and though he'd been as slow and patient as he could, she understood only that so far, the shop was paying for itself.

Until today. Today, his high-pitched sigh was deeper, his shuffling of papers more snippy, his patience with her ignorance more fleeting.

"Now look here, young woman," he said at last, causing her to blush like a teenager, "what it comes down to is this: You are on the verge of spending more than you are taking in. This cannot continue. Early winter is supposed to be the best time of year for a business that serves the public, but yours is actually doing worse than last month." His mouth formed a grim line. "Unless you do remarkably well this month, this will be the third or fourth worst Christmas since I have been keeping Crewel World's books."

Betsy felt a rush of defiance. "Perhaps if we checked, we'd find the bad Christmas seasons occurred for reasons beyond the owner's control, such as a bad economy or," she rushed to add, since the economy could hardly have been hotter, "bad weather?"

The old man glared at her, then his face wrinkled alarmingly as he began to cackle. "You are Margot's sister, all right!" he crowed. "I wondered if you would ever show your spunk, or if maybe your sister got it all."

Betsy smiled. "There's far too much spunk in our family for just one of us to hold it all, Mr. Hollytree. And I'm sorry we're not doing so well right now. But I'm doing the best I can, and I don't know what changes I can make."

"Since salaries are your biggest expense, you need to cut your employees' hours. Check what your competition is charging and charge less, even if it's only a penny less—and make sure your customers know your prices are lower."

Betsy nodded. "I'll talk to my employees about working fewer hours. Perhaps, with Christmas so close, they've got all their shopping done and won't be so disappointed in smaller paychecks. And I'll look into competition prices."

"Perhaps you should hold your after-holiday sale now. That means a special advertisement, but you'll more than make it up in extra sales."

Betsy hadn't done any advertising at all, and her face must have shown that, because he said, "I thought so, when I saw no expenses for ads. Some people may think Crewel World's gone out of business because its original owner is dead. I am sorry to add another expense to your burden, but advertising always pays, especially when there's a change of ownership."

Betsy hadn't thought about that. There had been so many people who rallied around her when her sister was murdered that it never occurred to her that there were people out there who didn't know about her. What a terrible thought; once-loyal customers who had found another source of supply! Customers who might still be loyal, who might keep Crewel World in the black, if only they knew.

Oh, yes, she must advertise, tell these people Crewel World was still here, ready to serve all their needlework needs.

But how, with money already in short supply? How much did advertising cost, anyhow? Where was the best place to put it? What should she say in her ad? She didn't want to make a further display of ignorance by asking her accountant. Maybe Godwin would know.

Mr. Hollytree was making a neat stack of her copies of his report. He paper-clipped his calculator printout to it before rising. Godwin brought his coat and helped him back into it.

Betsy answered his good-byes almost absently. Crewel World's logo, needle and yarn spelling *Crewel World* in cross stitch, should appear in the ad. And how deeply could she cut the prices of—what? What bargains would be most likely to bring customers in?

Though Godwin must have wondered what she was thinking, for once he didn't ask. Instead, he went to take inventory of the stitchery books in the box shelves toward the back of the store. Such books were a big favorite as Christmas gifts, and he wanted to make sure they weren't out of the most popular ones.

When the phone rang half an hour later, he was putting an order of little scissors, thimbles, and other items on a spinner rack near the back, so Betsy put down her pencil to answer it.

"Crewel World, good morning, how may I help you?"

A mild voice said, "Good morning, Betsy. This is Father John Rettger of Trinity. Are you busy at present? I can call back."

Betsy said, "Oh, hello, Father. Unfortunately, no, we're not busy. What can I do for you?"

"I don't know if you are aware, but we're about to start a major renovation of the church hall and business offices of our church."

Betsy had seen the story in the weekly *Excelsior Bay Times*. (What would it cost for a two-column ad in the Times?) "Yes, I read about it."

"Well, we're in a great uproar, moving furniture, cleaning out storage areas, and so forth. Not surprisingly, we are finding things we thought were lost or sold or given away long ago."

"Mm-hmmm," Betsy murmured. Her eye fell on the ad she had been designing. Would it cost a great deal more to put the word *SALE* in red?

"One of the things we're going to do is expand our library. We have found a tapestry in a basement storage closet that would be very appropriate. Unfortunately, the tapestry has been damaged by moths—not very badly, but noticeably."

"Mn-hmm." A tapestry, a huge ruglike thing people hung on castle walls.

"Patricia Fairland, who is a member of our vestry, has kindly volunteered to coordinate the restoration of the tapestry. She said I should tell you that it is not woven but stitched, a distinction I am afraid is lost on me. It is about six feet long and four wide, a beautiful thing, very appropriate for the use we hope to put it to."

That wasn't so enormous. But Betsy, mindful of those extra hours she was going to have to work, said, "I don't think I'll be able to volunteer right now, this is the busiest part of—"

"Oh, I wouldn't presume to make demands on your time. I understand that as new and sole proprietor of a business, your time is very limited. No, I was hoping you would be able to make a contribution of materials for the restoration."

This, on the heels of a warning of imminent failure

to break even, should have made Betsy refuse immediately. But wait—surely there would be more stories in the paper as renovation continued, and a big one on completion. If there was a photo that included the tapestry, perhaps Betsy could be mentioned as contributing to its restoration. *Free advertising,* whispered the merchant in her.

So even as she took a breath to say no, Betsy changed her mind.

But then in the second it took to change gears and say yes, Betsy had another thought.

"I'd like to see the tapestry, see what materials are required, and how much," she said, because "not badly damaged" could mean anything. "Would that be possible?"

"Oh, of course. It wouldn't be fair to ask for a donation of material without an understanding of how much and what kind. Mrs. Fairland has told me that she would be glad to come in at the same time and explain to you what is needed. I understand there is a group of needleworkers who meet at your shop, the, er, Monday Bunch? Mrs. Fairland is going to ask for volunteers from that group to do the work. I'm very pleased she has taken on this added responsibility, as I have no knowledge whatever about the needle arts. Shall I ask her to phone you? Or would you rather contact her yourself?"

"I'll call her, I have her number."

"I want you to know that we appreciate your agreeing to do this, especially since you are not a member of Trinity."

Was there a hint of rebuke in his voice? After all, Betsy had been raised in the Episcopal Church, and her sister had been an important member of Trinity. But perhaps she was being too sensitive. What she said was, "That's all right, it's my pleasure to be of service." Because it was. She enjoyed being generous—when she could afford it. And in this case she might actually injure herself by saying no and thus giving free advertising to a rival needlework shop.

Betsy worked some more on the ad, called the weekly newspaper and was shocked by their rates, but agreed a salesman might call, then made herself a cup of raspberry tea and dialed Patricia's number.

Patricia wasn't available this coming Wednesday, which, Hollytree notwithstanding, Betsy was taking off. Christmas was on the horizon, and Betsy had shopping to do. Funny how the less money she had, the longer it took to find gifts. After going through the calendar and failing to find any mutually agreeable time and day between Wednesday and mid-January, Betsy said despairingly, "I don't suppose you're free this evening?" And to her surprise, Patricia was.

2

It was dark when Betsy set off for Trinity at quarter to six, and cold. In San Diego—no, Betsy wasn't going to think about that. She lived in Minnesota now, and she liked it, really she did. If not the climate, then the people. They had taken her to their hearts when she'd come here all dispirited and unhappy, and supported her through the even worse time after her sister had been murdered. And they had encouraged her to keep her sister's needlework shop open, which introduced her to a subculture she'd barely realized existed. There were people, mostly women, who would rather do needlework than eat.

Betsy halted in the middle of the sidewalk. She could remember when she'd liked embroidery. And she could remember a time when she thought people who did lots of needlepoint or counted cross stitch were obsessed, possibly a little crazy. But now she thought about how, when she was really lost in the sweet rhythm of basket weave, she, too, was on the verge of loosing little knots that daily life tied in the back of her neck.

She started walking again, smiling at herself, until she came to Water Street. The foot of Water Street was open to Lake Minnetonka, and the north wind had a long, uninterrupted start down the length of the lake. She quickly turned her back to its bitter bite and went up Water, past the Waterfront Café and the movie theater, the bookstore, the pet store, and the imported gift shop, crossed and turned right, up the hill to the church.

Patricia met Betsy at the glassed arcade between the tiny stone church, the first church built in Excelsior, and the large building that was so modern it didn't look like a church at all. Standing next to Patricia was Martha Winters, another member of the Monday Bunch. Martha was a short woman with snow-white hair and a round, pleasant face that made her look like Mrs. Claus, an effect emphasized by the fur trim on her wine-colored coat and hat. She was an expert counted cross stitcher but did just about every kind of needlework. Though well into her seventies, Martha had an alert and vigorous manner. She still worked part time in the dry cleaners she owned with her grandson.

"Jill Cross says she will try to drop by for a while before she goes on duty," said Patricia. "Phil Galvin couldn't make it."

"All right." Phil was a regular customer, but Jill was Betsy's good friend. She was a police officer with a quiet manner that belied her strength of character—and she did exquisite needlepoint.

Patricia bent and unlocked the heavy glass door and led them into the arcade. To their left was a large room in front of the big, new church, made fragrant by a tall Christmas tree that had half a dozen paper ornaments on it. Betsy inhaled rapturously. Another reason to be glad to live in the north: Christmas trees were less of an artifice here. In this part of the world, the message they had brought Betsy's pagan ancestors—that the world in winter had not died—still had meaning.

On one wall of the hall was a row of black-framed photographs of bygone rectors. The last one had a broad, sweet face and a big nose, with white hair and intense eyes under shaggy eyebrows. His smile was sizzling enough to provoke an answering one in Betsy. On the picture frame was a little metal plate that said he was the Reverend Keane Abrams, and giving the years of the pastorship, which only amounted to seven. *I wonder what he was like as a person,* thought Betsy.

Patricia and Martha paused at the head of a stairwell to wait for Betsy. She came out of her musings and hurried after them, following them down into darkness. At the bottom of the stairs, Martha and Betsy stopped.

Patricia's footsteps went ahead, paused, and lights went on in a room off a narrow hall. Betsy and Martha walked into a severely plain and obviously elderly room with a high ceiling and a magnificent fireplace at its far end. Because the church complex overlapped the hill it was set on, the left wall had windows and there was a door at the far end leading outside.

But Betsy's eyes were quickly drawn to the only furniture in the room, a card table near a wall with a large piece of light-colored needlework draped over it.

She approached and saw, on a neutral background, a near life-size figure of Christ as the Good Shepherd, the design flat and stylized. Christ, deeply tanned and sporting long black hair and a curly beard, wore a white robe under a dark-orange mantle. A lamb rested complacently on his right forearm, and he held a crook in his left hand. Around his head was a halo of two bold lines of metallic gold, with a blue gray stripe between them. Six sheep crowded around him, their expressions benign.

The work was done in plain diagonal stitching. Martha stepped forward and laid bold hands on it, even turning a corner of it over.

"Basket weave," she said, meaning the stitching. "And whew, is it mildewed!"

"Smells awful," agreed Betsy, wrinkling her nose. "Is that moth damage?" she asked, gesturing at a spot where the stitches were missing, exposing the heavy canvas. "I mean moth larvae, don't I? It's not the moths, it's the grubs, right?"

"That's right," said Patricia, and she sneezed. "Eggscuse be," she said, and held a handkerchief to her nose.

There weren't a lot of bare places, and most were smaller than the palm of her hand. Betsy smiled. She could supply the wool to mend this with very little strain. But, "What about the mildew? No one can work on it like this. Is there a treatment we can use?"

"Sunlight is good," said Martha—surprisingly, because she owned a dry cleaning shop. "But also you can mix one or two tablespoons of sodium perborate in a pint of water and sponge it on the mildew. That will get rid of the mildew stains, too, and it's a mild enough bleach that it shouldn't hurt the colors. I'll see about treating it before we start work."

"Thanks," said Patricia.

There were footsteps, and the women turned to see a tall woman in a police uniform coming toward them, taking off her hat as she approached. Her jacket was thick, her utility belt weighty, and her gun large. Above all that was a lovely Gibson girl face surrounded by ash-blond hair, pulled back into a short braid.

"Hello, Jill," said Patricia. "Glad you could come."

"I can't stay long." Jill came up to the table. "I've been meaning to call you, Betsy. Anything you want me to bring to the party tomorrow?"

Betsy was giving a Christmas party to thank her friends and employees for their loyalty. Both Patricia and Martha were coming, so it was all right for Jill to talk about it.

"No, I have everything I need, thanks."

Jill leaned closer than Betsy had dared to examine the tapestry. "This doesn't look so bad," she said. "That ground color should be easy to match. Who's working on it?"

"So far, just me, Martha, and Phil Galvin," said Patricia.

"I'm too busy with the shop," Betsy said, feeling a slight blush warm her cheeks at this need to justify herself. "But I'll supply the wool, the needles, Febreze, anything you need."

"That's generous of you," Jill said, frowning at the bottom left corner, where a strand of tan yarn hung down. "Are you in charge, Patricia?"

"Yes, I told Father John we could do this at no cost to the church. But Betsy, I didn't tell him to ask you to donate the materials. I'm sure we could raise the money to pay you."

"Oh, that's all right. It won't break me to donate a few yards of tan wool. How old is this tapestry?" The style of the design made Betsy think of the 1950s or early '60s.

Patricia said, "Ten or twelve years. But it has never been displayed that I know of. Lucy Abrams designed it and worked on it with other members of Trinity. I called her daughter, and when I described it, she said she remembered her mother and some other women working on it shortly before she died. She said she thought it was lost, thrown away." Patricia explained to Betsy, "Father Keane Abrams was Father John's predecessor, and one of the best-loved rectors we've ever had. Lucy was his wife."

"What a character he was!" said Martha. "A diamond in the rough, certainly, but a twenty-carat diamond, at least. His sermons were down to earth, addressed to the common man, which made us refined types sit up and take notice. Pithy, that's how we described his sermons."

Jill said, "My father liked him. But my mother thought he was probably a reformed burglar who should be a chaplain down at the jail."

Patricia, laughing, said, "The first time he stepped into the pulpit, I thought, *O Lord, what have we got here?* He looked like a longshoreman or a retired boxer. But in five minutes, I was thinking how wonderful he—" She broke off, blinking.

"What?" asked Betsy.

Patricia continued, "He wasn't here long, and retired from Trinity all of a sudden, saying he hadn't felt well for awhile, and he had a massive stroke a week later at home. His wife Lucy found him and apparently tried to help him up off the floor and had a heart attack. She was found dead beside him by their daughter Mandy. It was dreadful, just dreadful. Mandy went to live with an aunt, and Father Keane has been in a nursing home ever since. Can't talk, can't walk, can't feed himself." Real tears glittered on her eyelashes.

"It was awful for her to come home to that, just awful," agreed Martha. "So sad."

Patricia said, "Father John agrees that if we restore this tapestry and persuade the rest of the vestry, he will not object to it hanging in the officially renamed Reverend Keane Abrams Library."

There was a gleam in the woman's eyes that shone through the tears. Betsy exchanged a smile with Jill and Martha, who actually winked. They all knew Patricia. Even if Father John objected, the deed was all but done.

When Betsy walked out of the church hall after the meeting, snow was coming down again, blowing sideways in a stiff wind. It stung her cheeks, flapped the skirt of her long coat around her legs, and made her walk crabwise. She staggered down to the corner of Second and Water, where it blew even harder. Her hat lifted itself, and she barely grabbed it before it went sailing out into the street. She'd seen snowstorms like this on television, after an afternoon at the beach. She unwrapped her scarf from her neck and tied it over her head.

It was a struggle, those few blocks down Water, then a lesser one up Lake to her shop and home. Once safely inside, climbing the stairs to her apartment, she was suddenly overcome with a feeling of elation, as if she'd climbed a mountain. She remembered blizzards in her youth in Milwaukee, and she found it even more exciting now in her maturity to discover they still couldn't overmatch her.

The snow stopped by bedtime, and plows must have worked all night, because by Saturday morning the streets were clear. Snow was piled along the curbs, in mountain ranges so high that from inside the shop, Betsy could see only the roofs of cars as they went by. She cleared the sidewalk yet again, adding her own peaks to the Himalayas. Then she cut a narrow passage through to the street so customers wouldn't need ropes and pitons to get to her shop.

A few minutes later, a shadow passed the front window. Betsy looked to see a woman in a wine-colored, fur-trimmed coat holding her gloved hand to her face—the wind was cutting sharply this morning. She ducked into the slightly recessed door of the shop, the hand came down, and it was Martha Winters.

"Hello, Betsy, Godwin," she said as she entered. "I've come to pick up that bellpull. Is it back yet?"

"I believe so," said Betsy. "The finisher brought a whole box of things in just before closing yesterday."

She stooped behind the big desk that served as her

checkout counter and brought up a large cardboard box with a sheet of paper attached to it. She looked down the list and drew a line through a name. "It says something of yours is in here."

Inside the box, rolled up like a fire hose, was a long, narrow piece of canvas covered with eggshell stitching. The finisher had sewn on a back of eggshell linen. Betsy unrolled the piece to reveal a scattering of chickadees and cardinals sitting on branches of holly and evergreen. "Very pretty," said Betsy.

"You think so?" said Martha with a little sniff. "My daughter-in-law hinted and hinted that this was what she wanted for her dining room."

"Don't you like it?" asked Godwin, coming for a look.

"Oh, it's all right," grudged Martha. "But no beads, no fancy stitches, no zing."

"Well, right now we're in an era of rococo needlework," said Godwin. "Someday people will find this very restrained and therefore particularly lovely."

Martha smiled. "So says the maker of the Christmas Stocking That Clatters When Touched."

Godwin laughed. "The pot pleads guilty, Mrs. Kettle! Still, I can't see a false stitch in this piece. Even the tassel at the bottom is perfect."

Martha had opted for that authentic finishing touch and had made it herself from red velveteen yarn. "How much?" she asked Betsy.

Betsy consulted the order sheet in a file folder. "Sixty-five dollars, including hardware." Which meant the stiffening dowel and string, and the hook and screws so it could be fastened to a wall.

Martha got out her checkbook. Signing with a flourish, she handed a check to Betsy and at the same moment her eye was caught by a sampling of tan, buff, neutral, and cream wools. "Are these for the Trinity project?" she asked.

"Yes," nodded Betsy.

"I've told some other Monday Bunch members, and they're thrilled at a chance to do something in honor of Father Keane. Even nonmembers."

Betsy said, "I thought I'd go over on Monday and see if any of these matched."

Martha said, "I'm glad you want to get right to it. There are volunteers in the church hall today, you know."

"There are? Doing what?"

"Taking down the old kitchen and making sure nothing's left behind in the rest of the downstairs. The contractor finished another job early and will be starting our renovation on Tuesday."

"Thanks for telling me. I'll go over on my lunch break today."

Mrs. Winters left, and the one other customer said she wanted to browse, so Betsy joined Godwin at the library table in the middle of the room. He had a project of his own back from the finisher, a magnificent Christmas stocking. It was the one Martha Winters had teased him about, stiff with beading and tiny bangles, ornate with fancy stitching. The design was of two children coming down a stairway to see Santa hiding behind a Christmas tree. Santa's beard was curled into French knots, the children's pajamas were of brushed satin stitching, the wallpaper was two-color gingham stitch, and the tinsel on the tree was made of microscopic glass beads. Across the top of the stocking *JOHN* was worked with silver metallic thread.

Godwin was arranging it in a shallow box draped with silver tissue paper.

"You're not going to hang it?" asked Betsy.

"I haven't decided yet," said Godwin. "John and I exchange gifts on Christmas eve morning, because he goes home Christmas eve and stays till late Christmas day. I suppose we could hang it after he opens it, but then I'd be tempted to put something in it, and I don't want to stretch it out."

"Do you have someplace to go to celebrate Christmas?" asked Betsy.

"I just told you about my Christmas." Godwin saw the start of compassion in Betsy's eyes and said crisply, "We have our own private and very happy Christmas, and then we do something truly brilliant for New Year's Eve. So please, don't feel sorry for me."

"Don't you have parents or a brother or sister?" persisted Betsy.

"My father and mother are—well, never mind. I don't think my darkening their doorstep would brighten the holidays for any of us."

"I'm sorry."

Godwin shrugged. "Their loss."

Indeed, thought Betsy, still miffed on his behalf. She reached under the table for the counted cross stitch Christmas tree ornament she was working on. It was a hippopotamus wearing a Santa Claus hat, fifth in a series of a dozen animals she'd ordered from a catalog. Betsy had nearly decided she didn't like counted cross stitch. Those customers who claimed it relaxed them were a breed apart; for Betsy, doing counted cross stitch was aggravating, frustrating, and full of traps for the unwary.

Still, it's very attractive when it comes out right, she thought, looking complacently at the grinning hippo.

In a while she sold one skein of DMC 725 perle cotton floss to the browser and eight hanks of bright pink knitting wool to a man who had signed up for the January knitting class and was needlessly afraid someone else would buy his choice of color. His purchase reminded Betsy, and she added her own name to the class list. Rosemary had brought a finished example of the sweater she was going to teach her class to knit, and

Betsy had always wondered how knitters got that twist of cable into their patterns.

Soon after the knitter left, a woman came in with a child about twelve years old and bought a yard of sixteen count canvas, two needles and a threader, a dozen DMC perle cotton colors, six needlepoint wool colors, and a copy of *The Needlepoint Book.* Betsy thought the child was the woman's daughter until the child addressed her as Aunt Jay.

"This is half your Christmas present," Aunt Jay said, handing the weighty blue plastic bag with *Crewel World* printed on it in little Xs to the beaming child. "The other half is me teaching you how to do the stitches in the book. Your present to me is your first sampler, which I will hold in trust for whichever of your daughters gets the needlework gene."

Two more customers came in to pick up finished projects, and then it was noon. Betsy put on her long, dark gray coat and the bright red scarf and hat she'd knitted herself. The hat fit a little loosely because she'd figured the gauge—how many stitches to the inch—on size six needles and then knit it on seven, but that was all right, because now she didn't get hat hair. She put the wool samples in her purse and set off for the church.

The wind had let up, the sun was shining, and it didn't feel all that cold out. No challenge to the walk today. She went into the darkened arcade, heard distant voices, and followed them down the stairs and into the hall.

A half dozen volunteers were carrying huge cooking pots and boxes of utensils, what looked like parts of an early-model gas stove, and—proverbially—an old, stained, porcelain kitchen sink. Three others carried boxes of books, coat hangers, and unidentifiable junk.

Father John Rettger was standing by the tapestry, still spread across the old table.

"Hi, Father John," said Betsy coming up from behind.

He'd been concentrating so hard on the movers that her voice startled him. He shied, then laughed at himself.

"Oh, hello, Betsy! I was wondering if you'd come over today. I've been standing guard over the tapestry, because I'm afraid someone will pack it up and take it away and it'll be lost for another decade." His voice was mild, like his eyes, as if he were used to going unheard or overruled.

"Are there people who would like that to happen?" asked Betsy, surprised.

"No, no, or at least I'm pretty sure not. It's just that the contractors are coming early, for a wonder, and we're not finished moving out yet. And I don't know about you, but every time I've moved, I've lost things. Once it was volume twenty-four of our *Britannica*, Metaphysics to Norway, though all the rest of the volumes were in the box, even the annuals."

Betsy nodded. "I once lost a hamster in a move across the street. But I think maybe our cat got him. She'd had her eye on him for months."

Father John laughed, then turned to the tapestry. "Well, what do you think?"

Betsy said, "Oh, I've already told Patricia I'll supply the materials. I brought some samples of wool with me to see if anything I already have matches." Betsy opened her purse and began laying out the wool in various places on the tapestry. Just having sat in the open overnight had diminished the mildew smell significantly.

"That's funny," she said after a bit.

"What?" said Father John.

"Well, Cool Buff matches up here, but Cafe Latte matches over here. I think they must have used different dye lots. Interesting."

"What do you mean by dye lots?"

"Manufacturers stir up a big batch of dye using various ingredients. That's a dye lot. And for some reason, even though they use the same recipe, the next batch doesn't quite match the first. The label will give it the same name, but stitchers know when they are buying wool or floss to make sure the dye lot number is also the same."

"But that didn't happen with this tapestry, you say. Is that good or bad?"

"Good. It gives me more chances to match colors." Betsy continued checking, tossing the samples that matched into a little heap on Christ's mantle. Finished, she reached for them. "Uh-oh."

"Uh-oh what?" asked Father John.

"Look at this." Betsy pointed to a small area of the dark orange mantle. It was next to a gray sheep, and the mostly horizontal slice looked at first like a part of the sheep's back. But moth larvae had eaten a small section down to the canvas.

Father John said, "So you'll need to give us a few inches of that orange color, too, won't you?"

Betsy, grabbing for her sinking heart, couldn't say anything at first. As she'd already noted, color was a variable thing. It was impossible that the orange colors currently in her shop came from the same dye lot as this twelve-year-old yarn. She could feel the priest waiting for her to reply. "Sometimes it's hard to match colors," she said at last. "And if I can't match that one, we'll have to redo the entire mantle." The mantle took up a large area. It was one thing to donate a skein or even a couple skeins of needlepoint wool; it was quite another to donate enough to cover a quarter of this large tapestry. Especially done in basket weave, which by design used a lot of wool, since it was meant to stiffen the fabric on which it was stitched.

"Don't despair before you find it can't be matched," said Father John. "I've been pleasantly surprised a few times in my life."

Betsy looked to see if he was speaking ironically, but his eyes were kind and his smile genuine. She smiled back and repeated something her father used to say to her: "Never trouble trouble, till trouble troubles you."

"That's right."

"Is there a phone down here I can use?"

"Back over here."

It was early issue Ma Bell, made of heavy metal with an old-fashioned dial instead of buttons. Betsy called her shop.

"Godwin? We've run into a little complication over here. Can you bring me samples of all our orange wools? I'm looking for a color I'd call burnt orange, but bring anything from russet to red. Needlepoint, yes. What? Well, don't we have a sign that says Back in Five Minutes? Then write it on something and get over here. Fast."

While they waited, Betsy looked again at the tapestry. She knew she was still a novice at needlework, but she'd seen expert work, and this seemed very well done. The stitching had a satisfying evenness. There were no beads or metallics.

Well, except in the halo. Betsy came closer. The mildew odor was still enough to wrinkle her nose, through which she took tiny sips of air.

Between the double gold lines of halo was a blue gray, slightly sparkly area. No, it wasn't the blue-gray that was sparkly, there was a tiny design stitched over it, or in between the stitches or something. Betsy frowned and leaned over the table, holding her breath.

"Is there another problem?" asked Father John.

She straightened. "No, I'm just wondering what that is."

"I know stitches have various names, but I couldn't tell you the name of even one."

"It's not a stitch," said Betsy. "See, there are little

pictures in the halo. You have to get close to see them,
they're—oh, they were done separately, then stitched to
the gray stitching. Appliqué, it's called. They're like little line drawings, see them? There's a clover leaf, and
then some kind of animal, and then a heart or something . . ."

"Where?" asked Father John, bending beside her.
"Oh, I see them. How very clever. They're attributes, I
believe. See? That heart is supposed to be on fire. It's
for Saint Theresa. And here, this is Saint Olaf." He was
pointing to a tiny double-bladed ax.

"I don't understand," said Betsy, straightening again.
"I mean, how is an ax St. Olaf?"

"Come, come, you know what I mean. For instance,
that first one. If I tell you it's not a clover but a shamrock, who does it make you think of?"

"Oh!" said Betsy. "Saint Patrick."

"Of course. And the lamb is Saint Agnes, and if that's
a chain, it's probably Saint Ignatius. Back before literacy
was common—but also because no one knew what almost any of the saints actually looked like—when a
statue or painting of a saint was commissioned, the artist
could put whatever face he found inspiring on it. But
then, to tell the viewer who it was supposed to be, he
would add some of the symbols attributed to that saint.
That's what they're called: attributes."

Betsy said, "Well, yes, of course! I remember learning
about that in Sunday school. Saint Lucy was a pair of
eyes on a plate, ugh! And the four evangelists were an
angel, an eagle, a lion, and—what?"

"An ox. And the Trinity was a triangle or three inter-
locking circles. We use both here at Trinity, one over-
laying the other. Not all of the attributes are for saints.
Some symbolize various aspects of God or of Christian
virtues. The horse means war, unless he's ridden, in
which case horse and rider stand for our Lord Christ."

"So what was the idea of using attributes in this tapestry?"

"Perhaps to give it an all-saints theme as well as Good Shepherd? Hmm, this looks like a rowboat. I wonder who that symbolizes. Mrs. Abrams seems to have been something of an expert on Christian symbology—unless, unless!"

"Unless what?"

"There's an old book up in my office on Christian symbols. Can you watch over this for just two minutes?"

"Of course."

Father John hustled out of the room. Betsy traced another of the attributes with a finger. A boar? Maybe Lucy was saying something about husbands. Betsy normally referred to her ex-husband Hal as the Pig.

Hey, here was a cat, and over here was another, one sitting and the other crouching. Was that significant? Perhaps more than one person worked on this, and they forgot who was doing the cat. Here were three crowns in a tight pattern; she remembered that three crowns meant Saint Elizabeth of Hungary. Her Sunday school teacher's name was Elizabeth, and so made a point about this Saint Elizabeth's attribute. And Betsy remembered because that was her name, too. But the other emblems were hieroglyphics to her. She hoped Father John could find the book about these symbols. She rummaged in her purse for a notebook and couldn't find one, so she pulled her checkbook out of its folder and started to copy the symbols onto the cardboard back.

"Hello, Betsy," said a woman's voice.

"Hm?" Betsy said, straightening and turning. "Oh, hello, Patricia! Look what we've found! Little pictures, saints' attributes, in the halo. I'm so glad we don't have to redo this part. That would take special skills."

Patricia took a breath, held it, then leaned forward to look very briefly at the halo. She straightened and said,

"Why, yes, I hadn't noticed that before. What did you call them?"

"Attributes. Father John has gone to get a book on them. I want to see who they represent. I know the three crowns are Elizabeth, and the shamrock is Saint Patrick, but here, who has a horseshoe? Isn't this interesting? Like a puzzle. And look, there are two cats. I wonder why."

But Patricia was taking two steps backward, fishing for a handkerchief in her purse. "That's very interesting and clever. I wonder what metallic she used for those, er, attributes that maintained its shine all these years? Real silver would tarnish, and anyway I don't think you could get real silver thread until fairly recently. Maybe aluminum . . . Such very fine stitching, too, looks as if it was done with a single thread."

Reminded, Betsy said, "Patricia, there may be another problem." She showed Patricia the moth-eaten section of mantle and was just starting to say something about twelve-year-old dye lots when Godwin appeared, breathless from hurry, with a dozen strands of wool in one gloved hand.

"This is what we have in stock," he said. "Hello, Mrs. Fairland," and added, "Customer waiting," over his shoulder as he turned and rushed out again.

Betsy tried each strand over the mantle. None of them matched. "See, this is what I was worried about."

"Oh, dear," said Patricia.

"Yes," said Betsy, her eyes estimating the size of the mantle. She wished she'd done what Jill had suggested, memorized the length and width of her hand, so she'd have a way to gauge size when she didn't have a measuring tape in reach.

"Now look, Betsy, if we have to redo this whole area, that will take a lot of wool, which I'm sure will be a real hardship for you. Why don't you just forget that offer of a donation? As I told you, I'm starting a drive to name the renovated library after Father Keane. He was so popular that I'm sure we'll succeed. We could even raise the money to pay for a professional restoration of the tapestry, I'm sure."

Betsy, surprised and grateful, opened her mouth to accept the offer, but to her even greater surprise what came out was, "But Martha has told the Monday Bunch, and they're all excited about the project. I'd hate to disappoint them. I'll check around for more samples—and so what if I have to supply enough for all the mantle? I hardly think even that much wool will send my shop into bankruptcy."

Patricia frowned doubtfully. "Well, if you're really sure . . ."

Betsy said, "I'm sure. Now, I'd better get back to the shop. Godwin needs his lunch break."

On her way up the stairs, she met Father John. He was carrying a thick book. "It took me awhile to find it on my shelves," he apologized. He opened it at random to display a page divided into six squares, each with a simple line drawing in it: a book pierced by a sword, a ship's wheel, a harp, a lantern, a Celtic cross, a pair of pincers. The facing page was part of a dictionary of saints' names with their dates and attributes.

"Oh, lovely!" exclaimed Betsy. "May I borrow it? I'll be working on the tapestry, and I've already written down some attributes I want to look up."

"Of course," said Father John, kindly neglecting to point out that he'd gone for the book because there were some attributes he wanted to look up himself. He handed the book over and went back to guarding the tapestry against those who might store it away so securely it was never found again.

3

"Why didn't you take her up on that offer?" asked Godwin.

"I don't know," said Betsy. "Especially since I got some really bad news from George Hollytree."

Godwin looked up from his knitting—another in his endless series of white cotton socks. "Um, how bad?"

Betsy took a deep breath but kept her eyes on her cross stitching. "He says I have to cut back employee hours and at the same time stay open longer. That means I have to work more."

"How can I work more hours? I'm already full time."

Betsy looked sideways at him. "No, you need to work *fewer* hours. *I* need to work more hours."

Godwin laughed. He laughed so hard he had to put down his knitting. When the laughter slowed, he would look at Betsy and start in again.

Betsy tried to wait him out, but Godwin's endurance was apparently bottomless. At last she said, "That's enough, Godwin," and he stopped as if she had clipped him one on the nose. "Now, why is that so funny?"

"Because, my dearest, most wonderful, and favorite living employer, you are learning both needlework and the art of owning a small business with breathtaking skill and speed, but you are a long way from accomplished at either. You may do well here in the shop all by yourself—or you may not. For example, Mrs. Hagedorn came in while you were mucking about with that tapestry to ask me if I could get her some *one hundred twelve count* silk gauze. I looked in our catalog, and sure enough it comes that high. But she also wanted to buy some needles to use in this project. An ordinary needle won't fit through the silk gauzes, so if you were here alone, what would you have told her?"

Betsy looked uncomfortable. "Well . . . I guess I would've got you on the phone."

"And if I'm not at home but in Cancun basking in the sun?"

"Okay, I'd look in that catalog that has every kind of needle you can think of."

"And it wouldn't help, unless you already knew where to look. You use the short beading needles; if you look them up, it says they are also for extremely high-count fabrics. Fortunately for you, Mrs. Hagedorn already knew that. I have ordered the silk gauze for her, but we already have beading needles in stock." Beading needles were thin as hair.

Betsy said, "Well, if she already knew—"

"But what if she hadn't known? Would you have known who to call? I would, because I know *almost* everything, including who to ask."

"Whom. All right, I know, too. I would dash upstairs and put the question on the Internet, to my favorite newsgroup, RCTN. I'd have an answer in about sixty seconds. Collectively, those people know everything."

Godwin nodded. "You're right, they do. But it's not good business practice to leave a customer alone in the shop. Admit it, boss, you need me here as much as possible. I only cost a dollar an hour more than the part-time help. Theirs are the hours you'll have to cut down on. If you can't do that, you'll have to cut some other expense."

"Which brings us back to my original question, doesn't it? Why didn't you *enthusiastically* jump on Patricia's suggestion that you back out on your offer to supply the material for the tapestry?"

Betsy said, "Because Mr. Hollytree also told me I should advertise, to let people know Crewel World didn't die with my sister. Which I am going to do. A salesman should be here on Tuesday. But if I get involved with this project, then the name of my shop will get in the paper as the supplier of materials. Before I knew we might have to replace a huge area of the thing, that seemed an easy, cheap way to get some publicity."

Godwin widened his blue eyes at her. "Then it was a *good* idea!" he said.

"Of course it was! I may be ignorant, but I'm not stupid!"

Godwin winked at her. "Honey, *no one* thinks you march with the stupid platoon, not after you beat our local police to the solution in two murder cases."

Betsy grimaced, looked for her place on the fabric, then consulted the pattern. She thought herself lucky, not bright, when it came to solving murders. But no one paid any attention when she said that. She stuck her needle in, pulled the floss through. "I was thinking of calling Picket Fence and Stitchville USA to see if they have any dark orange wool in a shade I don't have," she said, and put down her stitching again to reach for the cordless on the table.

Godwin nodded. "Another good idea."

But they didn't have anything different. Betsy was looking up more shops' numbers when a customer came in with a large cardboard box, its top folded shut.

"I'm hoping you can help me, Betsy," she said, dropping the box onto the library table. "My grandmother died a month ago, and when she got sick last spring, she said I should get her stash. But I already have a stash, and I may never get around to using this stuff."

"Are you saying you want to give it away?" asked Betsy.

"Some of it." She pulled the flaps of the box apart and began lifting out clear plastic bags filled with needlework projects, rolls of linen and Aida cloth in several colors, packets of needles, silk and perle floss, and balls of yarn. She gestured at one pile. "Look at all these needlepoint canvases! This one's stamped, but look, this one and this one are hand painted, so they're valuable. Thing is, I don't do needlepoint. And see this big bag of wool? Lots of colors but there's not more than a yard of any one color."

Betsy eyed the bag speculatively, but didn't see any dark orange.

"At least now I know where I get my squirrel nature. My mother throws leftover yarn away unless she's got another project that can use it, but I'll end up in one of those houses with paths winding among the stacks of newspapers, except my stacks will be patterns and projects waiting for me to find time to finish them, and leftover yarn and floss from projects I've completed."

Betsy said, "I hope you don't think your mother is the normal one. Almost all my customers save leftover cloth and floss." She picked up a needlepoint kit depicting a tropical sunset. The sky and sea were mauve and blue and lavender and pink, with palm trees making graceful black arcs in the foreground. She'd been to that beach, back in San Diego. But first things first: "Is there any dark orange wool? I need some for a project."

"Not in this box. If I find some, I'll bring it in. This

is only a quarter of what we found. About the stash I'm keeping: Can I store everything as I found it?"

"No, you can't," said Betsy. "You need to get it out of these plastic bags and into acid-free paper or cloth bags. Fibers need to breathe."

Godwin had come over for a look. "You know," he said to Betsy, "Margot would do consignment selling once in awhile. Some of this is very nice. Like this kit, which was never even opened." Then he picked up a completed needlepoint of a white horse rearing in storm-tossed surf. "This is beautiful," he said. "Do you know Diane Bolles, down at Nightingale's? She's looking for needlework to sell." Godwin reached for something else. "And look at this, too, Betsy." He was holding an un-worked canvas covered with hearts and cherubs. "It's a Patti Mann canvas. "We could sell this in a New York minute."

Betsy said, "All right. Are you willing to part with some of this on consignment, Katie?"

In half an hour, Katie left for Nightingale's with a gleam in her eye. Betsy spent another half hour putting the new items out, making sure they were artistically displayed, then properly marked and listed in the note-book Godwin showed her, in which Margot had kept track of consignment items.

"Do you have a stash, Godwin?" she asked, stepping back from the Patti Mann to see if it was hung straight.

"Honey, I'm at the point where I'm throwing out *clothes* to make room. *Everyone* has stash, but we're all too enamored of SEX to quit looking for more."

Betsy laughed; Godwin meant Stash Enhancement eXperience, one of the terms invented by her favorite newsgroup. Betsy was not herself immune to the lure of SEX; she set the tropic sunset kit aside for herself.

At five they locked the front door. Godwin and Betsy straightened up the shop: washing out the coffeepot and unplugging the teakettle, shutting off the radio, running the credit card machine's total, counting the take. Betsy made out a deposit slip, which Godwin took along with the cash and checks to the bank a couple of blocks away. "See you later at the party," he said. "I'll be the one with the tie that lights up."

Betsy and Sophie went upstairs, where Betsy took a quick shower and put on her prettiest party dress, the cranberry velvet, and stroked on evening makeup, more emphatic than her daytime wear. She put on her garnet earrings and necklace, inherited from her mother.

The apartment was sparkling clean, but Betsy went around putting breakables higher or into cabinets, leaving as much flat surface as possible for plates and glasses. Sophie followed her, whining until Betsy remembered she hadn't fed her pet.

Sophie was alleged to be on a diet. She was allowed two small scoops of diet cat food a day, which should keep even a lazy cat like Sophie at a svelte seven or eight pounds. Sophie, by dint of nonexistent metabolism and a lifestyle that "Less Active" overstated, had lost three pounds, gained one back, and now held stubbornly at eighteen. The problem was, she cadged treats from anyone who approached her in the shop, and would accept any offering. Betsy had needlepointed a little sign that read, "No, Thank You, I'm on a Diet," to hang on the back of Sophie's chair, but just today, a customer, still laughing at the sign, had fed Sophie a potato chip. Betsy had thought of a muzzle, but Sophie might find it very tasty, too. And Betsy couldn't stop the Iams feedings; Sophie's diet otherwise was too unhealthy.

"You could leave her upstairs," Godwin had suggested. But the thought of the friendly, ornamental, happy creature condemned to a life of waiting for Betsy to come home was too awful.

Two hours later, Betsy took off her slippers and put on her highest heels. The apartment was beginning to smell of hot hors d'oeuvres and rock gently to the jazz piano of Ramsey Lewis. The little table in the dining nook was laden with crystal goblets, bottles of good red and white wines, and a big punch bowl filled with something pink and fragrant. Beer and soft drinks were in the refrigerator. Betsy took a ceramic pie plate out of the freezer. Last night she had overlapped alternating slices of lemons and limes in a ring in the pie plate and scattered a few maraschino cherries on top. She had put a straight-sided bowl of water in the center, poured half an inch of water into the plate, and put the whole thing in the freezer. Now she dismantled the arrangement and put the ring of frozen fruit into the punch bowl, where it would serve to chill and ornament the punch.

By the time the first tray of hors d'oeuvres came out of the oven, three couples had arrived.

Betsy loved to give parties. Godwin was there, of course, with his lover John, a tall attorney with a distinguished profile and just the right amount of gray in his hair. He looked around her apartment and then at Betsy with the amused air of the *New York Times* home/arts editor visiting Archie Bunker's house. He was obvious enough about it that Jill Cross, Betsy's police officer friend, raised an inquiring eyebrow at her when they met over the punch bowl a few minutes later. Betsy rolled her eyes to show she didn't care what the jerk thought and went to get a fresh batch of cheesy, spicy hamburger on tiny rounds of rye bread out of the oven.

Shelly Donohue, an elementary school teacher who worked part time in the shop, came with an extremely handsome fellow she introduced as Vice Principal Smith.

Joe Mickels, Betsy's landlord, came. Betsy had an ironclad lease at a ridiculous rent on the shop, a mistake

Joe's late brother had made with Betsy's late sister. Joe had made numerous strenuous attempts to break the lease when Margot had run the shop, but they had stopped when Betsy took over. She didn't know why, and it made her uneasy.

Joe was a short-legged, pigeon-breasted man with enormous white sideburns and a great beak of a nose. His winter coat with its astrakhan collar was as anachronistic as he was—Joe should have lived in the era of robber barons.

He had an attractive woman his own age with him. "Still think you're going to stay the course?" he asked Betsy with an icy twinkle.

If Betsy had the occasional tremble for herself and Crewel World, she wasn't about to show it to Joe. "We're doing fine, thank you," she said with a determined twinkle of her own and took their coats to the back bedroom.

The part-timers came with spouses or significant others. The Monday Bunch, a needlework group that met at the shop, came mostly alone. The party divided into clusters, naturally, but Betsy went casually from cluster to cluster, taking a person from the Monday Bunch to introduce her to someone in the business discussion Joe was leading, and a person from the business world to introduce to the arts discussion, and so forth, making sure everyone got a chance to meet everyone else.

The five or six on and around the couch were into politics. "Do you think Mayor Jamison will run again?" asked Peter Fairland, Patricia's husband, a state senator contemplating a run for Congress. (The mayor, typically, was in the kitchen, helping stir up a new batch of that hamburger-on-rye hors d'oeuvre.)

"I think the job is his as long as he wants it," said Godwin.

"I think it's time for a woman mayor, don't you?"

asked Martha Winters, a refugee from the Monday Bunch.

Betsy paused to listen. She admired Patricia's smooth, classic exterior and wanted to see what her husband was like. Peter showed himself quick-witted and friendly, with piercing gray eyes and a great laugh. He was smooth in a practiced way, an intense listener, and Betsy found him not quite as intimidating as his wife.

Betsy left the political group to deal with a minor explosion in the business corner, where Joe Mickels was defending his latest attempt to squeeze yet more money out of a nonprofit group renting one of his buildings. "You all seem to forget," Joe growled, "that our great wealth happened *because* we use the capitalist system." Betsy asked Joe if he could help her open the sticky window in the dining nook just an inch, because it was getting rather warm in the apartment. He would have taken that as criticism of his maintenance until he recognized the look she was giving him. He came and opened the window and meekly did ten minutes of penance with the needleworkers, who were gathered around the punch bowl.

Betsy went to check on the quartet in the kitchen, who were telling favorite-pet stories while waiting for the hors d'oeuvres in the oven to come out. She stayed there only long enough to remind them that the oven ran a little hot and continued her rounds, this time bringing Mayor Jamison along.

She left him with Godwin's friend John, who was arguing probate law with Betsy's own attorney while three other guests kibitzed.

The group by the CD player were looking through the albums and not finding anything with words. "You collect only instrumentals?" asked Patricia as Betsy stopped by.

"I collect everything," said Betsy, "but I left only instrumentals out tonight, because singing competes with conversation. If you've got to have music with words, go into the back bedroom and boot up the computer; it has a CD player in it, and I put my other CDs in there."

To Betsy's surprise, Patricia went, taking another woman with her. Betsy thereafter checked the back bedroom twice. She didn't want them to get isolated, nor did she want anything messy or scandalous to happen. No fear; the first time she found four music lovers singing "Bar-Barbara Ann" along with the Beach Boys; the second time she found Jamison, retired railroad engineer Phil Galvin, and Alice Skoglund, who was a Lutheran minister's widow, looking through the book on Christian symbology.

They certainly are a moral bunch here in Excelsior, Betsy thought, remembering a couple of faculty parties from her old life in San Diego.

The doorbell rang. Had someone gone for a smoke and locked himself out? The apartment was too crowded to see if anyone was missing. She shrugged and pressed the buzzer that unlocked the door—there wasn't an intercom to ask who was there.

She opened her door to see who would come up the stairs. Her eyes widened. A handsome face appeared, tanned and smooth-shaven, with dark brown eyes, a square jaw with a cleft chin, and a mouth just begging for a pipe. It was topped with a smooth sheaf of nearly white hair with a dramatic dark streak near one temple. The head sat on broad, square shoulders, atop a torso that looked, even covered by a trench coat, to be toned and fit. The whole rode on slim, long legs.

The face looked sideways at Betsy and assumed an abashed air, a handsome comic caught with his hand in a cookie jar.

It was Hal Norman, Hal the Pig, Betsy's ex. The one who was ratted on by a college freshman after he dumped her too abruptly for another college freshman. Which turned out to have been a pattern of behavior dating back God knew how many freshmen, and all while married to Betsy. "H'lo, Betsy darlin'," he said. "I've come back to you."

"I—I *beg* your pardon?!?" said Betsy.

Hal began to chuckle. He bounced up the last few steps and strode quickly to her. He was smiling, which made his dimples extra deep. "No joke, darlin', it's *so* good to see you!" He would have taken her in his arms had she not stepped back inside. When she tried to close the door, he put a hand on it.

"Hey, what's the matter? Please, won't you listen for just one minute?" His voice was surprised and hurt, which amazed her.

"Who is it?" asked Jill, coming up behind her.

"It's my ex-husband."

"The one you left in California?"

"I thought I had."

"What does he want?"

"I don't know."

Hal's voice asked plaintively, "You mean you're going to leave me standing out here till the mice get round-shouldered?"

"What'd he say?" asked Jill.

"It's an old joke," said Betsy, then added to Hal, "Until they are positively hunchbacked."

"But, darlin', I don't have anyplace to stay!"

That surprised Betsy so much, she released her pressure on the door, which he promptly pushed open. She said, "You mean you actually thought you could just come here and I'd let you in? And let you stay *overnight?*"

"But why not? I drove all the way from California just to see you."

"That's too bad." Betsy started to close the door again, but he put his hand on it again.

He said in a humble tone, "You're right. I shouldn't have presumed anything. I should have stopped at a motel and phoned you. But darlin', the closer I got, the more I got to thinking about what it would be like to actually see you again, talk to you face-to-face, and I just couldn't put it off another minute. Say, what's the noise? Have you got company? That should make it all right for me to come in and use your phone, shouldn't it? I need to find a motel."

"No, you can't come in. I'm having a Christmas party for my employees and some friends."

"Really? Why, say, I'd love to meet them. I understand they were a real help to you when Margot died. I'm *so* sorry about Margot, by the way. I wish I could have been here to support you through that awful time—"

The idea of Hal here during those early weeks, making himself at home in this place, helping her with the funeral—Betsy heard herself make an odd sound and heard an inquiring noise behind her. She glanced back.

Jill, reading the look on Betsy's face, immediately stepped forward to say over Betsy's shoulder, with that wonderful authority cops can summon, "There's a motel back out on the highway. You can't miss it." And she gave the door a hard shove to shut it.

Betsy said, "Thank you! I think I was about to barf on his shoes."

Jill smiled. "That message might have penetrated."

Betsy laughed. "I can't imagine his turning up here. I wonder what he really wants?"

Jill said, "Have you told anyone in San Diego about the money?"

"Oh, the money! Of course!" Betsy's sister had turned out to be wealthy. In another month or so, when probate was finished, Betsy would be an heiress. "Yes, I told three friends. I wonder who let me down and told him."

"I suppose he lost his job at the college?"

Betsy nodded. "Despite his tenure, yes, and it got into the papers, so he won't find another teaching job anytime soon. Our house was supplied by the college, so we lost that, too."

"I'm sure that if one of your friends saw him flipping burgers somewhere, they thought they were doing you a favor by letting him know his loss was even greater than he thought."

"So here he comes, playing penitent, hoping he can worm his way back into my life!"

"Worm being the operative word here," said Jill. "Is he from California originally?"

"Yes, born in Redondo Beach."

"Then he'll probably take the next bus home. Native Californians don't transplant well to climates like this."

But Betsy, as she returned to the party, wondered. Three million dollars was an excellent incentive to learn to like snow.

4

Betsy woke with a dry mouth and a headache. She opened her eyes and immediately closed them again. The bedroom was flooded with painfully bright sunlight. Why was that wrong?

Because she'd been waking to darkness lately, hadn't she? It was December in the northlands, and on workdays she awoke before dawn. Was this not a workday? Or had the clock radio not gone off? Or had it come on and she'd shut it off and fallen back asleep again?

Last night—there had been a party here last night—*that's* why she had a headache. And the party was Saturday night, so this must be Sunday. The radio hadn't come on because this was Sunday, which was lovely because even late as it surely was, she wasn't ready to get up just yet. In fact, she could feel herself drifting back to sleep again.

The mattress joggled as about eighteen pounds landed on it.

Sophie, aware by the change in her breathing that Betsy was awake, had jumped on the bed. Betsy tried to feign the deep breathing of sleep. Another fifteen seconds and it wouldn't be fake.

Too slow. There was the imperious tap of a cat's paw on her shoulder.

"Go 'way," muttered Betsy.

But this further sign of consciousness only encouraged the cat. "Reeeewwwwww," she whined, her mouth close to Betsy's hypersensitive ear. Betsy flinched and pulled the covers over her head. The cat tapped again. And again. Her normal breakfast time was long past, and she was probably genuinely hungry.

Betsy groaned—softly, softly!—and began a careful struggle to free her legs from the tangled blanket and sheet. Sophie immediately jumped off the bed and hustled toward the kitchen, where the cat food lived.

Betsy was sure that somewhere deep in the cat's soul Sophie knew she was not starving nor in danger of starving. But probably she was equally certain that this was because of her own unending efforts to keep her mistress aware that The Cat Must Be Fed.

Betsy had been running a campaign of her own to Make the Cat Wait, but so far it was a series of strategic retreats. Sophie cleverly—her laziness apparently did not include her brain—didn't approach each target directly but went for the target beyond and accepted as compromise the one she was after.

Back when Betsy fed the cat *after* she got dressed, Sophie began nagging for food before Betsy got into the shower. Betsy compromised by feeding Sophie after she showered but *before* she got dressed. Now Sophie was trying to maneuver breakfast time up to right after that first and most necessary trip to the bathroom. And Betsy had actually been contemplating feeding her before she showered. Today the cat had crossed another line: waking Betsy up. Never before had Sophie ventured to wake Betsy. She'd always waited until Betsy woke up either by herself or to the music of the clock radio. And she normally included an interval of cuddling. Not today; today The Cat Must Be Fed *Now*.

Well, no more compromising; if Betsy wanted to sleep in on Sundays, she was going to have to hold the line at feeding the cat after her morning shower.

Betsy looked at her puffy morning-after face in the bathroom mirror and smiled. The Pig had come and been sent away empty-handed. It was great how Jill had backed her up, literally slamming the door in his face. Imagine his turning up here like that, thinking he would be welcome! When it came to nerve, the Pig took the cake.

The party last night had been good, Betsy thought as she brushed her teeth. Most of the guests had departed at a respectable eleven, but a final six remained. They, with Betsy, had settled into a discussion of modern culture (what was lacking and how to fix it) that went on until nearly three A.M. Joe Mickels was proven not to be the Fascist everyone thought, and the straitlaced Patricia had unbent so far as to be amused by Godwin, who had sent John home alone when he hinted for the fifth time he was bored. Alice Skoglund told the joke about the bishop on roller skates, which set off a sidebar on religion that for a wonder actually shed more light than heat. Betsy had opened another two bottles of wine, and after her third glass had given a lecture on college faculty politics. Perhaps after the Pig's brief appearance, that was to be expected. Her guests bore it patiently, and even offered cordial thanks for a good time when at last they'd gone home.

Betsy took a quick shower, then went to give Sophie her breakfast of diet cat food. She put the kettle on.

Half an hour later, she was eating dry toast, sipping a second cup of green tea, and thinking of tackling the Sunday Crossword of the *New York Times Online*. It was a little after eleven, and Betsy was still in her striped flannel robe. The phone rang.

"Hello?" she said into the receiver.

"Hello, darlin'," said a deep, warm, oh-so-familiar voice.

"Calling to say you've got to stay on campus for another staff meeting?" said Betsy.

"Now, hon," protested the voice, but Betsy hung up so she wouldn't have to listen to the rest.

"He's still in town, you know," said Godwin on Monday morning.

"Who?" asked Betsy, checking the sky out the front window. It was gloomy, and the forecast was for snow, but so far it had held off. Perhaps the flakes would hover in the clouds until the weather system moved over to Wisconsin.

"Hal Norman, your husband."

"He is not my husband." Betsy came back to the library table and sat down.

"He's telling people he has reason to hope for a reconciliation." Godwin's tone put a twist on the words, hinting he thought this wasn't going to happen but leaving a little wriggle room because the ways of love are passing strange.

"He needs a reality check," said Betsy, picking up the hippopotamus ornament she was working on. She'd made a mistake twenty stitches back. She'd seen it half a dozen stitches ago. Realizing it wasn't an important mistake, she'd tried to ignore it; but it kept mocking her until she couldn't bear it. Frogging, it was called, when you took stitches out. She said, "No, he should fall off that pink cloud of fantasy he's been riding and break his neck."

"I see," said Godwin. "You want to know who he's talking to?"

"No," said Betsy, her needle going rip-it, rip-it. But Excelsior was a gossipy little town. Pretty soon people would be dropping by and making remarks, so perhaps it was better to be forearmed. "Okay, who?" she said.

"Irene Potter," began Godwin, but Betsy interrupted him with a groan. Of all the gossips, Irene was probably the worst. She was a fanatical needleworker, fabulously talented, but passing strange, on her way to totally weird. Perhaps because she had no social skills, she was endlessly interested in what people said and did and loved speculating aloud what their motives might be. More than anything in the world, she wanted her own needlework shop and suspected darkly that Betsy kept Crewel World open mostly to keep Irene from taking it over and running it as it should be run. Her speculations about Hal and Betsy, therefore, would not be kind.

"Who else?" asked Betsy, pinching the bridge of her nose between her thumb and forefinger, trying toward off a headache.

"I understand he bought Patricia Fairland a cup of coffee at the Waterfront Café and talked to her for about ten minutes. Left her doing that thing women do with the back of their hair. He is rather good-looking."

"Looks aren't everything," said Betsy, the voice of experience.

"But they open a lot of doors," Godwin said, the voice of his own experience. Betsy nodded. Godwin was so handsome he was almost pretty. "He talked real estate with Joe Mickels," Godwin continued—real estate was one topic on which Joe was always willing to converse— "oh, and at church yesterday morning, he expressed surprise and disappointment that you weren't there."

Betsy groaned again. "*What* am I going to do about him?"

"Nothing," said Godwin. "People are already speculating. Some think he's here because he heard about your money, others that the father of one of the coeds he seduced has a contract out on him."

Betsy giggled and Godwin smiled. "Well, it's Irene who offered that one. If you really have to do something, sic Jill on him, why don't you? She could find an excuse to shoot him, maybe."

Betsy said, "No. I've read about what shooting a person does to the shooter."

"Not to mention the *shot,*" said Godwin, surprised.

"I'm serious," said Betsy. "I have a friend in San Diego, her name is Abbey, and she has a friend who is married to a cop, and he shot some teenage thug who was holding up a bank. He got a medal for valor, but he was suicidal for years afterward. So don't even joke about doing that to Jill."

"All right," said Godwin.

A customer came in looking for a needlepoint project and expressed disappointment that they hadn't marked down the Christmas stockings, now that Christmas was almost here.

"There's no need to mark them down," said Godwin. "Many customers give them as gift kits. And besides, it can take as long as *two years* to finish a project like this, so it isn't exactly a seasonal thing." He looked around as if to check for eavesdroppers and winked at Betsy with an eye the customer couldn't see—and then at the customer with the other eye. "However," he murmured, "we *may* be able to give you a special price on the wool or silk you select for the project, or on one of our scheduled classes on needlepoint. I *think* there's an opening in the one I'll be teaching, the one that starts the middle of January."

"Well," hedged the customer, "I always did want to learn beading, and Emily told me you do wonderful beadwork."

"I hope you will consider it. I was very impressed

with that sampler you worked. You do a beautiful mosaic stitch. In another year, you'll be teaching your own class for us. Just let me get the schedule."

Her brunette and his blond heads were soon bent over the calendar on the checkout desk, and then she was writing a check.

After the woman left, Betsy got out her employee list and their schedule of hours and tried to find ways to reduce them. But she had gotten to know her part-timers. Several spent the greater part of their wages on needlework projects—a saving to the shop all by itself, even considering the employee discount. The one young woman Betsy felt she could most easily spare was newly separated from her husband and desperately needed the little Betsy was able to pay her.

"I don't want to cut any of these people," said Betsy.

"Well, what else can you cut?"

"I don't know. Maybe I can cancel my medical insurance. Crewel World pays for it, and it's very expensive."

"Don't do that," advised Godwin. "The goblins of fate are just waiting to pounce on people who cancel insurance policies."

"Well then, what does Hollytree expect me to do?" she grumbled, throwing her pencil down. It bounced on its eraser and barely missed Godwin's ear on its way into a basket of fuschia wool.

The phone rang. Godwin was retrieving the pencil, so Betsy answered it. "Crewel World, good morning, may I help you?"

"Hello, Betsy, it's John Penberthy. How are you today?"

Penberthy was Betsy's attorney, a young man of great ability with an office on Water Street.

"Except for being in danger of going broke, I'm fine, thank you. What's up?"

"This may cheer you up. I've got some more figures for you on the estate. Thanks to a healthy stock market, it looks as if the final numbers will be closer to three million than two and a half. The first million is now exempt from inheritance taxes, but the rest will be taxed at forty percent."

"Forty percent, huh?" Was that good or bad? Betsy hadn't earned the inheritance, but neither had the government.

"It also appears that certificates of deposit, money market accounts, and other assets are generating between twenty-five hundred and three thousand dollars a month, which Margot was using as income. I assume you will want to continue that, and meanwhile, the money is being put into an interest-bearing account. Not a very high interest, I'm afraid, as I'm sure you will want it to be accessible as soon as the estate is closed."

So that was how Margot kept the shop in the black, by not paying herself a salary. "Yes, please," said Betsy, stifling an impulse to shout, "How soon can I put my hands on that money?" Instead she said, "I got your last letter, where you put in writing what you told me about the stocks and bonds, and I thank you. I'm getting better at this, but I'm afraid I don't understand what you said about a silent partnership Margot was in. I can't find any record of it at the courthouse. I wondered if perhaps you were acting as her representative so her name wouldn't appear."

"Oh, no, I couldn't represent her in that way. Why don't you stop by my office today or tomorrow, and I'll show you the file? You may find it amusing."

"Is it a lot of money?" asked Betsy.

"It's an irregular income, and right now there's not much action. But it is going to pay off majorly in short order."

"What is it, interest in a gambling casino?"

Penberthy laughed, but he only insisted Betsy should be looking at the file while he explained. "If I may make one more suggestion?"

"Of course."

"I think you should consider making a will. You said there are no relatives, so it would be a shame if you died without one and the government got everything, after the time and effort we've spent keeping them from taking most of it. Name a favorite charity or give some friends a happy surprise. I will, of course, be very pleased to talk to you about it when you are ready."

"All right," said Betsy. "I'll think about it." She hung up.

After she settled back into her project, Betsy said to Godwin, "It's different when you really become rich. I mean, instead of daydreaming about it. In the dream you get huge checks every week, which you cash and spend. In the real world, there are IRAs and investment properties and nonexempt bonds and taxes. I'm just grateful I have Mr. Penberthy to help me through it all."

"Well, I'm sure he'll be equally glad to hand you a substantial bill when you start getting those huge checks," said Godwin. "And may I add just one little point of my very own? Connect the fact that you're an heiress to the money problems you are having with Crewel World. Probate's about finished, isn't it? You could have stopped paying some of your bills last month, you know. Because well before your distributor refuses to ship any more DMC cotton floss to this address, you could *buy* that distributor and fire his smelly old credit manager."

Betsy smiled. "I would love to believe that," she said.

"Believe it," said Godwin. "About money, I am always right."

•   •   •

Toward one, June Connor came in, her shoulders covered with snow. It had started in around noon, falling in thick, heavy flakes.

June was an attractive young woman who did wonderful counted cross stitch. "Whew!" she laughed, pulling off a knitted cap and reopening the door just enough to shake it off outside. "It's coming down out there! How are you, Betsy?"

"Fine, Mrs. Connor. How are Steven and David?"

"Very well, thank you. Impatient for Christmas to arrive, of course."

"I bet I know what brought you out in this," said Godwin with a smile. "I warned you to buy six hanks of that wool, not five."

June laughed. "No, five was enough. Barely, but enough. I came to pick up my angel—you know, the one that was being finished as a pillow."

Betsy had a sudden sinking sensation. She'd gone through the box several times to find finished projects for other customers and didn't remember seeing June's wonderful angel pillow.

On the other hand, she remembered writing up the order and packing it for the finisher, so perhaps she'd just overlooked it.

But while June's name was on the list, the pillow wasn't in the box.

When she saw the dismay on June's face, she picked up the phone and dialed the finisher's phone number. "Hello, Heidi? Betsy Devonshire at Crewel World. Fine, thank you. But we have a problem. A pillow with an angel on it, a big one, counted cross stitch—yes, the Mirabilia. You do? Oh, no! Well, can you—Oh, I see. All right, I'll call you back."

"What?" asked June.

"It's finished, and it's fine," said Betsy, to June's relief, "but it's still there. She overlooked it when she packed our other finished projects. And she says she can't bring it in until late tomorrow, she's swamped trying to finish other last-minute projects."

"But we're leaving for Florida at noon tomorrow!" wailed June. "And that pillow is a gift for my mother-in-law!"

June was a very loyal customer who spent a lot of money in Crewel World. Betsy, feeling she could ill afford to lose a good customer, said impulsively, "I'll go get it today. I mean, when the shop closes, of course. It's not that far to Heidi's place."

June said doubtfully, "It's coming down kind of hard."

"*You* drove in it to come here and pick the pillow up," Betsy pointed out. "Besides, I heard it's supposed to stop in another hour or two. You can pick it up in the morning on your way to the airport."

"Well . . . thank you, Betsy."

But the forecast changed an hour later. The front had stalled, the snow wouldn't stop now until early evening. The wind was picking up, making driving hazardous.

Godwin said, "I think you shouldn't go, Betsy."

Betsy said, "Hey, I grew up in Wisconsin. I learned to drive on ice and snow! And I've been doing fine so far."

But the Monday Bunch was more alarmed than June or Godwin.

"Betsy, it's really very bad out there," said Alice. "Already the plows aren't able to keep up, and the radio is saying road travel is not recommended."

Betsy looked out the window. In the gap she had cut in the snow lining the sidewalk, she could see cars passing by. "No one is staying home yet."

"They're not driving out in the country on winding roads in the dark," Martha Winters pointed out.

"And the roads around here can be very confusing to an inexperienced driver," added Patricia.

"Now just a goldanged minute," said Betsy. "I've been driving for nearly forty years! Heidi lives less than five miles from here. Besides, it's for June Connor, and she has spent hundreds of dollars in the shop in just the past three months. The pillow is for her mother-in-law." There was a little silence as the women thought about daughters-in-law who came to Christmas gatherings with presents for everyone but their mothers-in-law.

"Well . . ." conceded Martha, and the talk moved on to the latest patterns in *Cross Stitch and Needlework* magazine.

Godwin asked Patricia, "Have you ever bought a counted cross stitch pattern on eBay?"

"Yes, why?"

"I saw a doll house rug kit on there I really liked. And the bidding wasn't very active. Is it a good place to shop?"

Alice asked, "Where's eBay?"

"On the Internet," said Betsy. "It's like an auction house that handles just about anything you can imagine. I've looked at some things but haven't ever bid because I've heard you can get stung."

Patricia said, "I've never bought needlework items there, but I have bought antiques. I never bid on anything unless there's a picture. Do you use a computer, Martha?"

"No, I'm too old for a computer. Jeff has one." Jeff was her adult grandson, her partner in the dry cleaning business.

"Nobody's too old!" said Godwin. "I know several people who share AOL accounts with their mothers so they can stay in touch. They send pictures of the grandchildren and the grandmothers send pictures of themselves and their new husbands honeymooning in Hawaii.

It's not hard to learn. I'd be glad to show you, or you, Alice."

Alice, her large face reddening, blurted, "Oh, I couldn't afford a computer," which might have caused an embarrassed silence except she went on, "Betsy, could I see some of that new floss, the kind that's a blend of silk and wool?"

Betsy said, "Of course," and brought a skein to the table. The Bunch, incorrigible fiber fondlers, handed it around and agreed the texture was marvelous. Neither computers nor the subject of Betsy driving in the snow was mentioned again.

After the Monday Bunch left, Betsy said, "Are you going to put a bid in for that rug kit?"

"Yes, but I probably won't get it. Too many things go for more than they're worth on eBay. I wouldn't even bid, except I can't seem to find it anywhere else."

"Godwin, what do you think about Patricia?"

"I like her, but I wouldn't get between her and something she wants. Why?"

"Well, I was thinking about when I get my money. I wonder if it would be a worthwhile project to buy used computers for people who can't afford them. Alice, for example. She's a lonely person, and the Internet can be a godsend for the lonesome. Patricia has lived here all her life, and she's active in her church, and I wonder if perhaps she knows other people who might benefit from a computer. But she's not the sort I'm comfortable working with, she has that kind of rich person's veneer that seems . . . I don't know, impermeable, impenetrable. Do rich people send their children to special schools to learn that attitude?"

"Well, yes. On the other hand, Patricia didn't go to one. I think she tried to marry rich, but her in-laws didn't approve of her. They thought their son was too young to marry and that Patricia didn't have the right background, so they cut him off, refused to help out, even when Patricia got pregnant before their son finished law school. Now his grandmother dotes on the boy she wouldn't acknowledge."

Betsy tilted her head. "Is any of this true, or is it just the usual Excelsior gossip?"

Godwin laughed. "It's true, really it is. Patricia used to talk about it, until her husband got into politics. Now you'll never hear a bad word about her mother-in-law. Not that it was ever all that bad, I guess. I think Patricia was just tired from the constant struggle, and Margot was a sympathetic ear—and I'm a gifted eavesdropper."

"I guess a really hard struggle can give you that veneer, too," said Betsy, feeling much more sympathetic toward Patricia and trying to put a good face on her own remarks.

A little after five, just as Betsy was locking the front door, Jill appeared, large and dark, on the other side of the glass. She was in uniform and carrying a big box wrapped in midnight blue paper with silver and gold stars on it.

"Betsy, the weatherman says the storm system is still stalled and there's a blizzard warning out from here to Fargo."

"So? I'm not driving to Fargo. Who's the present for?"

"You. It's your Christmas present," Jill said.

"Oh. Thank you," said Betsy, ashamed for the second time that day of her sharp tongue. Jill put it into her arms and Betsy was surprised at how heavy it was. She hadn't bought Jill anything remotely this substantial. "I'll take it upstairs."

"No, take it with you. It's a bunch of little things. If you skid off the road, you can open them up to keep from being bored waiting for rescue. Now I've got to get back on patrol. Good luck, and drive very carefully."

"I will. And thank you for the present." Betsy had to go upstairs to feed Sophie, who was already sitting impatiently by the apartment door, but decided it was less effort to carry the heavy box to her car than up the stairs. She took it out back to put it on the passenger seat.

Up in the apartment, she checked the map one last time, put on her heavy coat, her new leather boots, her hat and scarf, and, pulling on her driving gloves, went down the back hallway and out into the storm.

Her big mistake was probably at that first turn. She knew Route 19 turned sharply to the right, but since she was looking for a curve rather than an intersection, she went right on through.

She noticed soon after that her brakes seemed soft, but they went quickly from soft to virtually nonexistent. She had to shift down to control her speed on curves.

It was totally dark, of course, and the snow was coming down heavily, so she had to weave a bit, using her headlights to make sure she was on her own side of the road. The road's surface was a white blank, and slippery. And the bridge the map had indicated just before the turn to Heidi's house never came. This was wrong. She was lost.

Betsy was not the sort who wouldn't stop and ask for directions, but now, ready to do so, there didn't seem to be anyplace to stop and ask. When trees didn't closely line the road, she could see nothing but thick snow, blowing directly into her windshield. But surely, if there were a gas station or some other kind of store, its lights would pierce the storm. Betsy saw nothing.

After awhile, she looked at her watch. She'd been out for forty minutes, which was supposed to be the entire time of her journey. She decided to stop at a private residence if she could see one, and find out where she was. But she wasn't afraid, she told herself, only a little nervous and concerned.

She began to realize she hadn't seen another car in some while. She couldn't even see any trace of previous vehicles on the road.

She tried to think what to do. Lake Minnetonka dominated the terrain around here. It was a large lake, with an extremely wobbly outline. Some said it was a collection of bays, others said it was actually seven lakes and a couple of creeks. In either case, that meant a thousand miles of shoreline. And by now, she had no idea which part of the shore she was on.

A curve ambushed her, and as she went into it, the wind came sideways, pushing at her car like a huge, soft hand. Her brakes were useless, but she wasn't going fast, so the car spun gently. Betsy could only hold onto the steering wheel, watching the play of headlights on a whirl of white snowflakes. Then the world went upward to the left and there was a twisty, bumpy slide, then she slammed to a stop, tipped at an angle to the right.

Betsy sat still for a few seconds, trembling. Her engine was still running, no warning lights had come on, her headlights remained lit. She didn't feel any sharp pains anywhere. She was all right, everything was all right.

After a bit, she looked out the side window. She was against a pine tree. She could see the bark and branches pressed against the glass, which wasn't broken. To the rear was blackness. Forward was driving snow, piling up on the windshield even as she looked. Her wipers leaped up, smearing the view. The instant they settled back, snow piled on again. To her left was a steep slope upward, dim and lumpish and scrawled with the marks of her passage.

The road was up there, on top of that slope.

She put the car into first gear and tried to move forward, but the wheels spun. She shifted into reverse, lifted the clutch gently, and again the wheels spun. She could see nothing out her rear mirror, not even a reflection of her taillights on the blowing snow. She shifted back into first. The car moved a few inches, tires spinning. The bark of the pine tree groaned against the door. She backed up, then rocked forward again, pleased to find an old skill still existed. She put it in reverse, and lifted the clutch. There was resistance, then suddenly the car bounced hard over something and slid around the tree, tilting more obviously backward. That scared her, and she jammed on the brake pedal, forgetting it was useless. The clutch slid out from under her other foot, and the engine died.

She started it up again, but the car ran only briefly before choking and stammering. She twisted the wheel, pumping the gas pedal, then the stink of raw gasoline filled the car and instantly she turned the ignition off.

I'm okay, I'm still okay, she reassured herself.

She left the headlights on, set the emergency brake, and found a flashlight in the glove box. It had been a while since she'd needed it, and she was unhappy to discover the batteries were half dead. She opened the door just an inch. The gasoline smell was stronger outside, and snow came in with a rush, driven by the wind.

The tilt of the car combined with the push of the wind to make getting out a serious effort.

She tried to walk around the car. An old fallen tree blocked her way to the back, stubs of branches poking up through the snow. That's what she'd backed over, and apparently something sticking up had punctured her gas tank. The car's back end was buried in a sprawling evergreen bush, and the shaggy-barked pine tree was a big old monarch. She turned around and went back, looking for the skid marks she'd made coming down the slope. She found them and followed them upward, slipping and falling, until suddenly she was on the road. She turned and looked down at her car.

All she could see was a light twinkling behind curtains of whirling snow.

Betsy trudged up the road for five minutes, the dying flashlight not much help. She hadn't changed out of her work clothes before setting out for Heidi's place, and the powerful wind whipped under both her heavy coat and her box-pleated woolen skirt, chilling her halfway up her thighs. When she stopped and turned off the flashlight, she didn't see the lights of a store, a house, or a barn anywhere.

Then she turned around, and she couldn't see her headlights, either. Alarmed, she started back. The wind was strong, shoving and tugging at her as she walked. Staggering onto the slope was her only warning that she was not keeping to the road. This happened three times, and by then she was wondering if she'd gone past her car. She stopped to peer all around. An extra strong gust of wind stung her face and she turned her back to it. And there were the headlights, gleaming fitfully from down the slope. As suddenly as they appeared, they were gone again in the yellow swirl her dying flashlight's beam made of the snow flying all around her.

But having found her direction, she looked for the skid marks—they were nearly drifted over—and half fell, half slid along them back down the slope, until she reached her car. After another struggle, she got the door open enough to get back in. There, she shut off the headlights and sat in gasoline-scented darkness to catch her breath.

Now she was scared.

5

"Hello, Godwin? It's Jill. Say, do you have Heidi Watgren's phone number?"

"I already called her. Betsy never arrived."

"Oh, heck."

"My very words, or nearly. I was hoping she got there and Heidi had the sense to make her stay."

"Me, too."

"Is it too soon to file a missing person report?"

"Ordinarily, yes. But this is different. I hope she has sense enough to open that box."

Betsy's stumble back down the slope had warmed her up but left her caked with snow. She had knocked the worst of it off before getting back into the car, but her coat and skirt were now damp, even wet in places. And once she started cooling off, she kept cooling right into chilled.

The stink of gas wasn't as overpowering now. Maybe most of what had spilled had evaporated or run away downhill. Was there still some gas in the tank?

She turned the key to Utilities, then turned on the running lights to make the dash light up. The gas gauge indicated a little less than a quarter of a tank. She'd had close to half a tank when she started out, and she hadn't used that much driving.

And gasoline vapor was explosive. Maybe she shouldn't try to start the car. But she was freezing, and rescue seemed remote.

Take a chance, said a small but certain voice inside her head.

She unlatched the door in case she had to get out fast, took a deep breath, held it, and twisted the key in the ignition. The car cranked strongly, but the engine didn't catch. Nor did it catch on fire.

She released the key, exhaled. After a few moments, she took another breath and cranked again.

No joy.

There was gas in the tank, and the battery was working fine. Why wouldn't it start? She twisted the key angrily, pumping the gas pedal hard and fast. Still nothing.

She sat in silence for awhile, feeling a kind of weightiness, as if the snow was piling onto her head and shoulders instead of the roof and hood of her car. The gasoline stink was strong enough to make her feel lightheaded, so she cracked the window on the passenger side. What was the correct procedure when one was lost on a back road in a blizzard, with no stores, houses, or traffic, wearing a damp overcoat, sitting with the window open in a car that wouldn't start?

John heard a tiny noise of scrubbing and came to investigate. Godwin was doing what he usually did when he was frustrated: cleaning the bathrooms. John didn't like Betsy—she sometimes took Godwin seriously, and John liked him boyish—but here was his lighthearted boy so upset over the woman that he was scrubbing the grout on the floor with a toothbrush. John came in to lift him by the elbows and take the toothbrush away from him.

"Goddy, it's not like she's gone down the Colorado in a cabbage leaf. She's in a nice warm car somewhere, listening to the radio and missing her dinner, which she can well afford to do. She'll be found as soon as the snow stops and they start clearing the roads."

"I know, you're right. But I do wish she'd listened to me when I warned her about going out in the storm!"

John felt his usual reply to that complaint—"Why would anyone listen to a silly little goof like you?"— was inappropriate. Which later caused him to reflect that while his relationships tended to end when there were signs of maturity, he didn't want to end this one with Godwin. Interesting.

It had been a long time—not hours, though it seemed that long. The bones in Betsy's feet ached with cold, as did the tips of her fingers. She wished she'd brought mittens along. Each finger in its lonesome sleeve of the driving gloves yearned to snuggle against its fellow. Perhaps she should take the gloves off and put her hands in her pockets. Perhaps she should get into the backseat and huddle up under her coat, maybe go to sleep. She could escape this nightmare for a few hours and perhaps wake to daylight and the sounds of traffic.

No, wait, going to sleep in the cold was a very, very bad idea.

She began to move as violently as she could in her seat, stamping her feet and waving her arms. Her feet hurt when they hit the floor, but she persisted, and she felt the pain lessen. In a little while she was warmer. And the stirring of her blood made her thinking a little clearer.

Perhaps it would help if she took off her coat and

used it as a blanket. She could cover that little bare section of shin above her boots that way. Suddenly that seemed the most desirable thing in the world.

But trying to take off a full-length wool coat while seated behind a steering wheel of a car in the pitch dark is at best difficult. And the confusing lean of the car didn't help. During her efforts to get out of it, Betsy fell over sideways and knocked against the big Christmas gift Jill had given her. Suddenly a light went on over her head. There had been something significant in the tone of Jill's voice as she suggested Betsy bring it along, "to open if you slide off the road." She reined in the wild hope that rose in her breast, even as she decided the coat could wait and went through another struggle to get it settled back into place.

She turned on the overhead light and reached for the package. She'd forgotten how large and heavy it was; it took two tries before she got it pulled close to her.

The Christmas paper looked even more glorious in the dim light, though the bow was a little crushed. Betsy took a deep breath and then rapidly dismantled the wrapping. The box inside was a sturdy grocery store refugee printed with a soup maker's logo. With trembling fingers, Betsy pulled off the heavy gray tape holding it shut.

The top item appeared to be thin aluminum foil folded into a square eight inches on a side. But it was almost as flexible as cloth, and it kept unfolding larger and larger, until it was as big as a sleeping bag. It was a space blanket; Betsy had seen them on television. They were supposed to keep people warm even in outer space. She arranged it around her shins and thighs and lap, turning it down at the top so her arms were free.

Already she was smiling. God bless Jill!

Under the space blanket was a very odd assortment of items: a bright-orange toy snow shovel with a folding handle; a pair of empty coffee cans in two sizes; a very large chocolate bar; a can of salted cashews, two bottles of designer water, a box of wooden matches; a heavy flashlight with batteries already in it; a couple of votive candles; heavy, rough-leather mittens made of sheepskin turned inside out and stuffed inside a thick knit wool hat; a ten-pound bag of kitty litter; and, still in its box, a cell phone. Under the cell phone was a note in Jill's neat printing.

Dear Betsy, I hope you are opening this in front of your Christmas tree! This is a Winter Survival Kit. Keep it in your trunk all winter and if you don't use it, eat the treats for Easter and replace them next fall. If you get stuck in the snow, dig a path with the shovel and lay down the cat litter for traction. If you still can't get out, dial 911 on the phone. (It won't activate until you use it, so it won't cost you anything if you're not having an emergency. Clever?) Tell the operator where you are, and someone will come and get you. While you are waiting: Stay with the car! Run your engine five or ten minutes every half hour to get warm, then shut it off to save gas. Get out every time you start it and clear away the tailpipe so you don't fill up with carbon monoxide. No matter what, stay with the car. Even if you run out of gas and are stuck in a place where the phone doesn't work, stay with the car. Light a candle in the smaller can. It will provide light and a small amount of heat. If you run out of water, put snow in the bigger can and melt it over the smaller one. Wrap up in the space blanket. Think cheerful thoughts. Eat, drink, and be merry. Rescue will come before you know it. Jill

Betsy's eyes stung with tears. Jill knew what a fool Betsy was; she knew Betsy hadn't been giving this weather the respect it deserved. Betsy should have listened to her, listened to all of them warning her not to go out.

At the very least, Betsy should have put together her own winter survival kit. There had been an article about it in the paper weeks ago.

If she'd made up her own survival kit, then at least the candy bar would have almonds in it.

She smiled at this thin joke. It was the cellular phone, of course, renewing her courage. The worst that could happen now was that she'd have a whacking great towing bill. And so long as he was whacking at her wallet, maybe she could persuade the tow truck operator to make a little detour to Heidi's place to pick up that damn pillow. Betsy snorted and shook her head. Amazing! She'd gone from being afraid she was going to die to being concerned about June Connor's Christmas.

She wondered what the charge was for cellular phone service. And wait, it was possible that her car had mushed against that tree hard enough to be dented. If so, that might generate the biggest bill of all, because Betsy had a $500 deductible on her car insurance.

She tossed the shovel and kitty litter into the backseat; that solution was out. And with the smell of gas still permeating the inside of the car, she'd better not strike a match.

The directions pamphlet for the cell phone seemed daunting until Betsy realized it was printed in five languages. In short order she had the phone plugged into her cigarette lighter and was dialing, first a number to activate it, then 911, and pushing the send button.

Ring, ring, ring, ring, ring. "Nine one one, what is your emergency?" said a woman's voice.

"I've had an accident with my car. I slid off the road into a tree, and now I'm stuck."

"Are there any injured parties?"

"No. And I'm alone in the car."

"Is there another vehicle involved?"

"No."

"Where are you?"

"Don't you have one of those ID things that tells where the call is coming from?"

"All it says is that this is a cell phone."

Uh-oh. "Ah, I don't know where I am. I started out from Excelsior on Nineteen for an address in Shorewood. Let's see, I was driving for about forty minutes, and I made three or four turns. But that's not very helpful, is it?"

"No, ma'am. Can you see any landmarks?"

"No. In fact, I could barely see the road. I didn't see any lights, either, or I would have stopped to ask my way, even at a house. This may be a back road. There hasn't been any traffic for a long time, since before I skidded off it. I slid down a little slope, and I'm jammed against a big pine tree. I've been sitting here for a long time."

"Have you tried to drive out?"

"My engine won't start." Betsy had to stop at this point and swallow hard. "And, and there's a smell of gasoline, I guess I tore or punctured my gas tank. I have a winter emergency kit with me, with a space blanket and a candy bar and candles, so I'm all right for now, except I can't run my engine, and I'm scared to light the candles, and I'm getting really, really cold." Tears spilled over despite her best effort. "I'm sorry, I'm really, really sorry." Sorry for being an idiot, sorry for breaking down, sorry her last words might be to a stranger on the phone.

"Hang on, honey, you're going to be all right, we'll figure out a way to find you and get you out of there."

Betsy sniffed. "Yes, of course you will. I'm just a little scared."

"Sweetie, anyone in your situation would be scared! Now, you say you started out on Route Nineteen. When did you turn off it?"

"I didn't think I did, but I must have. The map said the road would go left so I did, except after that nothing matched the map."

"Do you have the map with you?"

"No. It was just a short trip, to pick up a pillow for someone. I never thought I'd get lost."

"I'm going to go have a talk with some people about this, so you need to hang up and be patient. I won't be long."

"All right. Oh, can you do me a favor?"

"What's that?"

"Could you notify Officer Jill Cross of the Excelsior Police Department about what's happened? She's a friend, and she'll want to be part of the rescue operation."

"Aren't you Jill Cross? That's who my phone ID says you are."

"No, she gave me this phone for emergencies. I guess she was willing to pay the first month's rent on it, bless her. My name is Betsy Devonshire."

"Oh, you're the woman who took over that needlework shop in Excelsior! I've been meaning to stop by."

"If you come by tomorrow, I'll give you a terrific buy on any item you want."

The operator said, "It's a date. Now, if I don't call you back inside of fifteen minutes, you call nine one one again and ask for me. I'm Meg Dooley."

Betsy broke the connection, turned out the overhead light, and sat for a bit in total darkness. Then it occurred to her to consult her watch in order to begin timing fifteen minutes. She pressed the button on the side of its face and it glowed its beautiful aqua color. Only seven past seven. It seemed much later than that.

The watch's face glowed a surprisingly long time after she released the button, but at last it faded to black. She sat with the phone cradled in both hands, waiting for it to ring again.

Jill called Godwin and told him what the emergency operator had told her. She told him she was going to the police station and would call him from there.

"Anything I can do?" he asked.

"Pass the word, I guess. Because all we can do right now is wait. Thanks."

She hurried out to get her car out of its garage and bully her way through the snow-clogged driveway into the street. Though she'd been aware of the weather reports, she was nevertheless alarmed at the depth of the snow and the strength of the wind.

The streets were deserted, streetlights dimmed by the thickness of snow in the air. A plow had gone down Water Street, burying parked automobiles. Drifting snow smoothed their outlines until they looked like the ghost of that carnival ride called The Caterpillar.

Jill drove up Lake Street, past Crewel World, and saw that Betsy had left a light on in her apartment over the store.

Didn't think she'd be gone that long, thought Jill. She turned onto Excelsior Boulevard, whose high-tone name belied its narrow ordinariness, and went down it to the new brick-and-stone building that housed the police department.

Jill had been prepared to like Betsy for her sister Margot's sake—Margot had been Jill's best friend for years. But her present sharp concern made her realize she had come to like Betsy for herself, for her courage and tenacity, her sense of humor, her unpredictability. Jill was braver and more tenacious than Betsy, but she was not in the least unpredictable, so it was odd that she should like unpredictable people, but she did.

I'm not going to let Betsy die. She stifled that thought,

shaken that it had even occurred. She parked and hurried into the station. Of course Betsy was not going to die! What a stupid idea!

The cell phone rang, sudden and loud. Betsy, startled, flipped it onto the floor and had to scramble for it in the slush and dirt. By the time she got hold of it, it was ringing for the fourth time. She pushed the button. "Hello?" she said a trifle crossly.

"I told you not to go out on the road when it's snowing like this."

Betsy laughed. "Hi, Jill! From now on, your word is law. Are you the one coming to get me?"

"Maybe. But not right now. I'm sorry, Betsy, but we can't come looking for you because the roads are closed."

"Couldn't you send one of those big snowplows?"

"The plows are working exclusively on the freeways, trying to keep them passable for emergency vehicles. We could probably get one to come after you, if he knew where to come. But he can't just wander around, hoping he'll come across you."

There was a pause. Betsy said, "So what do we do?"

"Right now they say the storm won't move out of the area till morning. Once the storm quits, we'll turn out in strength looking for you. You'll be easy to find in daylight. Meanwhile, you just sit tight."

"Daylight? Jill, I can't sit here in the freezing dark all night!"

"Of course you can. You'll be fine, now that you opened that box I sent along."

"But—are you sure? I mean, all night? That's scary."

"Well, did you wrap up in that metallic blanket?"

"Yes. And it works. I was surprised, but it does."

"You didn't walk out on the ice and fall in the lake?"

"No, of course not."

"So you're not chilled from a soak in ice water. Is the car far off the road, or only on the shoulder?"

"I'm completely off the road."

"Good. That means you won't get squashed by accident when the plow does come through. Are you out of chocolate already?"

"No. I haven't started on it, actually."

"I think you should eat some of it now. Chocolate has lots of energy, to help keep you warm. And it has that stuff that makes you happy. What's it called?"

"I don't know. Phenyl-something."

"That's the stuff. So forget your diet and eat some. Eat a lot. You'll be warmer and you'll feel better."

"All right."

"Is the passenger compartment tight? I mean, is snow coming in, or the wind?"

"Well, you see, that's the problem. I ripped open the gas tank or something. I tried to start the engine, and it turns over but won't start, and there's a strong smell of gasoline. Does that mean it's okay to light a candle? The smell is so strong I've got a window cracked, trying to air it out."

"Hmmm, maybe you'd better not, at least right now. If the smell goes away, then you can."

"That's what I thought. But I'm cold. I'm really cold."

"All right, that makes a difference." There was a weighty pause, while Jill thought. "Have you got any idea at all where you are?"

"No. I got so lost toward the end I didn't even know what direction I was heading—and I usually have a pretty good sense of direction. I started out on Nineteen, but I missed something, I guess. Or maybe I didn't. I thought I was lost, and then I thought I was all right, but the road was curving wrong, so I guess I was lost after all. There were sharp curves where the map says easy ones, and my brakes quit working..." Betsy wasn't crying, but only because she had stopped talking.

Jill wasn't one to encourage people to break down. "That must have been tough," she said briskly. "How strong is that gasoline smell?"

"Well, it was pretty strong for a while, but I think it's not as bad as it was. Or maybe I'm just getting used to it. If I can't run the engine, how am I going to keep from freezing to death?"

"You're not going to freeze to death, okay? You're inside, you have a heavy coat and boots, and that blanket. You have water and something to eat. But you've got a window open and you're cold, which means you probably shouldn't curl up and go to sleep. I have an idea about how we might figure out at least your general location. You just sit back and relax, eat, drink, think good thoughts. I'll call you again in a while, okay?"

6

Godwin was sitting on the couch, asleep. The television was murmuring about cookware and flashing an 800 number on the screen. He jerked awake when the phone rang. "Yuh?" he croaked into the receiver, having grabbed it on the first ring so as not to wake John. "Yes?" he said, more clearly.

"Godwin, it's Jill. I have the phone company trying to triangulate from the car phone signal to figure out where Betsy is, but it's taking awhile. Last time I talked to her, she sounded a little sleepy. I may get called in, so I'm forming a committee to take turns calling her. Want to come?"

"Sure. Where?"

"How about we meet at Crewel World? Will you go down now and open up?"

"I'm on my way." Godwin broke the connection and stood up. He hadn't undressed; all he had to do was add a few layers.

· · ·

Patricia Fairland was struggling with a bad dream. Her husband murmured "Pat?" reaching over to touch her shoulder and wake her.

"What, what? Oh, sorry, bad dream," she whispered. "Thanks, 'm okay now." She lay still until he went back to sleep, which didn't take long.

But she didn't want to reenter that dream again, so she slipped out of bed and went to the window. She lifted the heavy drape at its edge and looked into chaos. The line between air and ground had vanished into flying snow. She could see two blobs of blue-white light that were the miniature streetlights marking the gate to the pool, barely a dozen yards from the window. The lights didn't seem to have any stems, which meant the snow was drifted four feet deep right there. The big old elm beside the pool was waving its huge branches as if this were a hurricane, not a blizzard.

Nothing out in that can live, she thought, shivering. She dropped the curtain and turned her back to it. She felt a painful gratitude for the thick carpet under her bare feet, the almost inaudible hum of the furnace as it heated the beautiful house and her and the children safe asleep and her husband in the big, luxurious bed. It had been a long, hard struggle. The last hurdle had been Peter's mother, but her signal of acceptance had been buying this house as a very belated wedding gift last year.

The phone rang softly—its bell was turned all but off and could not wake people already asleep. But Patricia hurried to it anyway and lifted the receiver. "Hello?" she murmured.

"Patricia, it's Jill. We're meeting at Crewel World to help Betsy. Can you come?"

Patricia's heart leaped. It was all over town about Betsy; no less than four people had called her earlier in the evening with the news that Betsy was missing. "Has she been found?"

"Sort of. She's in a ditch out there somewhere, we don't know where, and her engine won't start. But she's got a cell phone and we're going to keep calling her. Temperatures are dropping, and we don't want her to fall asleep."

"Yes, of course. Oh, this is awful, she must be terrified! But I don't think I can get out of the driveway, much less drive eight miles to town." She gave a scared laugh. "You don't need to be trying to keep two of us awake."

"That's right, I forgot you live that far out now. So never mind, go back to bed."

"No, no, I was up anyway, looking out at the storm. And now I'm aware of Betsy's situation, I couldn't possibly sleep. I'm going downstairs to make a pot of coffee. Can you call me every so often, too, just to let me know how she's doing?"

"Sure. Say a prayer, okay?"

"Of course."

John and Godwin's house was about five blocks from Crewel World. Godwin decided walking would be safer than driving his little sports car. He bundled up, but not too much—walking in snow was hard work, and it wasn't bitter cold out. He added a light sweater to his cotton shirt, then put on his navy pea coat and covered his head with a knit hat.

It took him twenty minutes to get to the shop, even walking down the middle of the streets where the snow was not so deep. As he approached, hatless and perspiring, there was someone already waiting in the shallow shelter of the doorway. It was Martha Winters. She was wearing a long scarf that wrapped around and around, making a sloping line between her shoulders and her fur-trimmed hat, with several feet left over to wave at him.

"H'lo, Godwin!" she called. She was shuffling her feet to keep warm. That was the tricky part about dressing for weather like this. Any activity warmed you up, but standing still chilled you fast.

"Yoo-hoo!" he replied and hurried up to her. The wind altered suddenly, cuffed him from behind and then threw a handful of snow in his naked ear. The gray townhouse complex across the street stymied the gale after its rush down the lake and left it confused about its direction. The snow it carried whirled as much upward as down and likewise sideways, like one of those globes you shake to make a winter scene.

"Not a fit night out for man or beast," he opined in a W. C. Fields voice, crowding in beside Martha to unlock the door.

He'd barely gotten it open and stepped back so Martha could go in ahead of him when a deep voice came faintly: "Wait for me!"

He turned and recognized Alice's tall, mannish shape. He waved, then waited.

The snow was two feet deep in front of the door, and they tracked it in with them. December snow wasn't like January's. This snow was heavy, full of moisture. Godwin turned on the lights and hurried to the back of the store to get the snow shovel and a broom. He scooped melting snow back out and cleared the doorway while Martha swept behind him. Alice went into the back room and started the coffee.

They only cleared a space in front of the door; trying to clear the sidewalk was futile. Then Martha turned the broom on Godwin, who was covered with snow. They heard the snarl of a snowmobile. "Who is that?" asked Martha, trying to look down the street while still dusting Godwin down.

"*Whoops!*" whooped Godwin. "Watch where you aim

that thing!" Laughing, he stepped halfway through an opening in the snowbank along the sidewalk and peered up the street. "Hey, I think it's Phil Galvin! And he's got a passenger!" Godwin began to wave. "Yoo-hoo, Phil-ill!"

The dark figure on the black snowmobile waved back and came though the opening to the building's driveway onto the sidewalk. The machine, a shiny black and hot pink number, came up level with Crewel World's big, lit-up window and stopped. The engine shut off.

Phil's passenger got off first. "Hi, it's me!" she said. It was Shelly Donohue. She was wearing boots that looked safe for space travel, wool pants, and a ski jacket with a hood. She was carrying a plastic drawstring bag that Godwin recognized as a Crewel World bag. The bag was bulging.

"Brought a project?" he asked.

"And some snacks," she replied.

"Good thinking," he said, waving her and Phil into the shop. Godwin realized then just how rattled he was. He hadn't brought the sport bag with his own projects in it, the one he normally carried everywhere.

At first it was fun. Betsy would call, then half an hour later one of them would call. Jill came and talked to Betsy about her boyfriend Lars's hobby farm—two of his miniature goats were pregnant, and he was going to make cheese—and about the Christmas ornaments she and Betsy had both been working on. "I even donated one of them to the Minneapolis Art Museum," said Jill. "They're putting up a tree decorated entirely with locally handmade ornaments."

Shelly talked about the medieval unit her class was doing, how the children had set up a medieval court with a king and queen and knights—some of them girls— and a magician. "I'm teaching them how to spin wool into yarn," she said. "Then we're going to try weaving."

On her turn, Martha thanked Betsy for being so clever about murder investigations and talked about the tapestry project they would be starting soon. "Everyone seems enthusiastic about naming the library after Father Keane, and we're going to stitch Lucy Abrams's name onto the canvas—once we're sure she hasn't already done that."

Alice said she was making loaves of raisin-cinnamon bread as Christmas presents, and Betsy said she often gave loaves of an Austrian bread that had blanched almonds, grated orange rind, and two kinds of raisins in it. They agreed to exchange recipes.

Phil said he was thinking of tackling an authentic aran sweater and asked Betsy if she could special order the yarn for him.

"Tell Godwin to remind me," she said.

At two, Jill became worried about using up the car battery and limited the calls to five minutes. Then she got a page from the police station, asking her to come in and relieve Emily at the switchboard.

At four-thirty, it was Godwin's turn. He talked about buying another Christmas stocking for himself, and then about his first attempt at silk gauze. "I was doing a twenty-six-count linen and making a real mess of it, remember? So I thought I was crazy to try a forty-count silk gauze, but you know something? It works! I don't even get out the Dazor, I can work it sitting by the window! Silk gauze is almost like needlepoint canvas, the holes are that obvious. I'm doing that pansy bouquet. I'm going to make it into a box lid."

"Uh-huh," said Betsy, sounding not very interested.

"Are you all right?"

"I'm just tired, I guess."

"I think it's time we marched along with the teddy bears again." He started to sing in a fair tenor, "Picnic time for teddy bears . . . Are you marching? Knees up nice and high."

After a few bars he realized she wasn't marching and stopped.

Betsy said, "I'd like something warm to drink," as if she were giving an order in a restaurant.

"Are you out of water?"

"Huh?"

"Isn't there any bottled water left?"

"I guess so."

"Well, take a sip of that."

"Okay. Are they coming soon, Godwin?"

"Very soon, I promise. The snow is slacking off, and it'll be daylight pretty quick. They'll be knocking on your car window any time."

"It's not getting light over here. And it's still snowing."

"But not as hard, right? Hang on. It'll be over soon."

"Godwin, it's never going to be over."

At five it took four rings before she answered, and she wasn't tracking at all well. Martha, near tears, was afraid her fear would infect Betsy, and Alice was openly crying. Shelly was comforting them, and Phil had fallen asleep, head down on the table, so Godwin took the receiver from Martha.

"Now listen up, woman!" he scolded. "We've been at this for too long to give up now. I called Jill, and she told me what she's been doing. A few years ago, there was a woman in South Dakota in the same fix you're in. What they did was triangulate the signal as it went through the cell phone towers, and by measuring the signal's strength at each tower, they figured out how far she was from each one. Does that make sense?"

"No. I don't know. I guess not."

"Well, it made perfect sense when Jill described it.

But you have to keep talking, so they can trace the signal. All right?"

"You're lying to keep my spirits up. Nobody's coming."

"Me? Lie? Betsy, would I *lie?"*

"No. I don't know. I guess not."

But that was the last time she called them. They had to call her every time, now.

"Don't call me anymore," she mumbled at seven. "It's dark all the time. I'm going to die. I'm just too tired."

"Of all the nonsense—!" began Godwin, too tired himself to think clearly.

"Tell the Pig to go home and not to marry again," she said. "And I wrote this down, you get the shop. Don't forget to take inventory."

"Betsy, I'm not taking over the shop."

"Why not?"

"Because what are you going to do when you're home and safe? I don't know if I'd want you working for me. That's a joke, okay?"

"I'm not coming home. Because they can't find me. They'll never find me. Listen Godwin, you take the shop and run it, all right? And Jill gets half the money."

"Betsy—"

"Say you'll do it, Godwin. Say it."

"All right, when you die at age ninety, I'll take over the store and give half the money to Jill. I'll be twenty-nine by then and ready to settle down. That's another joke, Betsy."

"Keep the same part-timers, okay?"

"Why aren't you laughing?"

"And don't let Irene teach a class. She's a lousy teacher."

"Shall I tell her your last thoughts were of her?"

Behind him, Martha wept, "Oh, Betsy, Betsy!"

Alice shook Phil awake. "Betsy's dying, wake up!"

"She is not. Don't say that!" cried Shelly.

All four stared at Godwin, who was listening hard. "Who'll take Sophie?" fretted Betsy feebly.

"Boss lady, what is this all about? It's morning! I can actually see daylight outside, honest I can! And the snow has stopped. The sky is clear, the snow has stopped! Snowplows are already on their way! They'll be pulling up any second, and be running up and down the road, calling your name. They've got hot cocoa in a thermos with them, and you'll be just fine. And there you sit, worrying about your spoiled cat. Now stop it, okay? Just stop such nonsense. Betsy, I think we should do some foot stamps. You haven't done them in a while. Ready? If you go out in the woods today—Betsy?"

"And how can it be light where you are? It's still dark here."

"No, really, it's starting to get light, can't you see it? It's going to be a beautiful day."

"No sun here. No sun."

"Snow on the windshield," suggested Phil.

"Well, of course! Betsy, that's because there's snow on your windows. You need to roll your window down so the snow will fall off. Then you'll see it's getting light, and you can wave at the snowplow when it comes along. Roll your window down. Betsy? Roll your window down, now."

" 'S too cold. Don't let 'em put her t'sleep, 'kay? Promise."

"Yeah, yeah, I promise. Roll your window down, Betsy, and you can see the sun come up. Okay?"

"In a minute." After a very long pause, "In a minute."

And that was the last anyone could get out of her. No amount of shouting, cajoling, ordering, or begging got a reply.

•   •   •

Jill exploded into the shop. "We know where she is!" she said, her face alive, her eyes sparkling. "A snowplow is on its way to her right now!"

"Jill," said Godwin, coming to take her by the arm, "we can't raise her. She's not answering."

"What?" said Jill. "Where's the phone?"

"Maybe the battery's dead," said Shelly, holding it out to her.

Martha, fending off despair, agreed. "These cell phones will drain a car battery right down if you don't run the engine and recharge it." Her face was pale, her eyes red-rimmed.

"She's fine!" said Jill, grabbing the phone. "Betsy, this is Jill. Betsy? Listen, they did that triangulation thing—Did you tell her about it?"

Godwin nodded.

"And Betsy, they know where you are. A snowplow is on its way to you this minute. Betsy? Betsy! *Betsy!*"

Jill turned on Godwin. "How long since she talked to you?"

Godwin looked at his watch, though he knew almost to the second how long it had been. "Twenty-seven minutes. How long till they get there?"

"Forty minutes, maybe? Less than an hour. But she's in a white car covered with snow and completely off the road. If she could flash her lights or blow her horn when she hears them coming, that would help." She lifted the phone again. "Betsy, this is Jill. We're coming to get you, but you can help us find you. Are you listening? Turn your headlights on. Do you hear me? Turn your headlights on, right now! Betsy? Have you done that, have you turned your headlights on? Talk to me, say something!"

She wasn't cold anymore, but she was muddled and very, very tired. She felt her head fall sideways, onto something hard. She thought very briefly about moving it, but it fit her ear. Besides, it was making a noise that sounded like her name, which was pleasant. She wanted to make a noise back, but she was just too tired.

The door went *bing* and everyone looked up to see someone standing just inside. The sun on the snow made a blinding halo around the figure, so they couldn't see who it was.

A mild voice said, "I heard. Is there anything I can do?" It was Father John, muffled to the eyebrows, with an old fedora on top.

"We can't raise her," said Jill.

Godwin added, "We know what road she's on, and just about where along it she is, and the snowplow led an ambulance out there, but they can't find her. We think her car is buried under the snow. They're walking up and down the road, but it's taking a long time."

"She's dying," said Alice. "Or already dead."

"Who are you talking to on the phone?" asked the priest, approaching, hat in one hand, unwrapping his scarf with the other.

"Her, sort of," said Godwin. "The line is open, but she's not answering."

"May I try?" asked Father John, taking the receiver. "Betsy, this is Father John Rettger of Trinity." He was speaking slowly and firmly. "Can you hear me? We are going to pray for you and for your rescuers. Let us pray. In the Name of the Father, the Son, and the Holy Spirit, Amen." He crossed himself. "Our Father, who art in heaven, hallowed be Thy name. Thy Kingdom come, Thy will be done—" He began nodding hard, and gestured at the trio standing around the table, and his voice slowed further, as if to give a slow-speaking person time to catch up. "—on earth, as it is in heaven. Give us this day, our daily bread, and forgive us our trespasses, as we forgive those who trespass against us. And lead us not into temptation, but deliver us from evil, for Thine is the Kingdom, and the power, and the glory, forever and ever. Amen. Betsy, lean forward and make your horn blow." He said to Jill, "Tell them to listen for it!"

"Is she doing it?" demanded Shelly. "Is she doing it?"

Jill grabbed the mike attached to her shoulder and said, "Fifty-six ten."

"Ten fifty-six, go."

"Tell the plow to shut all engines off, tell them to listen for a car horn!"

"Ten fifty-six, copy."

Father John said, "Again, let us pray," and started in on The Lord's Prayer again. This time, both in prayer and psychic encouragement to Betsy, everyone joined in. At the end, he said, "Are you blowing your horn, Betsy?"

Godwin, standing beside him, leaned toward the priest's ear. Very, very faintly, he heard a sound that could have been a car horn blowing steadily. Or it could have been static.

Then there was a wait that went on forever—or about ten minutes' worth of forever.

Jill's radio suddenly crackled, "Ten fifty-six."

Jill lifted the microphone fastened to her shoulder and barked, "Ten!"

"They've located the car, and Ms. Devonshire. They're putting her in the emergency vehicle now. Transport will be to Hennepin County Medical Center in Minneapolis."

Jill was the only one who understood the crackling transmission, but when she translated, the room broke into cheers. People slapped one another on the shoulder or shook hands or hugged. Father John was roughly handled, but he kept grinning.

"How did you know what to do?" Jill asked, when she could be heard.

"All priests visit the dying, of course, and often, as the end approaches, the dying person will sink into unconsciousness. They don't respond when you talk to them, won't squeeze your hand when you take it. But when you start to pray, and you come to The Lord's Prayer, very often they will surprise you by suddenly joining in. If they're Christian, that is. I understand that Jewish people on their deathbeds will equally often join in on the Sh'ma—you know, 'Hear O Israel, the Lord your God is one God, and you shall love the Lord your God with all your heart, with all your soul, and with all your mind.' I wonder if there's a deeply familiar prayer in the Muslim faith that would work the same way. I know there is that statement that starts all their services, 'There is no God but Allah, and Mohammed is his prophet.' But that's rather short to rouse an unconscious person and give him or her time to join in. Perhaps there's something longer. I should look that up sometime."

7

Betsy had little memory of what was done to warm her up, save that it was unpleasant. By the time she was able to pay attention, they had taken the noisy part away, or put her in another room, one or the other.

Then she slept for a long time.

She woke and it was night. She felt clear-headed and able to take an interest in her surroundings. A nurse came in and took her temperature and pulse and had a nurse's aide bring her a cup of cocoa. Betsy turned on the television and watched the second half of a movie with such a strange plot that the next day she wondered if it had been a dream. She slept again.

She woke famished. It was daylight, and someone brought her toast and coffee. Then a nurse came to tell her she was going home. *This sure isn't like television,* she thought, signing papers. On sitcoms, whatever brought the hero or heroine into hospitals as a patient quickly faded into the background and he or she was soon joking with visitors and/or enjoying the ministrations of kind and attentive nurses.

The nurse gave Betsy copies of the papers along with a lengthy list of things she should do (eat lightly, get plenty of bed rest) and shouldn't do (operate heavy machinery) for the next twenty-four hours. There was also a list of symptoms to watch for. If any appeared, Betsy was to call her doctor immediately.

Oh, and Betsy wasn't to drive a car for forty-eight hours.

As if, thought Betsy, whose car was, so far as she knew, still crumpled against a pine tree somewhere.

As she handed the pen back, she said, "If I'm in such precarious condition, with dangerous symptoms threatening, maybe I shouldn't go home just yet."

The nurse laughed. "No, you'll be fine recovering at home. The only people who go home well from the hospital nowadays are the doctors."

Betsy chuckled obediently and asked, "But what about my clothes?"

"They're in this closet here," said the nurse.

"Oh, no," said Betsy. "I'm not putting that underwear back on again."

"Then you'll have to call someone who can bring you fresh underwear."

Reluctant as Betsy was to have anyone but herself rummaging around in her lingerie drawer, she called Godwin at his home. Not that she would allow him to do it, but he had Jill and Shelly's phone numbers. When she got an answering machine, she left a quick message asking him to call her at the hospital—she had to consult her wrist to find out what room she was in—and then tried the shop.

"Of course we're open!" said Godwin, when he answered. "My dear, you wouldn't believe how many women woke up this morning desperate to find a Christmas gift for Aunt Mary, who never does anything but needlepoint! And, of course, there are the curious, who want to hear all about your adventure in the storm."

"Thank God for Aunt Mary," said Betsy, who then explained her dilemma. Godwin said at once, "I'll call Shelly. She's already asking if there's anything she can do."

Betsy told him to tell Shelly she wanted a complete change of clothing. "There's a spare key to my apartment in the bottom drawer of the desk," said Betsy.

"Winter break starts today," Shelly said an hour later, when Betsy asked why she wasn't at school. She had brought lingerie, jeans and a sweater, socks and walking shoes. And that ugly secondhand coat from the shop's back room, Betsy's only other winter outerwear. And a big garbage bag for the used clothes.

She walked beside Betsy as a nurse wheeled her down to the main entrance, and then left her there while she went to get her Dodge Caravan from the parking lot. The vehicle, a purple so dark it was almost black, pulled up under the wide, tall portico. Betsy abandoned the wheelchair the nurse wanted her to stay in and walked the few yards to the vehicle. Getting up and in was a problem, but Betsy gritted her teeth and managed. Shelly had turned the heat on high, it was like July in the Mojave in there. Betsy unzipped the coat.

But it was definitely December in Minnesota outside. Even the parking meters wore thick caps of snow, and every sharp angle of brick and glass and steel was softened by drapes and mounds of white. As they pulled out into light traffic, their tires chewed a brown sugar mix of snow, salt, and sand. Once they got onto 394, the lanes were already mostly clear, though about half the cars they saw wore slabs of snow on their roofs, which trailed thin comets' tails behind them.

For a wonder almost everyone was driving only forty-five or fifty miles an hour. In Betsy's experience, Minnesotans took speed limits under advisement.

They took the exit onto Highway Fifteen, just past
Wayzata, where there was mostly countryside. The road
was covered with snow, and the fields were a dazzle of
white, with shadings of gold, pink, and lavender under
the trees. Evergreens were trimmed in white, and the
crotches of leafless trees were filled with snow. Not a
footprint marred the surface anywhere.

"Very Christmasy," noted Shelly.

"I don't like snow as much as I used to," replied
Betsy, looking at young pines bent almost double under
their burdens.

"You'll get over that," said Shelly. "By the way, you
won't have to cook for days, everyone's bringing something for you."

"Including you?" asked Betsy hopefully. "I just love
that casserole thing you do with chicken and noodles
and cream of mushroom soup."

"Casserole? Is that what you call a hot dish?"

Betsy laughed. "No, hot dish is the name Minnesotans
gave to what everyone else calls a casserole."

"Well, I'm glad you like them, because that's what
almost everyone is bringing. There were four lined up
on the counter when I got there. Pick the ones you want
for today and tomorrow, and I'll put the others in the
freezer."

The road narrowed and ran between a large bay on
one side, already frozen over, and a steep slope upward
on the other. "Some nice houses up on top of that,"
remarked Shelly. "We'll have to bring you out here in
the spring and show them off."

"You know, I think I've been on this road," said
Betsy. "Doesn't it connect with Nineteen and take us
back to Excelsior?"

"There you go!" said Shelly. "You're learning your
way around."

"I thought I was," said Betsy. "But obviously, I'm not

as good at navigating around the lake as I thought."

"Betsy, the way that snow was coming down, *no one* could find their way. People from out of state think we laugh at snow. We don't. We listen to the weather reports, and when a blizzard blows in like it did Monday night, we stay at home. We close schools and businesses until it's over and the roads get plowed, and if we take the kids sledding or skating, we all wear serious cold-weather gear. I can't believe Godwin and the others let you go out in that."

"What should they have done, locked me in a closet? I was going. I was sure I knew what I was doing. Besides, no one knew the storm system was going to park itself over us and keep dumping snow."

Shelly sighed. "I suppose so. But if people scold you about this, remember, they're really scolding themselves. I think it was divine providence that made Jill insist you take her present along."

Betsy said, "Have they towed my car yet?"

"I don't think so. Why?"

"Because I keep thinking about it, up against that tree, buried in snow. If Jill hadn't given me that cell phone, I'd be sitting in it yet."

Shelly had to pull over to the side of the road and hug Betsy for a minute.

Back on their way, Betsy said, "I guess it's like people who live near deserts know the rules, like to tell someone where you're going and when you'll be back, and to fill your gas tank and take a couple gallons of water along."

"Exactly. Mother Nature can be a merciless bitch. But once she gets over her tantrum, isn't it beautiful?" Shelly nodded out toward an expanse of Lake Minnetonka, where the snow piled up in exotic, glittering, wavelike drifts, the tops of which appeared to be steaming as the wind continued its work.

Betsy shivered. "It's like a dead planet."

"But it's not dead," Shelly countered. "Just wait till spring, when the land jumps up green and blooming again. I love living in a place where there are seasons; I don't think I could live in the tropics. How would you know when it's Christmas?"

"Look in the store windows or at a calendar," said Betsy, remembering Christmas in San Diego. "Listen to the radio or watch television, look at the lights on the houses next door, or—"

"All right, all right, all right," laughed Shelly. "I get your point. But look over there, isn't it just like a postcard?" She gestured toward a point of land extending into the bay, where a yellow log cabin crouched among evergreens, the snow piled like sugar frosting all around.

But Betsy was far too close to her recent adventure to appreciate the view. Nor did she like any of the other unpeopled, silver-gilt scenes that presented themselves around every bend on the road to Excelsior.

Once they got to town, that was different. Betsy looked with pleasure at the flower shop, the tiny jewelry store, Leipold's Antiques, the bakery, the pet shop, the bookstore, and Haskell's on the corner, its decorative marine pilings buried under snow. Christmas lights and decorations underlined the season. People were out, walking, shopping, greeting one another. This was lovely; this she liked. There were warm cookies in the bakery and hot cider in the Waterfront Café. One could not possibly sit down and freeze to death on a crowded street like this.

Shelly made the turn onto Lake Street, and in another block they were in front of the old redbrick building that housed the sandwich shop, the used book store, Crewel World, and Betsy's apartment over it. Home. Betsy was suddenly very tired. She sighed and reached for her purse, fumbled in it for keys.

"You go right on up and get into your jammies," said Shelly, helping her through the narrow pass in the mountain range of snow along the curb. "No one expects you to stop in the store."

"All right."

Betsy went through the door that led directly to the upstairs apartments. She walked up the stairs, Shelly close behind, and unlocked the door to her place. The first thing she saw was Sophie ambling unhurriedly toward her.

Betsy stooped and stroked the animal, who arched her back and purred. Shelly went around her into the kitchen, and Betsy heard the refrigerator door opening.

"She's been fed," said Godwin from behind her, and she rose. "Sophie, I mean," he added. She came to hug him.

"I knew someone must have taken care of her," said Betsy in a minute. "Otherwise she'd be giving orders."

Godwin laughed. "You go straight to bed, all right? Shelly's handling things in the kitchen, and I just wanted to say a quick welcome home. We're staying open late tonight."

"Who's helping down there?"

"Who isn't? Half of your employees volunteered to work for nothing! I've got them lined up until Saturday, by which time you should be able to either come to work or make other arrangements."

"You didn't accept the offers to work free, did you?"

"No, of course not. But while they're in that mood, I'm lining them up for inventory."

Betsy said, blinking away tears, "You are the best."

"Aw, shucks, no one has said that to me for years."

"Not even John?"

"Oh, well—that's different," said Godwin. And he left.

Betsy defied everyone's instructions and took a long,

hot shower before climbing into bed. Sophie joined her in bed, purring loudly, snuggling close, for once seeming more interested in giving comfort than seeking it. Betsy stroked and murmured to the cat, profoundly happy and grateful to be there with her. She thought she wasn't the least sleepy, but before she knew it, she was dreaming.

She woke to the sound of someone knocking on her door. Her *bedroom* door. "Whosit?" she said, struggling with the words. Sophie padded heavily across the bed and jumped down.

"Relax, it's just me," said Jill's voice. She came in wearing her uniform, looking immense in her bulletproof vest and thick winter jacket. "How are you?"

"Okay. What time is it?" Betsy hadn't the strength to lift her arm and consult her watch.

"Almost two in the afternoon. You were asleep, I guess."

"I guess. But I'm glad you came. I was having a bad dream. Come on in. How did you get in, anyhow?"

"Your door's unlocked. Godwin is sending people up through the store. Unless you want me to tell him not to."

"No, it's all right, I s'pose." Betsy still wasn't completely awake. "What, through the shop and up the back way? Should I get up? Is there company out there?"

"No, no. Stay in bed. They're just bringing things, to judge by what's on the kitchen counters. Apparently they hear you snoring and just sneak right back out again."

"I don't snore!"

"Godwin said someone told him you were snoring, so when I came in and didn't hear anything, I decided to check on you."

Betsy sighed, "Huh. Thank you, I guess. Well, yes, thanks for checking. And Jill, thanks for that survival kit. I mean—" Betsy found, to her distress, that her eyes were watering. She tried to blink the tears away. "Thank you for saving my life. If you hadn't insisted I take that box along—" Betsy rubbed her eyes with both hands, like a child. "And all I got you was that book on hardanger you were looking at!" If Jill had come over and hugged her, Betsy would have broken down. But Jill, being Jill, only stood there, so Betsy pulled herself together again. "I'm glad you're my friend."

"I'm glad I was able to do the right thing for you." Jill smiled faintly. "Now, I've got to get back on patrol."

"Wait a minute, I thought you were on nights."

"We're working double shifts until everything's back to normal. There are still roads closed, and we've got a pair of thieves on snowmobiles hitting summer cottages around the lake. I'm cruising in a four-wheel-drive vehicle, hoping to surprise the little buggers."

So much for that serene cottage in the snow. "Good luck," said Betsy.

Someone knocked on Betsy's bedroom door again, and Betsy, who thought she'd only dozed off for a minute, opened her eyes and said, "Sorry, Jill."

But it was a man's deep, warm, familiar voice that replied, "Hello, darlin."

Betsy groaned. "Oh, no, it's the Pig."

"No, it's me, Hal, the world's greatest fool."

"You got that right." Betsy hauled herself into a sitting position again, glad she'd worn her thickest flannel nightgown to bed, and hoping her hair looked awful. "Go away, Hal." She looked at her bedside clock. It was a little past seven. She'd no idea she'd been asleep five more hours!

"Not till you let me have my say."

"Nothing you say could possibly interest me."

"There's a saying, 'Experience keeps a hard school,

but a fool will learn in no other.' I've been to experience's *grad* school, let me tell you."

"It seems to me, since you're standing upright and have all your limbs and both eyes, it wasn't hard enough."

Hal's voice took on a pleading tone. "What can I do to show you I mean it when I say I'm sorry? That I've learned my lesson? What do you want from me?"

"Besides your head on a pole? Nothing. And all you're going to get from me is a hard kick to a delicate place if you don't get out of here. Now."

"Please, let's talk! I really want a second chance!"

"To what? Hurt me again? Never! If you don't leave, I'll call the police." When he didn't start immediately for the door, she picked up the bedside phone's receiver and glanced at him, fully prepared to dial.

Betsy had read in English novels about a person "going white to the lips," but had never seen anyone actually do that before. In the blink of an eye, he went from hurt and contrite to ferocious, his dark eyes blazing at her from that white face, his lips a thin slash. But he didn't say anything, only turned on his heel and walked out of the bedroom. Seconds later, she heard the door to the hall slam.

"Whew!" she said, replaced the receiver, and slid down under the covers again.

But the excitement of that visit had left her wide awake. She huffed a bit, trying to work up a sleepy yawn, but no good. So she twisted over and picked up the bedside phone again, dialed the shop.

"Godwin?" she said when he answered. "If Hal comes back, don't let him upstairs again, okay? I don't want him up here. Thanks."

She hung up and realized she was hungry—no, famished. When had she last had a real meal? Yesterday? The day before? She went out to the little kitchen and was touched to find the counter space crowded with baskets of fruit, a large selection of Excelo Bakery's cookies, and a loaf each of their beautiful herb and multigrain bread. In the refrigerator were a six-pack of Diet Squirt, a liter of V8 Extra Spicy, three brand-new quarts of milk, and four kinds of casserole—er, hot dish—plus two orders of her favorite chicken salad made with red grapes and cashews, a plastic bowl of homemade potato salad, and a whole banana cream pie. She checked the freezer and, as Shelly said she would do, there were more no-longer-hot dishes waiting in there.

This was ridiculous. And vastly touching. She stood there sniveling until cold air spilling out of the refrigerator started to chill her toes.

Then she got a dinner plate out of the cabinet and made an enormous and peculiar dinner by taking a sample of every hot dish that wasn't frozen. She washed it down with milk.

She washed the plate, glass, and fork and wandered into the living room. Normally eating an enormous meal made her sleepy, but having slept so much already, Betsy was in no mood to go back to bed. She looked around for something to do. She didn't feel up to the concentration it took for counted cross stitch. She was about to pick up the scarf she was nearly finished knitting for Godwin, when she remembered the mystery of the tapestry.

Those little symbols, the shamrock, the flaming heart, the pig. Attributes, Father John had called them, because they identified certain saints. Was there a pattern to the ones selected?

She went into the back bedroom where she had her notes, and the book on attributes Father John had loaned her. The book was there, on the computer desk, but her notes weren't. Betsy could be absentminded, moving things and forgetting where she'd put them, so she looked all around the room. No luck. She even went into the two-drawer file cabinet, though she knew perfectly well she hadn't been so organized as to make up a file folder and put the notes in there. She started to boot up her computer, then remembered she hadn't saved the notes, just printed them out.

She expanded her search to her own bedroom, then the living room. The doorbell's ring found Betsy on her knees in the kitchen, looking under the sink. She answered it warily, afraid Hal might have talked his way past Godwin again. But it was Jill.

"I saw your lights on and thought I'd check on you," said Jill, who looked barely able to stand.

"I'm feeling pretty good, but you look terrible," said Betsy. "When were you last in bed?"

Jill thought. "I can't remember, though it wasn't all that long ago. I'm just tired. Driving on icy roads after a storm like this isn't much fun."

"Have you eaten?"

"You don't have to feed me."

"Okay, how about I let one of my many friends feed you?" Betsy went to her refrigerator, brought out one of the hot dishes, and spooned half of it into a Tupperware bowl. "Here," she said, "take this home, put it in the microwave, and hit your soup button twice."

"Thank you. I didn't even think I was hungry until you started spooning it out. Then I had to keep swallowing so drool wouldn't drip off my chin. Whose is it?"

"Patricia Fairland's. It's got shrimp, pea pods, mushrooms, and three kinds of cheese."

"Golly," sighed Jill.

"It tastes as good as it smells, too."

Jill said, "Well, thanks so much. I'll call you tomorrow morning. *Late* tomorrow morning."

After Jill left, Betsy gave up her search and sat down to knit. Knit two, purl two, fifty times, with an odd one at either end of the row. There were only a few inches left to do, so she turned on KSJN and finished it to Schubert's Unfinished Symphony—she had to get out her *Learn to Knit in One Day* booklet to remind herself how to cast off—then, to the odd cadences and plaintive harmonics of medieval music, used all the colors of yarn that were in the scarf to make a long fringe at either end.

Tired at last, she went to bed and read enough of the book, which was actually called *Attributes and Symbols of the Christian Church* and was nearly a hundred years old, to put herself back to sleep.

8

Betsy came down to her shop around ten-thirty on Thursday morning looking bright and chipper.

Godwin was explaining how to use blending filament in counted cross stitch to a customer, so Shelly hurried to intercept her, exclaiming in an undertone, "What are you doing down here? Why aren't you in bed?"

"I feel fine. I couldn't stay in bed any more without being tied down. How are things?

"Fine, really, just fine. I'm here with Godwin, so why don't you go shopping or something?"

"I don't know if I'm up to shopping. Too much walking."

Betsy went to the library table. "But I feel odd not coming down to work. How are we doing? Has it been busy? Did that ad salesman come in? Anything going on I should know about?"

"It's been fairly busy, enough so we're glad there are two of us. We had three people waiting at the door for us to open. Godwin's just winding up the last one. And the ad salesman came in yesterday, so we showed him the ad you designed and he should call you today with prices. Are you going to advertise in all the weeklies around the area?"

"Depends on the price. Maybe only the *Excelsior Bay Times*." Betsy leaned right, then left. "Is my project down here?"

"What, the ornaments?"

"No, the needlepoint one, the kitten asleep in the basket of yarn."

Shelly came to pull out a chair. "Here, sit down. What's it in?"

Betsy sat. "The basket with the lid." She bent again to look for it, but Shelly had already picked it up. She put it on the table, her movements hasty and her face anxious. "What's the matter, Shelly?"

"Nothing, I guess. I mean, Betsy, we were afraid you were going to die, and you still looked awful when I brought you home. I can't believe you think you're well enough to go back to work already."

"Plus," drawled Godwin as he closed the shop door on his customer, "Shelly wants that Wentzler Camelot sampler, and is afraid you'll send her home before she earns enough money to buy it."

"Goddy—!" scolded Shelly, but her face was pink. "It's not true!" she said to Betsy. "Well . . . not altogether."

Betsy laughed. "I want you to stay. I don't think I have the stamina to work a full day."

Godwin said, "I don't think you should work at all. Aren't you supposed to stay in bed until Saturday?"

"No, I'm supposed to rest until Saturday. And if I have to stay upstairs, I will start climbing the walls, which isn't very restful. I'd rather be sitting down here with you."

The shop door went *bing,* and Godwin said, "Who's sitting?"

It was Martha Winters. "Well, I'm so glad to see you up and about, Betsy," she said. "I'm here to see if you have any of those Rainbow Gallery 'Wisper' colors."

"Yes, we do," said Godwin. "They came in yesterday."

The two went off to the back. Shelly said to Betsy, "You might want to try them for your kitten. They're fuzzy, and if you brush the stitching, they look just like fur."

"Sounds great," said Betsy. "But let me figure out this stitch for the yarn first. What do you think of—"

Just then the door sounded, and Joe Mickels came in. He nodded at Betsy and said, "You should be in bed."

Betsy, beginning to get annoyed at this insistence she shouldn't be at work, snapped, "Why, do I look sick?" She had taken some care with her appearance this morning, and thought she looked at least healthy.

He frowned at her, taking her invitation seriously. "I guess not. I came by to see if your help can tell me if you're recovering on schedule. I can see that you're ahead of predictions." Joe managed not to sound pleased, but on the other hand, he didn't sound like his usual blustery self.

"I'm fine, thank you," said Betsy, frowning at him. This was the second time Joe had passed up an opportunity to bluster.

As if reading her mind, he swelled his chest and said more strongly, "You let me know right away if what happened makes you decide to move to a warmer climate, all right?"

"Yes, I'll be sure to do that," retorted Betsy, and he turned on his heel and left.

"What was that all about?" asked Shelly.

"The usual," said Betsy with a shrug.

"You know, it's odd how he hasn't gone after you like he did Margot. He was in here growling at her or serving her with some kind of legal paper practically every week for a long time."

"Maybe he has a mad, secret crush on me," Betsy joked.

"More likely it's some new trick. You watch out for him, Betsy. For Joe, everything comes down to money, and with your lease, he's losing money every day."

Betsy got out a piece of scrap canvas and consulted her book of needlepoint stitches. Someone on the needlework newsgroup had suggested the stem stitch for the balls of yarn, and though her book showed it only in straight lines, she set out to see if she could curve it just a little to make the balls look round. And maybe if she used a slightly darker shade around the edge . . .

She'd only done a few stitches when the phone rang. Godwin, who had just sold Martha four packs of hairy yarn, picked up and said, "Crewel World, good morning, how may I help you? Oh, hello, Vern!" He listened and said, "Great!" and to Betsy, "It's Miller Motors. They towed your car in and Vern wants to talk to you."

Betsy reached for the cordless on the table and pushed the talk button. "What's it going to cost me for the tow?" she asked. Miller Motors was a shabby old place, located in a converted stable, and Vern Miller was a retired army sergeant who had learned about motors by repairing tank engines. Betsy had no intention of allowing him to work on her car.

"We ain't got that figured, yet," replied Vern. "What I want to know is, who's got it in for you?"

"What do you mean?"

"I mean your brake line's been cut. Did you notice your brakes goin' soft while you was out drivin' in the snow?"

Betsy said, "Well yes, and then they quit altogether. That's why I went off the road. But I thought it was my gas tank that was punctured."

"It wasn't your gas tank, it was your gas line; it got ripped loose back near the gas tank. That was an accident that happened while you was wallowin' around that pine tree. I'm talking about your brake line. It was cut, like with a box ripper or a good pair of scissors. And you're supposed to be smart, so think: If your brakes went out while you was driving, it was done *before* the accident. Which means it wasn't an accident."

Betsy sat perfectly still for a few seconds. "You're sure?"

"You want to come and take a look for yourself? I'm tellin' you, the line was cut!"

"All right, all right," said Betsy. "I believe you." She thought, then said, "Okay, just park the car someplace. Don't let anyone touch it, and don't start any repairs; I want someone else to look at it. I'll call you back."

"Storage is twenty bucks a day."

"Fine." Betsy hung up and picked up her canvas. But she only stared at it without making any stitches.

"What?" demanded Godwin.

"Mr. Miller says someone cut my brake line."

"You mean when they were hauling it back up on the road?" asked Shelly.

"No, before I went into the ditch. My brakes failed, that's why I went off the road. He's very sure it was cut, like with a box opener, deliberately."

"Nonsense," said Shelly. "Why would someone do that?"

Godwin said, "That, my dear, is a very good question."

Shelly said, "Oh, Godwin, you don't mean—Oh, *Betsy!*"

There was a little silence. Betsy said in a small voice, "I can't think of anyone even miffed at me right now."

Shelly said, "Joe Mickels?"

Godwin said, "It's silly to think anyone would seriously want to hurt you for any reason, even Joe."

The silence fell again, then Shelly said lightly, "Who didn't you invite to your party that you should have?"

Godwin stared at her, scandalized, then started to laugh. "Yes, and you haven't held a pre-Christmas sale. That's bound to upset at least some of your regular customers."

Betsy giggled. "Maybe it's Sophie, angry because I put her on a diet."

"Yeah," said Godwin, "I can just see her sneaking out to crawl under your car and rip that puppy loose with her hind claws. That'll teach you."

"How would she know—" Betsy paused, frowning.

"What?" asked Godwin.

"How would anyone know? I mean, if it really was cut, who do I know who knows what to cut? I don't know what a brake line looks like. I don't think I know anyone who would know; most of my customers are women. Well, except Phil Galvin. Or Steve Pedersen, or Donny DePere." These were her three most faithful male customers.

"Trust me, Donny wouldn't know, either," said Godwin.

Shelly said, "You're wrong; a lot of us women know, Betsy. Remember that course, Godwin? Introducing Your Car, it was called. It was aimed primarily at women. Open U taught it four years in a row. I took the first one, and it was so great I told everyone, and a lot of women from around here signed up. Four or five of the teachers at the elementary school did. And Patricia did, she said she was sick of being taken by car repair shops. And Martha, and June, and Eloise, and Heidi, and—gosh, a lot of your customers. Mandy Abrams took it. We learned how to change the oil as well as flat tires, and we studied all the parts of the engine and transmission. It was very interesting. I kept all my notes, and I haven't felt intimidated by car repairmen since. Though I never did change my oil after that one time. I thought I'd never get my fingernails clean!"

Godwin nodded. "I think two used-car dealers went out of business while they were teaching that course."

"Only one," corrected Shelly. "And he was already notorious."

"Hmmmm," said Betsy.

"You don't think Vern is right, do you?" asked Shelly.

"Probably not," said Betsy, "but I'm going to call Mike down at the police station anyhow."

Detective Sergeant Mike Malloy, somewhat to Betsy's surprise, took her report seriously and said he would stop by Miller Motors and look at her car.

He stepped into Crewel World less than an hour later, a slender redhead with freckles spattering a thin-lipped face. "All right, what are you mixed up in now?" he growled.

Betsy said, "You mean Vern Miller was right? The line was cut deliberately?"

"Yes. You didn't discover another skeleton did you? Maybe under that old tapestry they found at Trinity?"

"No, of course not," said Betsy.

Godwin said, "What she means is, she hasn't figured out yet what her new case is about. Though obviously *someone* has."

"Goddy, go help Shelly with that customer back by the counted cross stitch patterns," ordered Betsy, and he sniffed and walked away.

"Don't listen to Godwin, Mike," Betsy said. "There isn't anything to figure out. I was thinking after I called you that if Vern is right, if the brakes were tampered with, then perhaps someone got the wrong car. People park back there once in a while while they visit someone who lives across in the condos." Mike turned to glance out the front window at the gray eminence across the street—a large complex that blocked what once must have been a lovely view of the lake.

"All their parking is underground," continued Betsy, "and you need one of those magnetic keys to access it. So visitors have to park on the street. And with the snow emergency rules being so confusing—what are they? Something like you can only park on the even-numbered sides of the streets on odd-numbered days—anyway, people who don't want to get towed try to park off the street."

"And you're telling me someone across the street wanted to kill a visitor?"

"How would I know? I'm just looking for an alternative to the explanation that someone wants to kill *me*. Because no one does. I don't know about over there, I don't know anyone who lives over there." She smiled suddenly. "Well, except John Penberthy. And attorneys are too valuable to the law breakers to get murdered, aren't they?"

Mike laughed. "Unless they lose a case. But I see your point. Some stranger hustles back there, it's dark, it's snowing, your license plate is covered with it, and they're in a hurry. Makes sense to me." He wrote something in his notebook, tapped it to his forehead in a kind of friendly salute, and departed.

He had to sidestep out the door because someone half hidden behind an enormous plant bundled in green florist paper was coming in. The delivery man put the plant on the table and lifted a finger in a warning to wait and went back out again. When he came back, it was with a big, long white box, the sort roses come in.

"Wow, who loves you?" asked Godwin.

"They're more likely for you," said Betsy, nevertheless continuing to peel back the green paper to reveal a huge, deep, deep red poinsettia.

"Ooooh, pretty!" said Shelly. "I think that's the biggest one I've ever seen!"

Betsy began poking among the leaves for a card and found one on a clear plastic stick. It had her name on it.

She opened the envelope and found written on it, in a familiar hand, *"Remember?"* "Oh, damn," she muttered.

"Why? Who's it from?" asked Shelly.

"My ex-husband." She tore the card in half and tossed the pieces into a wastepaper basket under the table.

"Then I suppose this one's from him, too," said Shelly.

Godwin said, "It might not be. And it might not be roses, either. To fill a box that size would take two dozen roses, at least. Was the Pig one for spending big time on flowers?"

"Sometimes." Betsy sighed and opened the box. Inside were at least two dozen red roses. She picked up the card in its little envelope and opened it. In the same hand was written, *"My Love is Like the Red, Red Rose."* She sighed again, tore the card in half, and tossed it after the first.

"Maybe you should talk to him," said Shelly.

"No."

"But he spent a lot of money on those flowers."

"If they were made of rubies, I still wouldn't want to talk to him."

"Since they're only real roses, shall I put them in water?" Shelly bent to inhale the fragrance.

Betsy started to order them thrown away when she was forestalled by Godwin. "Let's give them away. A Christmas rose for every customer until they're gone."

Betsy nodded. That's a nice idea, Godwin. There's a bucket in back, Shelly. Fill it halfway with warm water, cut the bottoms off the stems, and put them in there."

"What about the poinsettia?" asked Shelly.

"Do you want it?"

"No, I've already got one."

"Godwin?"

"No, ever since I saw them growing like weeds in Mexico, I don't think of them the same."

"Me, too," said Betsy. That was what Hal was reminding her of with his card. She smiled. "I know, let's give it to—to Irene Potter. Poor lady, she spends half her salary in here, and I bet she's never gotten flowers in her life. Godwin, can you remember the company where she works?"

Godwin could. Betsy called and, handed along to the shipping department, got Irene on the line and said, "Irene, someone brought in a big, beautiful poinsettia and there's no room for it in the shop. Would you like it?"

"How much?" asked that suspicious woman.

"For free. You are one of our best customers, and I would like for once to give you something."

Irene came in from work a little after five and stood a moment staring at the plant. "It's awfully big," she said.

"I didn't think of that. It's too heavy for you to carry," said Betsy. "How about I drop it off after we close? We're open till nine tonight."

"And every night till Christmas," added Godwin with a little sigh.

"Why," said Irene, torn between suspicion and pleasure, "that's very kind of you, I'm sure. Thank you. It is a beautiful thing, and we wouldn't want it to freeze its little leaves off, would we? Which it might do if I were to carry it home. Yes, thank you. Thank you." She backed toward the door, then turned abruptly and hurried out.

"Poor thing," said Shelly. "Thinks it's some kind of prank, I bet."

When Betsy carried the big plant, wrapped again in

its green paper, to the front door of the elderly boarding house where Irene lived, she was waiting in the parlor. Betsy, looking through the half-glassed front door, could also see four other roomers sitting on the two couches and three easy chairs that filled the room. But they all waited while the owner, a very old woman, answered the door.

"Why, Betsy Devonshire, how nice of you to come in person!" she said in her creaky voice. "Do come in! Irene, you have a caller, and look, she's brought you something!" This was said in a patently false voice. Obviously, Irene had told everyone about her gift.

So Betsy made a little ceremony of it, putting it on an end table and carefully unwrapping it. She said, "Irene is such a talented needlepointer that her work is an advertisement for us. I thought it would be nice to reward her loyalty and applaud her talent, so I am bringing her this little gift."

As the "little gift" was unwrapped, it spread like a red and green avalanche. The man sitting on the end of the couch beside the table had to scoot over to keep it from draping across his lap.

"Oh, my, that is just *gorgeous!*" said the landlady. "I've never seen one so large or beautiful! I just hope Irene will let it stay down here at least for tonight, so we all can enjoy it."

"Yes, of course," said Irene, and it was a pleasure watching her be magnanimous. Her cheeks were pink and her little dark eyes glowed as she raked in the smiles. She said to Betsy, "Will you come up to my room for a bit? There's something I want to tell you."

"Of course."

Irene's room was about what Betsy expected: small and inexpensively furnished. Except for the Dazor light, of course, and the magnificent needlepoint cover on the bed. Every possible surface was covered with needlepoint or with needlepoint supplies, but there was a ruthless order to everything and not a speck of dust or dirt anywhere.

Irene sat on the bed and Betsy took the only chair, which had a petit point cushion.

"I hear someone cut the brake line on your car," said Irene.

"Yes," nodded Betsy. Unlike most native plants, the Excelsior grapevine did not go dormant in winter.

"Have you thought that it might have something to do with that tapestry they found in Trinity?"

"How could an old tapestry make somebody want to commit murder?"

"Well, I've always said it was suspicious how Lucy Abrams died on the same day her husband had that stroke," said Irene. Which was probably untrue, as Betsy had never heard anything of the sort from her, or anyone else, either. "And then this tapestry, which she was working on just before she died, got put right out of sight. Now it turns up, and someone tries to murder you. I think there's a connection."

"But I'm not the one who found it," protested Betsy.

Irene leaned forward, eyes shining. "No, but you're the one with a talent for discovering murderers, aren't you?"

9

Godwin expected to find Betsy already in the shop when he arrived the next day, Friday, at about ten minutes to ten. But he had to unlock the door and turn the lights on himself. Shelly arrived a few minutes later and, seeing Betsy was not there, said, "She's probably still in bed. I thought she was pushing it, staying till five yesterday."

"Mm-hmm," said Godwin. "Still, she didn't look tired when she left for Irene's place. I was hoping to get the morning off. I've got some errands to run. If I have to stay all day, I can't work this evening. Two eleven-hour days in a row is too much."

"Well, I'll see who's willing to work this evening," said Shelly, going to the big desk that served as a check-out counter. "Where's the list?"

"Top drawer on the left. Do you have the opening-up money?"

"I thought Betsy gave it to you."

"She must have taken it upstairs. Maybe we should call her."

"Okay, after I get someone to work this evening. Or would you rather have this afternoon off, and come back this evening?"

Godwin shrugged. "Stores are less crowded during the day, but it would be hard to come back here once I get into full shopping mode. On the other hand, fighting crowds after an eight-hour day isn't fun, either. Since either choice is vile, get who you can when you can."

Shelly was still talking to the first part-timer when Sophie came trotting out from between the box shelves that marked off an area in the back of the shop. "Wait a second, I think Betsy's here," said Shelly.

And she was. She paused in the opening, blinking blearily and looking truly ill.

"Oh, my God, what happened to you?" exclaimed Shelly. " 'Scuse me, I'll call you back," she said and hung up.

Godwin hurried to take Betsy by the arm. "Here, sit down." He led her back between the shelves to a pair of little upholstered chairs on either side of a small table.

Betsy sank gratefully into a chair. Her hair was sketchily combed, her clothing was an old pair of jeans, a faded cotton sweater, and bedroom slippers. Her complexion was pale, except under her eyes, where it was dark gray.

Godwin said, "If you feel as bad as you look, you shouldn't be down here."

"I *told* Godwin it was too soon for you to come back to work!" said Shelly, coming to look with concern at Betsy. "You obviously wore yourself out yesterday."

"No, I was still feeling pretty good right up to when I went to bed last night," said Betsy. "But I woke up sick in the middle of the night, and I've been getting sicker and sicker. I'm so sick now I'm scared to be up there alone."

Godwin said, "Then we're glad you came down. What

do you think, Shelly, a delayed reaction to frostbite or whatever she got from spending the night in the cold? Or maybe to the drugs they gave her at the hospital?"

Betsy said, "No, I think it's something I ate." As if saying that reminded her, she rose and made a wobbly dash for the bathroom in the storage room. When she came back, she looked, if that were possible, even worse.

"I'm calling your doctor," declared Shelly, starting for the phone. Then she stopped and turned back. "Who is he?"

Betsy sighed. "Melody McQueen. Isn't that the silliest name? I've only seen her once, but I like her. Well, maybe twice; I think she came to the hospital. Don't call her. I'm too sick to go to the doctor's office. Do doctors in Minnesota make house calls?"

Godwin said, "I don't think so. Call her anyway, Shelly. Her phone number's on the Rolodex." He felt Betsy's forehead, which was cool and clammy. "If this is food poisoning, it's the worst case I've ever seen. What was it you ate?"

"Cashew chicken salad with red grapes, my favorite. There were two cartons of it in the refrigerator, they came with the hot dishes. I don't see how it could have gone bad so quickly. I came back from taking that poinsettia to Irene—you should have seen her, Godwin, she was so *proud* that we gave her a gift, it nearly made me cry. And you know, she said the oddest thing—" Betsy got a sudden, inward look, and leaned forward a little. "Cramps," she muttered. "There's nothing left in there, but my body still keeps trying to shove it out."

Godwin reached for her hand. It was alarmingly cold. He chaffed it gently between his own for a bit. "Have you got her doctor yet?" he called to Shelly.

"I'm on hold for her," replied Shelly.

"Change places with me, I want to talk to her," said Godwin.

Shelly came to sit with Betsy. "Have you had food poisoning before?" she asked.

"Yes, years and years ago. I think it was fish that time, not ch-chicken salad . . ." She fell silent, swallowing ominously.

Godwin called, "Betsy, Dr. McQueen wants to talk to you!"

Shelly helped her to the phone.

"Yes?" said Betsy. Between pauses of various lengths, she continued, "Yes. About ten last night. Yes. No. No. Do you really think—yes, all right. Yes, I will." Betsy hung up. "Since I can't keep even fluids down, she says I should go back to the hospital."

"I'll drive you," said Shelly.

"All right. But first go up to my apartment and get both cartons of that salad. She wants to see what kind of bug it has." Betsy reached into the desk drawer, got the spare key to her apartment, handed it to Shelly. "Bring my purse, too, will you? They're going to ask for that darn medical insurance number."

"That wonderful medical insurance number," corrected Godwin firmly. "I'm glad you listened to me when I told you not to cancel your medical insurance."

As Godwin was helping Betsy up and into Shelly's big purple SUV, she stopped and said over her shoulder, "Call Jill when you think she's up, will you, Goddy? Tell her I want to talk to her."

Jill joined Betsy in the emergency room an hour later, where she was still waiting for treatment.

"There's two heart attacks and a hand shredded by a snow blower ahead of me," said Betsy. "They say this is the usual result of a bad snowstorm."

The waiting room was large but dimly lit, with four

television sets hanging down from the ceiling, all tuned to the same soap opera. The dozen people in the room bent under the sound as if being beaten.

Jill sat down on the chrome and plastic chair beside Betsy. "What do you think you've got?" she asked.

Betsy pointed to the paper bag between her feet. "I came home around ten last night and I hadn't had any supper, so I ate some of this chicken salad, and I woke up a little after midnight, very sick." She hesitated, then asked, "Can you, as a police officer, order them to test this salad for poison?"

Jill blinked and replied, "What kind of poison?"

"The kind that makes you lose everything you've eaten since the Fourth of July, makes your inside hurt like you've got ulcers, makes your fingers and toes tingle, and gives you a headache and chills."

"Sounds like bad mayònnaise to me," said Jill.

Betsy nodded. "It probably is. But Vern Miller says my brakes failed Monday night because someone deliberately cut the brake line."

Jill searched Betsy's eyes. "Does Mike Malloy know about this?" she asked.

"Yes. He checked it out and says it does look as if the line was cut. I told him I haven't made anyone mad at me lately, so it was probably somebody after someone else's car. But I don't think someone mistook my refrigerator for someone else's."

Jill touched Betsy on the arm. "You stay right here." She went back to the treatment area and used the authority of her badge to get Betsy seen right away. Then, because she could not require a test for poison on her own authority, she took the paper sack to a phone and called Malloy.

"If I hadn't seen that brake line with my own eyes, I wouldn't do this, you know," he said.

"I know. But she's really, really sick, Mike, bad

enough that they're going to admit her. Besides, her doctor's having the food tested anyway, for botulism or *E. coli* or whatever."

"What kind of poison is it supposed to be?"

"She doesn't know. You're the detective, what kind of poison appears to be serious food poisoning?"

"I'll call someone at the toxicology lab."

Jill thanked him and hung up, then went to see how Betsy was doing. They'd started an IV line—she was seriously dehydrated—and were going to admit her under a preliminary diagnosis of food poisoning. Under the white sheet on the narrow gurney, Betsy in fact looked very sick. But as they wheeled her away, Jill heard her joke to the nurse's aide, "Can I have my old room back?" Which Jill considered to be a good sign.

It was toward evening when Dr. McQueen came into Betsy's room. She was a Viking princess, nearly six feet tall with very pale blond hair pulled back into a French twist and a cool, assured manner. She was wearing a pale blue jumper over a thin white wool sweater. With her was a nurse carrying a little tray with a green cloth over it. "We'll be treating you for arsenic poisoning," said Dr. McQueen.

"Arsenic—Is that what it is?"

"Yes, and I congratulate you for recognizing the symptoms all by yourself. One of the two samples given the toxicology lab contained arsenic, and your urine sample also was positive."

"Could it be accidental? I mean, I remember reading there's some kind of poison in nuts."

Dr. McQueen replied, "Cyanide occurs naturally in peach pits and almonds. But you'd need to eat a bushel of almonds at one sitting to get sick. And in your case, the poison is arsenic, which is a mineral—an element, actually, almost but not quite a metal." Dr. McQueen gestured at the nurse, who uncovered her tray and picked up a hypodermic that looked suitable for an elephant.

"If you will roll over, please," said the nurse.

"Are—um, I mean, that's a really big needle," said Betsy.

"The dose is large," admitted Dr. McQueen, "and this is only the first in a series. Plus we have to go deep so you don't get site abscesses. The nurse will stay with you for a while after the injection, because there can be other reactions to Dimercaprol."

"Like what?" asked Betsy, allowing herself to be rolled onto her side. "Ow, ow, ow!" she added.

"You may feel a burning sensation in your mouth and throat or experience muscle cramps, tingling extremities, tightness in the chest, or nausea. You'll probably get a headache fairly quickly and may feel a little dopey."

"I already feel most of that," said Betsy, rolling back over gingerly.

Dr. McQueen took Betsy's pulse, and the nurse sat down on a chair beside Betsy's bed.

Betsy tried to relax, but alarm over possible side effects took most of her attention. And other thoughts were leaping and waving in a panicked attempt to get her attention.

Who wanted to kill her?

And why?

Two hours later, the door opened again, and a slim redhead in a dark suit, white shirt, and conservative tie came in, his charcoal-black coat over one arm. With him was Jill, in uniform.

"Hi, Malloy," sighed Betsy. "I've been expecting you."

"Have you figured out yet what you've got yourself into?" he asked, his thin mouth pulled into a little smile.

"I can only repeat that I am sure I haven't done anything to provoke this. Nothing."

Jill asked, "Are you feeling better yet?"

"Yes, the IV really helped."

Malloy hung the coat on a chair and reached into an inside pocket for a notebook and pen. He searched the notebook until he found the right page. "Only one of the chicken salads taken from your refrigerator contained arsenic. But it was enough to kill you if you'd eaten all of it."

Betsy felt a shiver run down her entire body. She had been really hungry by the time she sat down to her very late supper, but eating heartily just before bed was a guarantee of a restless night.

Not that she hadn't had one anyway.

Malloy asked, "I take it these salads were brought as gifts?"

"Yes. When I got home from the hospital, people brought me all kinds of food."

Malloy nodded. "Who brought the chicken salads?"

"I don't know."

"You mean you don't remember?"

"No, I mean it started coming while I was still in the hospital, and continued after I got home. I went to bed and to sleep. Godwin may know who brought it. He was running the shop and sent the people up. A lot of people know I love Eddie's cashew chicken, so it could have been anyone."

Malloy smiled. "Except for the ones who brought you something else." He made a note, then went back a few pages. "Jill says she remembers you told her Patricia Fairland brought a hot dish, and that Godwin and Shelly also mentioned Martha Winters, Kate MacDonald, Alice Skoglund, and Phil Galvin as people who brought food. Do you know these people?"

Betsy nodded. "Good customers. Friends, some of them."

Malloy said, his eyes amused, "What, you're so broke you're accepting charitable donations?"

Betsy rolled her eyes. "Come on, Mike. People want to do something for someone who's been in the hospital, and when they don't know what else to do, they bring food, God bless them. It was a revelation, seeing my kitchen. I didn't realize I had so many friends."

"And one enemy," Malloy reminded her. "Any idea who that might be?"

Betsy shook her head. "I told you, no."

"You sure? Nobody mad at you for any reason right now?"

She started to shake her head again, then said, "Well, my ex-husband was. But he wouldn't do anything, he's trying to get me to come back to him."

"Why?"

She frowned at him. "What do you mean?"

"Why does Mr. Norman want you back?"

"I don't know, maybe he needs someone to do his housework. But more likely it's because he found out I'm an heiress."

"You're sure he knows that?"

"I can't think why else he'd come all the way here from California to try to make up with me."

"Why did you divorce him?"

"He started it, filing for divorce after he fell in love with one of his students. But another student he'd dumped for her blew the whistle. And that started a chain reaction of whistle blowing that went back years. His true love dumped him, the college dumped him, and I dumped him."

"So things really came unraveled for him," said Jill.

Betsy nodded. "He lost his tenure, his job, his house, and me. Now he says he's learned his lesson and is very sorry and wants me to forgive him and take him back."

"And you are willing to do that?" asked Malloy.

"Remarry Hal the Pig? Not in a million years!"

"You told him that?"

Betsy, remembering the white, furious face, nodded. "He came to see me on Wednesday, trying to apologize for his behavior, and got very angry when I told him to get out."

"So he was in your apartment, then. And you exchanged words. Did he bring you a food gift?"

"He didn't say. Godwin may know."

"Did he threaten you?"

"No. He was really angry when I told him I'd call the cops if he didn't leave, angrier than I've ever seen him." She grimaced. "But his goal is to win me back, so why try to kill me?" She nodded at the enormous bouquet of mixed flowers on the shelf in front of the window. "See? Latest in a string."

But Malloy persisted, "Would he profit in some other way from your death? I mean, is there a life insurance policy he might still hold with your name on it?"

Betsy shook her head. "No. I changed the beneficiary—" She stopped.

"What?"

"I just remembered; I made Margot the new beneficiary. I'll have to change it again."

Malloy went through her current circumstances with her in some detail. "Shelly Donohue pointed out Joe Mickels hasn't gone after me like he did my sister," said Betsy at one point. "He doesn't like me, but he seems content now to wait out the lease." She frowned, remembering the last two times she'd seen him. "I think there's something on his mind, though."

"Do you know what it is?"

"No, but it's not me or the building the shop is in.

It's almost like I don't matter much anymore. Otherwise, why isn't he trying to evict me?"

Malloy smiled. "You haven't heard of the law passed by our city council?"

"What law?"

" 'No building in the City of Excelsior shall exceed forty feet in height.' So he can't put up the six-story Mickels Building. I hear he's looking around for a site outside Excelsior now."

"Oh-ho! That explains it. I guess I've been too busy to notice that new law, though it's funny none of the town gossips dropped by to tell me about it. But surely they didn't pass that law just to keep Mickels from building in Excelsior?"

"No, it's this vision thing they've got hold of. There are a lot of people who live here because it's their ideal of a small town," said Malloy.

"Mayberry of the North," nodded Betsy.

"Right. They like the small-town feel, and they want to preserve it. So they elect representatives who feel the same way, and this is one way they've chosen to preserve the ambience they like."

Betsy remembered how comforted she'd felt coming down Water Street on her way home from the hospital, as if she'd stepped into a Norman Rockwell painting. "Yes, but—" Betsy began, and stopped.

"Yeah, I agree," said Malloy. "It means taxes stay high. Still, it takes Mickels off the list. What about Irene Potter?"

"What about her?"

"You know she was angry with Margot because she thought your sister was deliberately keeping her from her dream of owning an embroidery store or whatever you call it."

"Needlework," said Jill.

"And you wonder if she's transferred that anger to

me." Betsy smiled, remembering the pride and delight with which Irene had accepted the gift poinsettia. "No, she's not mad at me. Though she may see me as incompetent and is just biding her time until the shop goes under, at which glorious moment she'll take over."

"Are you incompetent?"

Betsy chuckled. "In a lot of ways, yes. But I've got good help. And I'm learning fast. Irene hasn't realized that yet."

Malloy wrote something down, then went back two pages in his notebook. "A cut brake line and now arsenic poisoning. That's two attempts on your life, Ms. Devonshire."

Again, Betsy felt that chill, but all she could do was shrug helplessly. "Do you have any ideas?"

"I'm thinking you sent some people to jail charged with murder," said Mike. "Very few people are pleased by that."

"Well, yes, but both of them are still in jail."

"They've got friends and relatives."

"Oh. I hadn't thought about that. Do you know who these friends and relatives are?"

"Not yet. But I'll find out."

Jill said, "I still think it might be Joe. He was fit to be tied when it turned out Margot's death didn't give him back his building. Even if he can't build something bigger, he can at least raise the rent."

Betsy chuckled, but not wholeheartedly. It was no joke, having someone murderously angry with you.

Mike said, "But we can still eliminate people. It's someone who knows Betsy pretty well—she's still new in town, remember."

Betsy nodded. "It's also a person who knows how to get hold of arsenic—and there can't be many sources around, can there?"

Jill said, "I shouldn't think so. Do you know of any, Mike?"

"No. It's not a street drug. I know it's used in some manufacturing processes, like in preserving wood."

Betsy said, "In old-fashioned mysteries, you soaked it out of fly paper or went to a chemist and signed a poison book—but that was England in the thirties. I have no idea where you'd get it in modern America. Dr. McQueen said it also has medical uses."

Mike asked, "How well do you know Dr. McQueen?"

Betsy replied, "Not very well, why?"

"So she has no reason to be mad at you?"

"No reason at all."

Malloy closed his notebook and shook it lightly. "Still, here's a start," he said. "We'll find this crazy person, and meanwhile, we're not going to let anything happen to you. I'll arrange for an officer to stand guard around the clock."

"Wait, Mike, that'll pull an officer off every watch," said Jill. "And we're shorthanded as it is. Besides, he can't follow her everywhere—like I can. So how about you assign me? I can move in with her, and we can put out the word that she has an armed, live-in guard with a real snarky attitude."

Betsy waited for Mike to say something against that— he almost never agreed with Jill's ideas—but he didn't.

But Betsy didn't want a roommate and tried to say so politely after Joe left.

Jill replied, "All right, then we'll have to let Mike take you into custody. Do you want to spend Christmas in jail?"

"Jail? He can't arrest me, I didn't do anything!"

"What do you think protective custody is? His job is to enforce the law and to protect the public. You're a member of the public, and he has the power to do whatever it takes to protect you."

Betsy glared at Jill, who looked back with that serenely adamantine Gibson-girl face. So Betsy unclenched her own face and sighed. She seemed to be doing a lot of that lately.

10

The next morning Betsy, who was feeling pretty good now her reaction to the Dimercaprol had settled down, said to Jill, "Okay, I'm ready to see what you brought from my place. How did you get in, by the way?"

Jill replied, "I called Godwin, and he came over to the shop and gave me the key to your apartment." She put a lidded basket on Betsy's legs. "In light of what's been happening to you lately, I think that key is a bad idea, so I brought it along." She held it up by its needle-pointed tag, then dropped it into Betsy's purse on the bedside table.

"Then how's Sophie going to be taken care of?"

"She's in the shop. I brought her down, and her dish and some of her food in a plastic bag. You'll probably be sent home this afternoon, so not to worry."

"Was Godwin miffed at being asked to come in early? I don't like asking him to do more than he already does, which is a lot."

"It wasn't Godwin who was miffed, it was that lawyer

he lives with. He treats Godwin like a boy toy, you know."

"Yes, I got a glimpse of that when Goddy brought John to the Christmas party. I wonder what will happen if Godwin starts acting more grown up?"

"Godwin will *maybe* turn twenty-three just before he dies eighty years from now."

Betsy laughed and opened the lidded basket, which sat heavily on her legs. On top was the reason: the thick old book on Christian symbology Father John Rettger had loaned her.

"What'd you bring this for?" asked Betsy.

"It was on your bedside table. I thought you were reading it."

"Well, I was, but I'm not as interested since I can't find my notes on the tapestry. You know, it's the darnedest thing..." Betsy had started to put it aside, but now paused, frowning.

"What?" asked Jill.

"Maybe I've been a dope. Did I tell you the notes I put into the computer and printed out have gone missing?"

"When did this happen?"

"Last week. Hand me my purse, will you?"

Jill did, and Betsy dug around until she found her checkbook. She opened it and pulled out the tablet of checks. "Gotcha!"

Jill said, "Now what?"

"Here are my original notes, the ones I made while looking at the tapestry. I wrote them on the back of this, then copied them into the computer. Then I added more stuff from memory and printed it out. That's what disappeared, the printout. I could kick myself for not saving it, but at least I put this back where it belonged. We can maybe start over. I suppose you've got a pen and notebook on you?"

Jill did. It was a small one, with the pages sewn in, and to be used for official business only. "But taking care of you is my official business."

Betsy paused in her search for a blank page. "It may be more official than that. Irene Potter told me I should wonder why Lucy Abrams died the same day her husband had that stroke. And it's suspicious that this tapestry went missing right about then, too."

Jill said, "If I thought a tapestry pointed to me as a criminal, I wouldn't hide it. I'd burn it or bury it."

"Yes, that would make sense. But maybe they just meant to hide it temporarily, and the room got sealed off, and they decided it was as good as gone. Or Lucy herself hid it."

"Why would she do that?"

"I don't know. Is there anything suspicious about her death? Did they do an autopsy?"

"I don't think so. You want me to find out?"

"Please." Jill took her notebook back, wrote herself a note, and handed it back to Betsy.

Betsy looked at the thin cardboard back of the checkbook. There was a flock of little drawings: a shamrock, then a calf or a fawn, then a heart with—something. An M? No, a heart aflame, she remembered now. And there was an ice cream cone, a candle . . . Betsy began copying the drawings into the notebook. She wished she were a better artist; it wasn't easy figuring out what her original hasty sketches were supposed to be. Of course, the original stitching wasn't always clear, either. That slanting line with the three lines coming down from its tip, for example. She remembered wondering at the time what that was supposed to be. On the other hand, "Saint Olaf," she murmured, as she copied the ax.

"Who?" said Jill, turning her head sideways to take a look at the tablet.

"Father John told me the double-bladed ax is an attribute of Saint Olaf. Like the shamrock is for Saint Patrick."

"Oh, yes," nodded Jill. "I remember those from Sunday school. The shamrock is also for the Trinity. And crossed keys are for Saint Peter. Are there crossed keys on there?"

"No," said Betsy, "but there's a single key. I wonder who that stands for. And who is the cat?" She had written "cat" rather than drawn one, and had written "2" beside it to remind her that there were two of them. That was interesting enough that she put down the pen and notebook to open the big book and search down to the section where symbols were listed alphabetically. "Ahhhhhh, cat, cat—here. It says Saint Yvo, and it also means witchcraft. Did you know there's a witch in town?"

"Yes, but she wasn't a witch back then, she was an astrologer. And before that she was into tarot cards."

"Hmm. Then I guess Lucy wasn't telling us to hang all the witches. I remember the last item was a hangman's noose." She hadn't drawn that on the checkbook, so she drew one now on the notebook page. "There was a star, too, a Star of David, the kind you make with two triangles." She drew one of those. "I didn't copy all of the attributes on the tapestry down," she explained. "Now I think about it, there was Saint Elizabeth of Hungary." She drew three crowns, one above two. "And a horseshoe, I'm pretty sure there was a horseshoe, unless it was omega, the Greek letter. Omega is the last letter of the Greek alphabet, and if you combine it with the first, alpha, it's an attribute of God." She drew a horseshoe like an upside down U, in case it was omega. "And Father John said there was the attribute of Saint Agnes, though I can't remember which one it was."

"You really think there's a message in all this?" asked Jill.

"Maybe." Betsy looked again at the book, still turned to the section on symbols. "Did you ever know anyone named Yvo, spelled Wye-vee-oh? Maybe these attributes are members of the church back then."

"No. But there was an Elizabeth. And I think there was an Agnes. And I knew a Mr. Ives, he taught Sunday school. Is Saint Yvo the same as Saint Ives? I bet it is. Remember that old riddle: As I was going to Saint Ives, I met a man with seven wives, each with seven sacks, each with seven cats, each with seven kits."

Betsy was already looking up Ives in the section that had saints alphabetically. "No, his attribute is a fountain flowing from a tomb. Ugh."

"Ick," agreed Jill.

The door opened and an attractive, dark-haired woman in a headband and beautiful swing coat came in, closely followed by three children.

Jill, who had swung to her feet in one swift movement, relaxed.

"Well, hello Patricia," said Betsy, surprised and pleased.

"Hello, Betsy," said Patricia. "We were on our way to Christmas-shop at the Mall of America and decided to stop in and see how you're doing. But I see you already have a visitor."

"That's all right, come in," said Jill, "come in and talk." She moved away to the window.

Betsy said, "I'm glad you came by. Are all of these yours?"

Patricia laughed a fond parent's laugh. "Yes, all three. This is Brent, who is eleven." She pushed forward the oldest child, a very handsome dark-haired boy with hazel eyes that looked back at Betsy—a woman in a nightgown in bed—with a warm interest that was surprising in one that age. *Knows he's good looking, too,* thought Betsy.

"And here is Edith Ann, who is nearly six." Edith Ann had her mother's light brown eyes and a gap-toothed smile. She was very thin and a little shy.

"And this is Meryl, who is three." Meryl was round and blond and ravishingly pretty. She smiled at Betsy from behind her mother's left leg.

"What are you doing?" asked Brent.

"Oh, I'm trying to figure out a puzzle, but I don't have all the pieces." She looked at Patricia. "I didn't write them all down, so I'm having trouble figuring out if Lucy hid her name in those attributes."

"Well, I hope you aren't straining yourself over it," said Patricia. "You should just rest and get well."

"I'll be all right in a day or two," said Betsy.

"Are you very, very sick?" asked Edith Ann, who must be named after her grandmother, because no one named a child Edith Ann nowadays.

"I was, but I'm only a little sick now," said Betsy. "I may go home today."

"That's good news," said Patricia. "So I suppose I needn't offer to bring you something."

"No, but thank you."

"I'm going to buy my grandmother a present today," said Brent. "We're going to fly to Phoenix for Christmas. That's where she lives. There isn't any snow there."

"It sounds wonderful," said Betsy.

"We're going in a airplane," announced Edith Ann.

"Yes—oops, come here, Meryl," said Patricia. She went to pull her youngest off the empty bed nearer the window and continued, "My mother told me there are two ways to visit someone in the hospital. First, don't sit down, and when your feet start to hurt, go. Second, bring a small child, and when the child gets bored, go. Either way, you won't overstay your welcome. So that's it for now. Say good-bye, children."

"Good-bye, Ms. Devonshire," said Brent, offering another of his charming smiles. "I'm glad you feel better."

"Good-bye," smiled Edith Ann, who might be thin because so many baby teeth were missing. Meryl used that adorable just-the-fingers wave as her mother herded them out the door.

"Awwwww," said Betsy, when they'd gone.

"That boy of hers is a born politician, just like his father," remarked Jill, coming back to sit beside Betsy's bed.

"Phoenix, where there isn't any snow," sighed Betsy. She picked up the checkbook and finished copying her notes into Jill's notebook, then looked them over. "Phil said she also sometimes put a family member's name in her work. Maybe she had a sister named Agnes." She frowned and tapped the notebook with the pen. "How about she spelled her name with the first letter of these things?" She looked but couldn't find any symbol that started with an L. "Wait a second, I think Father John said this was a lamb, not a fawn." Betsy tapped the lying-down animal. "Now, U, U, U . . . Not here."

"Unless you're wrong about the horseshoe," said Jill. "Turn it right side up, and it's a U."

"And if the shamrock is really a clover, that's a C! All we need is a Y, now."

"Oh, Yvo, of course. But there's a lot of stretching to make it fit. Horseshoe is H, not U. Plus I know the horseshoe was upside down, or why would I think it could have been omega? Ach, this is giving me a headache." Betsy gave the notebook back to Jill and put the book on the bedside table. She lay back and closed her eyes. After a minute she asked, "What was Lucy like?"

Jill composed herself to think. "She was almost as tall as her husband—though he wasn't really tall—and very slim, with a narrow face and a long nose. She had gray hair and very nice gray eyes. She was quiet and dignified, and never said 'ain't' or 'swell' like he did. I used to wonder about them as a couple—you know, what they saw in each other. He was loud and friendly, and, now I think about it, she was probably shy. She was polite to everyone and she carried hard candy wrapped in cellophane in her purse, and sometimes she'd give one to a toddler. I remember my cousin got one and for months he kept a close eye on that purse in case it opened again when he was around."

Betsy laughed. "Did it?"

"No, she only did it once in a rare while, which made it special."

Betsy settled deeper into her pillows and said, "Go on, tell me more."

"Well, she always wore dresses, long and flowing and far out of date. She made them herself. I remember my mother talking about how well made they were. And she always wore a hat to church—and this was when nobody wore hats. She was a little too nice to join the Monday Bunch, but I admire her more now than when when I was a kid. Father Keane was more fun. But he had his dignity, too; like he never wore shorts in public." Jill smiled. "But he did have some pretty raggedy old trousers he'd put on to repair the roof or mow the lawn. And he had this straw hat with a big brim . . ." She stopped, having wandered from the topic of Lucy Abrams.

But Betsy, smiling too, said, "Go on, tell me about Father Keane now."

Jill's voice took on more color. "I adored him. We all did. He was one of those tough-guy priests, intelligent in a low-brow sort of way. He could bluster and shout, but everyone knew he was marshmallow inside. He never had any trouble with the vestry or with anyone in the congregation, which is amazing when you think about it. He was a soft touch, too; when he left, there was a scramble to rebuild some of the funds, especially the rector's discretionary fund. Not that he'd give money to everyone with a sad story, but if he thought someone was in real need, he was very generous."

Betsy, remembering that photo of the craggy face with the bright eyes and sweet smile, nodded. But she nevertheless asked a hard question. "Could he have used some of that money for himself or his family?"

"I never heard that, and you know how gossip is around here. He certainly didn't live beyond his means—the opposite, in fact. I remember Margot doing a fundraiser to get him into a nicer nursing home, because they didn't have any savings. The church owns a rectory—that big old house on Center Street with the really huge silver maple in the front yard. It's in bad shape, and Father Keane did a lot of repairs himself to save on bills. It has five bedrooms, and Father John simply rattles around inside. The vestry keeps saying we ought to sell the place and give our rector a housing allowance. Which I wish they would; with property values what they are, the church could pay for the whole renovation just from the sale of that house. And Father John would love to live in a nice little apartment; he can't even change a lightbulb."

"I thought he was married," said Betsy.

"A widower," said Jill. "He has children, but the youngest is studying music at Julliard. I think he's actually afraid of the power lawn mower, he always hires local kids to mow his lawn. He's really different from Father Keane. I can see our old priest now, painting the windows or mowing the front lawn in that straw hat, sleeves rolled up, pants legs, too. And barefoot, with cut grass sticking to his shins. And Lucy bringing him ice tea on a tray. Some of the older members didn't think that was nice, him working on the lawn barefooted or climbing up on the roof, but those're hardly the acts of a man living high off stolen funds."

Betsy rubbed a forefinger under her nose, her sign of frustration. "Why the noose?"

"Why not?"

"Surely no saint has a hangman's noose as an attribute." She opened the book but at first couldn't find a hangman's noose. She finally found it under rope, hangman's. "It means betrayal or treason, and it's the attribute of Judas."

That set off a search for more attributes' meanings. Even the ones that had a negative symbology, like the cat, performed double duty as a saint's attribute. There didn't seem to be a Saint Amanda though, or a Saint Keane.

Then she tried to see if some combination of the initial letters of the attributes would spell Keane, or thief, cheat, or adultery, without success.

Jill said, "You know what I think? I think Lucy picked out the attributes she did because they're easy to stitch." Jill took the heavy book and opened it at random. "Look here, Saint John the Baptist's attribute is a lamb on a book of seven seals and here, Saint Lawrence's is a thurible. What's a thurible?"

"Beats me."

"I bet it's more complicated than a cat or an ax. Remember, she was working with a single strand of silver metallic on a space less than an inch square. She saw that blank blue space in the halo and thought it needed something, and an all-saints theme is nice and theological, right? And I bet you were right when you said members of the congregation have the names she picked."

"But the hangman's noose," protested Betsy.

"Oh, it was probably some kind of joke, like my grandfather calling his best friend 'you old horse thief.' But we'll never know what Lucy's joke was, because she's dead, and Keane's got the mind of a houseplant."

"We could ask Mandy."

"All right, when you get out of here, we'll do that, since it's bothering you."

Betsy smiled at Jill. "Yes, thank you for understanding. As soon as we get home." She gave the notebook back to Jill, put the checkbook in her purse, and began searching the basket for some needlework.

But it was hard to let the idea go. Soon, while pausing to count stitches, Betsy said, "We should find out if anybody else connected with the tapestry has been attacked."

"Mike already checked on that. Patricia, Martha, Phil, Father John, everyone is going about his or her daily business with no problem."

The electronic *bing* sounded, and Godwin looked up to see Malloy standing inside the door.

"Hi, Malloy," Godwin said.

"I understand you were the one sending people upstairs with food for Ms. Devonshire Tuesday and Wednesday."

"Yes, that's right."

"Do you remember the names of everyone who brought something?"

Godwin assumed a thinking pose, tilting his head back, wrapping a slim forefinger around his chin, and closing his eyes. "Martha Winters brought a hot dish. So did Shelly Donohue, Alice Skoglund, and Patricia Fairland." He spoke slowly, assuming, correctly, that Malloy was writing this down. "Katie MacDonald brought a fruit basket, and so did Phil Galvin. June Connor brought a hot dish and Annelle Byford brought a tropical fruit basket. Ellen Rose, Ingrid Leeners, and Rayne Hamilton brought hot dishes, and Gabriel Anderson brought a banana cream pie. And Betsy's ex, Harold Norman, came in and asked what Betsy liked. I said she was crazy about that cashew chicken salad the sandwich shop next door makes, and he went and brought a take-out order. But after he took it up, Betsy called and said not to let him come back up again."

"Did he come back?"

Godwin nodded. "Yes. This time he had a live Christmas tree with him, a big one. And when I told him he couldn't take it up to her, he got in my face until I told him it was her orders. Then he took his tree and went away, and I haven't seen him since." Godwin was smiling at the memory.

"It's my understanding that two people brought chicken salad."

Godwin thought. "I only remember one, the one Hal Norman brought."

"Could he have brought two orders?"

"Sure, but he didn't. I saw him with just one."

"Could someone have gone through here without you seeing him or her?"

Godwin, shaking his head, opened his mouth to say no, then shut it again. "I don't think so. I mean, I'd be helping a customer, and people would interrupt to ask me if I'd take something up to her, and I'd unlock the back door and tell them the door to her apartment was unlocked. Then, when they came back down, I'd lock the door again. I thought leaving her door unlocked was okay, because the other doors to upstairs were locked. And because I knew the ones I sent up: they were friends or good customers. That's why I know who brought what. I was careful about keeping the back door to the shop locked, and we weren't so busy that someone could sneak by. At least, I don't think so. I mean, Irene Potter came in with her Peter Ashe canvas and we got into a pretty intense discussion of stitches, and I suppose someone could have walked through during it. But that takes two coincidences, that I was distracted *and* I left the back door unlocked. Which I don't think I did."

"Did you bring her a gift of food?"

"Are you kidding? There was enough food going up there to feed an army!"

"Did Irene Potter bring something?"

"No. Nor Joe Mickels."

"I thought Joe Mickels was being a lot nicer to Betsy than he was to Margot."

"Well, it's more like he isn't doing things to harass her, like lawsuits. On the other hand, it's not like he's asking her out to dinner. He still looks at her like he looks at everyone, like we're burglars on parole."

The owner of Eddie's Sandwich Shoppe next door was a blocky, middle-aged man with dark, tired eyes and large hands in clear plastic gloves. He couldn't remember how many orders of cashew chicken salad he'd sold on Tuesday. He sold between eight and a dozen orders on any given day, it was one of his most popular salads, so probably it was between eight and a dozen.

Irene Potter? Oh, yeah, that crazy lady with the dark, curly hair. No, she hadn't bought anything from him lately.

But yeah, now that Malloy asked, his landlord was in this week, he was pretty sure it was on Tuesday. Joe came in two or three times a month, and he usually picked either the cashew chicken or the orange coconut dessert. Last time he came in, it was the cashew chicken, and that was earlier this week. Yes, he was sure.

Betsy was working on her stem stitch when the door opened. Quick as thought, Jill was on her feet, standing between Betsy and whoever came in.

It was the Viking Princess, standing very still in surprise. "Hello, Ms. Devonshire," she said over Jill's shoulder.

"Hi, Dr. McQueen. This is my bodyguard, Jill Cross."

"I see. How do you do?" The doctor nodded, and Jill stepped aside. Today she was in blue wool slacks and a white cotton turtleneck with tiny blue flowers on it. A stethoscope was slung sideways around her neck. She came to plug it into her ears and listen to Betsy's heart. Satisfied, she asked, "Feeling better?"

"Yes, thank you. Are you going to send me home?"

"Not today. We need to keep you here another twenty-four hours, monitoring your arsenic levels while we continue treatment."

"Poor Sophie," said Betsy.

"You have a child?"

"No, Sophie's my cat."

"Ah. I've heard animals become lonesome for their owners when separated." Dr. McQueen said that as if she wanted to see a study before she would believe it. "You may get up and walk the halls, if you like. A little exercise may make you feel better."

But Jill said, "Since she's here because there have been two attempts on her life, I don't think she should leave this room, doctor."

"Where does arsenic come from, do you know?" asked Betsy.

Dr. McQueen said, "It's a mineral, so you mine it. There is, or used to be, an arsenic mine in France, and there's one in New Jersey."

"Another reason we're all so fond of New Jersey." Betsy nodded and Jill laughed.

Dr. McQueen didn't crack a smile. "Hundreds of years ago it was called inheritance powder," she continued. "It's tasteless and odorless, and its symptoms can be confused with severe gastritis."

"Very reassuring," said Betsy.

Oblivious, Dr. McQueen continued, "Of course, since they developed a simple test for it, people are less likely to use it to murder. It has commercial and medical uses. It was one of the first cures for syphilis."

"Brrr!" said Jill, surprised.

"The body quickly dumps most of what you ingest, but what little remains can kill you. That's why we're giving you Dimercaprol. It's a chelating agent that apparently binds to the remaining arsenic, rendering it harmless while the body excretes it."

"Apparently?" echoed Betsy.

"Well, we know chelating agents work, we're just not sure how. Any arsenic we can't get rid of winds up in your hair and fingernails. We can dig up a body buried for centuries and find it. It was found recently in a lock of Napoleon's hair."

Betsy said, "I'm so glad you didn't have to dig me up to find out I'd been given a dose."

"That wouldn't have been me, that would have been the medical examiner," explained Dr. McQueen seriously.

When she left, Jill said, "With that sense of humor, she should have been a surgeon."

It was a shabby motel room, with a big television attached to rabbit ears instead of cable and the remote bolted to the bedside table. It had an antique microwave oven, a plug-in coffeepot, and a tiny refrigerator that leaked. Hal might have done better, but flowers here in the frozen north were expensive, and he was afraid it was going to be a long siege.

He lay back on the queen-size bed. He was familiar with the literature that portrayed Midwesterners and Southerners as inbred folk suffering from mad jealousies and inflamed libidos. He'd never thought to actually find himself among such people.

What a place this was! Excelsior, Minnesota, land of ice and snow—and people who seemed to think there was nothing wrong with living that way. Coolly polite ice people, crazily jealous when an outsider comes in and makes good. Because that was what this stuff happening to Betsy was all about, right? She moves here from San Diego and gloms her sister's money and her sister's store and her sister's friends, and they just can't stand it. Tennessee Williams would have loved it.

Someone knocked on his door. Hal rolled to his feet in one easy motion—he was in remarkably good shape for a man his—that is, he was in really good shape.

He opened the door to find a slender man a few inches shorter than himself, a redhead with freckles and very chill pale blue eyes. Something about him set off alarms in Hal's mind, but he said calmly enough, "May I help you?"

"I'm Detective Sergeant Mike Malloy, of the Excelsior Police Department. May I come in?" And suddenly he was holding up a leather folder with a badge and a photo ID in it.

Alarms now sounding loud indeed, Hal took the trouble to note that the photo and name matched the name given and face on display, then he stepped back and said, "Come in. Don't mind the mess," though the place wasn't all that messy; it was more that it was dilapidated. Hal didn't mind good furniture that showed wear, but he didn't like cheap, seedy furniture.

He sat on the bed, gesturing the investigator to the only chair in the room, a wooden armchair. "What can I do for you?" he asked.

"Were you once married to Betsy Devonshire?" Now there was a pen and a notebook in the man's freckled hands.

"Yes." Hal wanted to say more but held his tongue. He tried to look friendly, harmless, and curious—but not too curious.

"You know she's in the hospital?"

"Yes, I sent her flowers. Someone told me she got hold of some poison somehow. She's having a serious run of bad luck lately."

"It may not be just bad luck, Mr. Norman. It appears someone is trying to murder her."

"I can't believe that! She's a fine person, not the type to get involved with people who do that kind of thing!"

"Are you aware that she's been involved in the investigation of three murders since she arrived in Excelsior?"

Hal, genuinely startled, asked, "You mean, she's been a suspect?"

"No, she's taken a role in solving them."

"She has? How . . . peculiar. She never did anything like that back home."

"Well, since she's come here, she has shown a positive talent both for getting involved in crime and tracking down perpetrators."

Bewildered, Hal said, "I thought she was running a needlework store. Has she also taken out a license as a private investigator?"

"No, she's working as an amateur. How long were you two married?"

Hal, still frowning over his ex-wife's peculiar choice of spare-time activity, said, "Eighteen years. Back in San Diego, her hobbies were photography, embroidering aprons and other articles of apparel, and volunteering at the local animal shelter."

"You sent her flowers at the hospital during this stay. Did you bring her a carton of cashew chicken salad when she came home from her first stay?"

Hal nodded. "That fellow who works in the needlework store said it was her favorite. I bought it at the deli next door to her store, and he said I could bring it up. So I did."

"And she thanked you kindly, I suppose."

Hal laughed. "No, she told me to leave and never come back, and she instructed the fellow in the shop to bar me. Which he did." Hal's grin disappeared. "I hurt her badly, and our divorce was entirely my fault. I came here without an invitation, and instead of finding her heartbroken, I find she's made a new life for herself. She wants no part of me, and I can understand that. But I'm hoping that if I stick around for a while, she'll remember the good times and let me have a second chance."

"Arsenic was found in the chicken salad," said Malloy.

Hal found he couldn't breathe in. He sucked and sucked, and finally managed to get just enough air to croak, "What did you say?"

"I said, arsenic was found in the chicken salad. There was enough to have killed her twice over if she'd eaten all of it, but fortunately, she took only one small serving."

Now able to breathe again, Hal couldn't think of anything to say except, "I didn't poison the salad. I didn't even open the carton. I just brought it up and put it in her refrigerator. Why would I poison the salad?"

"Because she won't take you back. Because she left you and came here and has found, by your own description, a new and better life for herself. While you have lost your career and your new girlfriend and your standing in your community. Because she is going to inherit a great deal of money in a few weeks, which you will have no share in. And because when you came up to see her with that little offering of food, she told you to get stuffed, and you were absolutely furious. So you added your own herbal flavoring—"

"Now wait, now wait!" said Hal, an idea coming to him. "What kind of poison is arsenic?"

"What do you mean?"

"Because if you can't buy it at a grocery or drugstore, I didn't do it. I don't know anything about poisons, and I'm not familiar with what's for sale on street corners around here, or even who to ask. I certainly didn't come here expecting to poison Betsy; I came hoping to be reconciled with her, to beg her pardon and ask if she would give me a chance to prove I am worthy of her forgiveness."

"Do you have a pair of scissors or a box cutter in your possession?"

"Huh? No, I don't. I have a pair of fingernail clippers and a fingernail file. I'm doing day labor—painting the interior of houses—and cleaning up is hell on my hands. But at least it's not shoveling snow. Are your winters always like this? My God, I can't imagine living in a climate like this. I haven't been warm since I got here."

Hal could sense he was winning Malloy over, but the cop's next question showed he was still suspicious. "Do you know what the brake line of a car looks like?"

Hal gritted his teeth and told the truth—nothing else would do in his situation. "Yes, I do. But I've never so much as changed a spark plug or the oil or anything but a tire. What was she doing out in a blizzard, anyhow? I would have thought Betsy had more sense than that. After all, she grew up in this part of the country, or practically. Milwaukee is just down the road, isn't it?"

"Milwaukee is six hours south of here by freeway."

"My God, that far? Minneapolis must be practically in the arctic circle, then."

The detective grinned. "Nothing between us and the north pole but a barbed wire fence."

Relieved, Hal grinned back. When the cops started joking with you, things were going to be all right.

11

Jill drove Betsy home from the hospital the next morning, right after doctors' rounds. The trackless snow-scape of the last ride home was now filled with snowmobile and cross-country skiing trails. The roads were wet but bare, and there were splashes of grime on the snow where it dared approach the road.

"I see two ways to go with this," Jill told her, sitting relaxed behind the wheel of her elderly Buick. "You can go into hiding—move to a new town, rent an apartment under an assumed name, and get an unlisted phone number. Run the shop by E-mail, and have Godwin send any profits to a post office box. But who knows when Mike will find out who's doing this? It could be weeks or even months."

"Or never," said Betsy.

"Or never," acknowledged Jill. "Alternatively, you can stay where you are. It may be that, having failed twice, he won't try again. For sure it will be a lot harder for him to get to you now you're aware of him and traveling with me. But if he does try again, our chances of identifying him are improved."

"So Mike thinks of me as bait?"

"No, Mike thinks of sushi as bait."

Jill knew which she wanted Betsy to choose, but shut up and let the silence last.

At last Betsy said quietly, "I'm not running."

Jill did not venture to comment on that, but she did smile, just a little.

They stopped off at Jill's apartment so she could pack a bag. They stopped in at the shop to a warm welcome from Shelly and Godwin—and Martha Winters, who had come in to buy a packet of gold needles. "I broke my last one without realizing it was my last one," she said. "Oh, Betsy, I'm so happy to see you looking well! I hope this is the end of that terrible business!"

"Thank you, me too," said Betsy. "Godwin, I've got some things to do today, but I'll be at work tomorrow, if you want to take that as a day off."

"Bless you, I do."

Shelly said, "You want me to come in?"

"Yes, thanks. And find at least one part-timer to work with me tomorrow evening, can you? I might as well start to make up for some of the time I've been away. Sophie looks comfortable. Shall we just leave her here for now? If I don't come and get her by five, just push her into the stairwell." Sophie was familiar with this procedure and would make her way up to the apartment to be let in.

"Will do. Here, take her bowl up with you."

When they got upstairs, Betsy said, "The back bedroom will be yours." It was the bigger, but it had been Margot's, and Betsy couldn't bring herself to move in there.

While Jill settled in, Betsy looked up Mandy Abrams Oliver in the phone book. Jill had told her Mandy's husband's name was Dan and they lived in Golden Valley, so all Betsy had to do was decipher GldnVly in the phone book. But there was no answer.

Betsy brewed coffee for Jill, who was a true Scandinavian in her love for that beverage, and made a cup of herbal tea for herself. The two sat and sipped and sketched out such things as who got the bathroom first in the morning, and whether the one who cooked dinner did the dishes.

That settled, Betsy asked, "Jill, what are the odds? How sure are you that you can keep me safe?"

"I'm more than reasonably sure. But you have to take some precautions. Let me drive you around, for example. Which isn't a hardship on me; I like to drive. Don't eat anything somebody else prepares for you—and that includes restaurant meals. The stuff currently in your refrigerator is a notable exception, since Mike had me bring samples of all of it in to be tested. Oh, and you've got to let me open your Christmas gifts."

"Now, *just* a *second!*" Betsy put her heart into her fake objection, and noticed with satisfaction that Jill had trouble keeping her deadpan in place.

Jill said, "Oh, I don't mind; in fact, I love opening presents so much I don't care if they're not mine."

"I always suspected you were a burglar at heart."

"Hey!" Jill's expression broke and she began to laugh. "I object!"

Betsy smiled, glad to lighten the topic, even if only for a moment and pleased to be mean to the person who insisted on talking about getting killed.

But Jill was relentless. "Speaking of opening things," she said, "let Godwin or me or one of your other employees unlock the shop in the mornings and open any orders that come in. Most important, make sure you tell people about these precautions. No need to let one of your employees get killed."

"Oh, no, I hadn't thought about that! No, Jill, I can't

let other people do dangerous things for me! I couldn't
live with myself if you or Godwin or one of my part-
timers got killed over this. Maybe I should just cut
and—No, no, *no!* I won't go into hiding! Okay, suppose
I just announce loudly and often that I'm not going to
open anything or eat any gift foods? Then I could go
ahead and take care of it myself, right?"

"No, because someone will see you opening a box or
eating the fudge someone else made, and word will get
around. You have to close that route absolutely. And,
from now on, before you do anything, *anything*, ask
yourself: Can someone possibly use this to hurt me?
Could this be a trap? If the answer is yes, don't do it.
It sounds awful, but I know a man who has lived like
this for years, and he said it got to be a habit pretty
quickly. And other people hardly notice how he is unless
they already know."

"I hope I don't have to do it long enough to become
a habit. I *wish* I knew why someone wants me dead!"

"Think about the why. If you figure that out, we'll
probably know who."

Betsy added more sugar to her tea and stirred restlessly. "Okay, the first attempt was Monday. What did
I do last week or over the weekend that scared or an-
gered someone? There was the Christmas party, but I
don't remember a dark look or poisonous hint from anyone. Hal came to town, but he wants my forgiveness,
not my funeral. I offered to go pick up that pillow—
which reminds me—"

"Their flight was canceled, so Mrs. Connor went and
got the pillow herself."

"Good. All right, the only other new thing in my life
is that tapestry. On the other hand, if it was the tapestry,
why am I the only one being attacked? Lots of other
people have seen it. What do I know about the tapestry
no one else does?"

"The attributes?"

"No, I showed them to Father John and Patricia. I can't imagine them plotting together to do me in. But maybe if I talk to Mandy, she'll know something. I wonder where she is."

"Christmas shopping," said Jill. "Want to go, too?"

"Love to, but if I don't do laundry, I'm going to have to go braless tomorrow, and that's not a pretty sight on a woman my age."

Betsy found laundromats depressing. When that money finally arrived, she'd already decided, she would install a washer and dryer, then hire someone to do the laundry anyway.

Was three million enough to have "people"? She'd known someone really wealthy back in California who had people to do his laundry, take care of his lawn and garden, clean his house, cook his meals, pay his bills, decorate his Christmas tree, sort his mail, keep his calendar. That was why he always had time for the important things, like taking impulsive trips to Paris and keeping himself beautifully tanned. How absolutely lovely it would be to have people!

While Betsy was getting her laundry together, the doorbell rang. She came out with the heavy bag bumping her legs, and Jill, already at the door, gestured her back out of sight.

Jill went out on the landing and came right back to ask, "Did you order a Christmas tree?"

"No, why?"

"There's a big one coming up the stairs. A man carrying it."

"Maybe it's the guy from across the hall."

"Then why is it your doorbell he's ringing? Wait here." She went out in the hall again, and Betsy heard her call down, "Who is it?"

"It's me," said a man's voice, somewhat strained.

"Stop where you are," ordered Jill. "What's your name?"

"Who are you?" demanded the man.

"You first, mister."

"I'm Harold Norman, if it's any of your business, and I'm bringing this up for Betsy Nor—er, Devonshire."

"Wait there."

"I *can't* wait, this damn thing's heavy!"

Betsy was behind Jill by then, and she called, "What's the big idea, Hal?"

"You used to wish for a live Christmas tree, darlin', so I'm bringing you one."

Live Christmas trees had been politically incorrect at Merrivale. Still, "I don't want anything from you."

"Now don't be hasty, I—Ai!" There was a thump, a swishy sort of crash, then a series of stumbles, and finally a crunch. "Ow, ow, ow, ow, damn!" said Hal from successively farther down the stairs.

"You want to talk to him?" asked Jill.

"No."

"Then go back inside, and lock the door. I'll take care of this."

A few minutes later, Jill called out. Betsy opened the door and had to back down the little hallway to allow a large and fragrant spruce tree in, with Jill somewhere close behind it. The tree was a little crushed on one side. "He fell on it," explained Jill. "Did you really used to wish for a live tree?"

"Yes."

"Well, Hal has lost interest in this one. It seems a waste to just toss it."

"What did he say?"

"That he couldn't have it in his motel room, and with it damaged, he couldn't take it back, so the hell with it. He stuck it into a snowbank and walked off."

Betsy looked at the tree for a few moments. Apart from the damage, it was a beautiful tree.

"I'll get the stand," she said.

Though Betsy had pictured her tree standing in front of the trio of living room windows, that wasn't possible because of the broken branches. They put it in a corner, damaged side in. Betsy brought out the boxes labeled Lights and Ornaments. They strung the lights first. They were the old-fashioned, big-bulb kind. "Margot always had a real tree," said Jill. There were even two strings of the kind with a bulb hidden in a base under a stem full of colored liquid, which Betsy remembered from her childhood. They were new to Jill, however, and the look on her face when the liquid started bubbling was a pleasure to Betsy.

There were two big boxes of ornaments. But Betsy turned away from them, saying, "Laundry first."

The laundromat's windows were dripping with condensation. Four washing machines and three dryers were in use, and a girl in her mid-teens was hanging blouses and shirts on the stainless steel rod over a wheeled basket. A thin young man was deep into a Grisham paperback, and a grandmother type was futilely calling after two toddlers who ran and yelled around the place.

Jill ran a professional eye over the group and said, "I don't think any of these people are a threat."

They started two washer loads and sat down on a pair of orange plastic chairs that wobbled.

Betsy said, "Tell me what you know about Mandy."

"From back when she lived here? Hardly anything. She seemed to be just an ordinary, average kid. She's six years younger than me, so we didn't go to school together. She was about thirteen when that mess with her parents happened, and I hardly saw her again after that. As for nowadays, I already told you her husband's name is Dan, and they have a little boy whose name I can't remember. Her husband manages a garden supply center in Golden Valley. I know all this because your sister told me. Margot was involved in getting Father Keane moved to a better nursing home, so she was kind of keeping track of the family."

Betsy said, "Doesn't sound much like a murderer to me." She reached into the bottom of her laundry bag and pulled out the thick tome on Christian symbology.

"Want to see my notebook?" asked Jill.

"Yes, please."

Jill pulled it out of a pocket and found the page where Betsy had been copying her notes. "Got a new idea?"

"No," admitted Betsy. "But it hangs in my mind. If Lucy was going to put her name on there, I think she'd put the letters in the right order. And if she was going to spell something with saints' attributes, then why stick someone who was about as far from a saint as you can get at the end?"

"Maybe she just wanted to show it was the end of the line. Hanging means that, too, you know. Like newspaper reporters used to put '30' at the end of a story."

Betsy considered that. She looked at the list in Jill's notebook, squinting as if distorting her view would reveal a plan or outline or . . . something. A pig, a horseshoe, an anchor, a whip. A shamrock, a lamb, a heart, an apple, a star. An apple for a teacher. A Star of David—but Lucy didn't have a son, let alone one named David.

Jill went to move wet clothing from the washing machine into the dryer. A dog, three crowns—there used to be a British coin called a crown. It was worth five shillings. There were twenty shillings in the pound, but that didn't seem relevant here.

The cat was Saint Yvo. Why were there two of them? As Jill said, *Beats me.* Betsy put the notebook in a pocket and went to help Jill.

They'd barely gotten back to Betsy's apartment when the phone rang. Betsy answered, and it was Godwin. "Can you come down? There's someone here who wants to talk to you."

"Who is it?"

"Mandy Oliver."

"Hurray, we'll be right down!"

In the shop was a young woman with a handsome tumble of chestnut hair around a broad face set with a strong nose. She was tracing the intertwining of cable stitch on a sample sweater with a slim forefinger when Jill and Betsy came into the shop. Godwin indicated her with a tilt of his head. Betsy stepped forward and said, "Hello, I'm Betsy Devonshire. You wanted to see me?"

The young woman turned and said, "Hello, I'm Mandy Oliver, Lucy and Keane Abrams's daughter."

"How may I help you?" asked Betsy.

"May I speak with you in private?"

Betsy glanced around at Jill, who said, "Ms. Devonshire isn't allowed to meet with anyone in private right now. But I assure you, anything you tell her won't be repeated by me. Unless, of course, it has bearing on some crime."

To their surprise, Mandy turned white and would have fled if Jill, in one swift move, had not gotten to her and taken her by the elbow. "What's this all about?" Jill said.

"Take your hand off me!" said Mandy.

"No, I think you'd better stay and explain yourself," said Jill.

Mandy gave her arm one unsuccessful yank, then said, "Oh! Do you think *I* have something to do with what's happening to Ms. Devonshire?" She looked sincerely horrified. "No, no! This isn't about *that!*"

"Then what is it about?" asked Jill.

Mandy looked at Jill a considering second or two. "It's about—about my father. And that plan they're working up to hang Mother's tapestry in the Trinity library."

"What about it?" asked Jill, and Betsy came closer.

"I can't believe nobody's said something already. I really don't think they'll be happy when somebody finally does say something."

"Something about what?" said Jill.

Mandy bowed her head and said so quietly Betsy had to strain her ears to hear, "My father was a thief. He stole money from his discretionary fund, and when that was gone, he started another fund, saying it was to help poor people pay their rents in emergencies, but he kept that money for himself, too."

There was an odd noise. Betsy looked over to see Shelly staring at Mandy with big, avid eyes.

"Shelly . . ." Jill said.

Shelly gestured. "Fine, I won't say a word to anyone. But *somebody* better tell the people at Trinity, and soon. And then Patricia is just going to *die!*"

12

Betsy said, "But is it true? Who knew about this?"
Mandy said, "The old vestry knew, they fired
Dad for it. My mother knew. She was furious. I heard
her tell Dad he had to pay back the money. The church
took every penny of our savings, but it wasn't enough
to pay back all he stole. Dad and Mother were terrified
he was going to go to jail."

"But he didn't," said Jill.

"No, he had that terrible stroke and Mother found him
and had a heart attack trying to lift him off the floor.
And they—the vestry—thought the scandal would be
too awful, so they forgave him."

"What did your father tell you about all this?" asked
Betsy.

"Nothing, he never got a chance. We moved out of
the rectory into another house. It was just three days later
when—when I came home from school and found
them—" Suddenly she put both hands over her face and
broke into noisy sobs.

"Here now, here now," said Betsy, coming to put an

arm around the young woman's shoulder, removing her from Jill's grasp. "Come with me, there's a nice chair back here out of the way." She led Mandy to the area behind the box shelves. She gave Shelly and Godwin a look that warned them not to follow, then seated Mandy on one of the upholstered chairs. "Would a cup of coffee help? Or tea? Or cocoa?"

Mandy shook her head. "I-I'm sorry for losing control," she said with an effort.

"That's all right. Did your mother have a weak heart?"

"Oh yes. She'd been sick for over a year. She couldn't climb the stairs anymore, so she moved into Dad's den on the ground floor. I had to do the heavy housework, like mopping and laundry. She was taking pills, and the doctor had talked to us about a heart transplant, but Mother said she wouldn't consider it."

"And your father?"

"Oh, that came with no warning. He was fine when I went to school that morning . . ." She stared at nothing, or perhaps at what she'd walked into, coming home from high school a dozen years ago.

"I'm sorry, Mandy," said Betsy, putting her hand over the young woman's.

"Thanks," she said. "It was a long time ago, and I'd pretty much gotten over it, and then—I wish Patricia hadn't found that tapestry!"

Betsy said, "Actually, it wasn't Patricia, it was Phil Galvin. He found it in a basement room off the church hall that had been closed off. Have you any idea how it got there?"

Mandy grimaced. "Probably someone from the vestry stuck it back there. I mean, they were willing to forgive Dad, but I don't think they wanted any reminders of us around once he was gone."

"What made you decide to come to me about this?"

"Well, I remember how busy priests get when Christmas is coming, so at first I decided I'd wait until after Christmas to talk to Father John. But it's been like a balloon getting bigger and bigger inside my head. I just had to talk to someone. I called Trinity, but Father John is at a luncheon in the city with the bishop, and Patricia isn't at home, either, so at last I came here." She looked up at Betsy. Mandy was more handsome than beautiful, but there was character in that face, and her hazel-brown eyes were lovely, even spilling tears.

"You were right to come to me," said Betsy firmly. "We'll think of some way to handle this without an explosion, you'll see. Everything will be all right." She went into the bathroom and brought back some tissues for Mandy to blow her nose into.

"Oh, I don't think it will ever be all right," said Mandy. "I loved my father's church, but I joined my aunt and uncle's so I wouldn't have to face the people at Trinity. And I joined my husband's church for the same reason. I was so sure lots of people knew, when I heard about this plan to name the new library after Dad, I was just amazed. I thought at first of not saying anything, but I knew the farther along the plans got, the bigger the mess when they found out. Shall I try again to get hold of Patricia?"

"If you like," said Betsy, "but they're getting ready to go out of town. Patricia told me they were flying to Phoenix to spend Christmas with her mother-in-law. Perhaps they've already left." She looked inquiringly at Jill, who shrugged.

"I haven't heard anything."

Mandy said, "When my father went from the hospital to a nursing home, it was as if he'd died. I thought it was because everyone knew, the way they stayed away. The nursing home wasn't very good, and it got worse as time went on. Margot—" she smiled through her tears at Betsy—"your sister was so wonderful! She held a

fund-raiser to get him moved to a better place, and that
shamed the bishop into finding some money somewhere
so Margot didn't have to keep on raising money. But
still hardly anyone came to see him." She wiped at a
fresh flow of tears with her fingers.

Jill said, "But he wouldn't know anyone anyway,
would he?"

Mandy nodded. "They tell me that. But I think somewhere, down deep, he's aware that something terrible
has happened to him, and he wonders where all his
friends went."

"Nobody visits him except you?" asked Betsy.

"Patricia comes once in a while. I don't know if you
know this, but there was a time when she and her husband were really struggling. She was trying to put him
through law school and worked practically till labor
pains set in, and then went back to work almost the day
she got out of the hospital. I remember my mother saying how tired and sad she looked, and Dad said he'd see
what he could do. He said there was money in the Fairland family, and it was a shame that Peter's parents
wouldn't help out. I don't know exactly what he did,
but Patricia is still grateful all these years later."

"Does anyone else come to see him?" asked Jill.

"Well, Father John, of course. And Phil Galvin. Dad's
grandfather was a railroad engineer back in the 1800s,
and Phil loved to hear Dad talk about him. Now, Phil's
the one talking, and I think it does Dad good. I don't
know if there's anyone else, certainly no one else comes
regularly. I kind of assumed it was because they all
knew Dad was a thief."

"That tapestry your mother made for Trinity," said
Betsy. "When did your mother make it?"

"She designed it before I was born, when Dad was
rector at Saint Boltolph's in upstate New York. The
Trinity vestry started talking about installing a colum-

barium, and she remembered the design and decided to make it to hang there. It took years to stitch. She called it her therapy piece. She said that doing needlework was better—and cheaper—than a visit to a shrink. She was often unhappy but would never say why. I wonder now if my father had stolen money before. I remember that other women of the parish would come over a couple of afternoons a week to stitch on it and talk. It was finished just before Dad resigned. Well, actually, it was finished a week or two before, but Mother was doing that thing needleworkers do, you know, going over it and finding missed stitches and so forth. I never saw it once we moved out of the rectory. I don't think it was ever hung in the church."

Betsy asked, "Have you talked with anyone else about it? Or has anyone come to you with questions about it?"

"No."

Jill said suddenly, "I hope the restoration project continues. The tapestry doesn't have anything to do with your father, and it's a beautiful thing, very appropriate for the columbarium."

Betsy said, "But maybe it does have something to do with Father Keane. Maybe that's what that all saints theme in the halo is about."

"What all saints theme?" asked Mandy.

"She worked tiny attributes of various saints on fabric and applied them between the double gold lines of the halo."

"She did?"

"You didn't know that?"

Mandy shook her head. "I don't remember seeing anything like that. But I was a teenager and didn't like needlework. Maybe Mother talked about it at supper three nights a week. I was full of teen angst and not paying attention to anything but myself. Then our whole world crashed in, Mother died, and Dad—well, all that would just run things like her tapestry out of my head."

"I understand. Now, this may sound like an odd question, but did your mother ever hide a message in her needlework?"

Mandy grinned. "Did you find one in the tapestry?"

"No, but I think there may be one."

"What she would usually put is just her name, my name, or Dad's name and sometimes the year into the pattern. More than once she did it by using a color barely a shade darker, so you couldn't see it unless you knew where to look. Once, she did a Noah's ark for my bedroom, and the animals coming up the ramp were monkeys, aardvarks, newts, donkeys, and yaks."

"Oh, that's clever!" said Betsy. "And were they in that order?"

Mandy frowned a little. "Of course. Why not?"

Betsy sighed. "Yes, why not? How else would you know it spelled Mandy?"

"That's right. It was clever, but some of my friends thought the newts were salamanders and the aardvarks looked a lot like pigs. Why are you asking me this? Is there a name hidden in those symbols?"

"If there is, we can't find it. Would she always put just a name?"

"When Uncle Will was young, he was a radioman in the navy. He used to send my mother letters that had some of it written in dots and dashes—Morse code. She got a book on Morse, to translate and to write some things back to him. So when she made him a scarf, she knitted a pattern down one edge and up the other that said something like Thoughts of You Are Warm as a Good Wool Scarf. If you didn't know, it was just a broken line in yellow on the green. Are you thinking she hid a message like that on the tapestry?"

"I was hoping you knew if there was," said Betsy.

"There are twenty-some attributes on the halo, enough for a brief message."

Mandy shook her head. "I'm sorry, I can't help you. She must have been upset, but she never said a word, so I think she probably just picked things at random to fill the space."

"Well!" said Betsy after Mandy left. "So the sainted Father Keane wasn't such a saint after all."

"And where does that leave us?" said Jill.

Betsy replied, "I think it depends on who knew. It was only ten or twelve years ago. Surely most if not all of those vestry members are still around. I wonder why they decided not to tell the parish. There must be a record somewhere, like minutes of their meetings or something."

"If they left a record, where is it?" asked Jill. "Because this is all news to me, and I've been a member of Trinity since I was baptized. I never heard a word. Patricia's a member of the current vestry, so she certainly should know, but she's the one gung ho about renaming the library after him."

"Then they must have decided not to tell anyone," said Betsy. "And having decided that, I can see why they'd be upset if it got out now. But what I don't see is why they're coming after me." Betsy gnawed at her bottom lip. "Maybe it's Patricia trying to keep us from finding that out. He's her hero."

"But then the person to kill is Mandy, not you," Jill pointed out.

Betsy said, "She'd better act fast. Mandy will get hold of Father John or Patricia—or both—later today." She looked at Jill. "Uh-oh."

Before she could say anything more, Jill was out the door. She came back a couple of minutes later, breathing hard. "I caught her. She's going straight home and won't talk to anyone about this until we tell her she can. I asked her what she said to the receptionist at Trinity, and she only told Crystal that she'd call back."

Though Godwin and Shelly were obviously eaten up with curiosity, Betsy refused to tell them more. And to keep them from speculating together, she sent Shelly on an errand. A little Christmas tree on the checkout desk that had been decorated with donated needlework ornaments was to go to a patient at a local nursing home. "Better get that over there now," Betsy said.

Back upstairs, Betsy said to Jill, "All right, let's look at the actual attributes, copy them all down in order." She called Trinity. Father John was doing hospital calls. Betsy said to Crystal, "I've got some more wool I want to try to match to the tapestry. May I come over and see it?"

"I'm sorry, Ms. Devonshire, but I don't know where it is. It was in the church hall, but they cleared that out. I know they didn't take it with them because Mrs. Fairland called yesterday wanting to see it, and when I said it wasn't in the church hall anymore, she called all the people who volunteered to help clear things out, and none of them had moved it. Our janitor says he didn't move it, either. She's pretty upset, but I could only tell her what I'm telling you: I don't know where it is."

"Well . . . ah . . . thank you." Betsy hung up and turned, frowning, to Jill. "Remember when you said that if the tapestry had a message that accused you of something, you'd get rid of it? Apparently someone has."

13

Betsy tried to call Patricia, but there was no answer. "When are they leaving for Phoenix, do you remember if she said?" Betsy asked Jill.

"No."

"So what do we do now?"

Jill looked around the apartment and said, "Finish decorating the tree?"

But while doing that, Jill, still picking at the case, asked, "Are you sure it isn't Hal Norman doing all this? There are a lot of weird men out there who decide, 'If I can't have her, no one can.'"

"I know. But don't they tend to shoot themselves after shooting their women? The Pig doesn't strike me as the suicidal type. I mean, how would the world get along without him?"

"Well, then let's call Mike and see if he's found any suspects among the friends and relations of the murderers you've unveiled lately."

Jill placed the call to Mike's pager, and when he called back, she asked if he'd developed any new suspects. "I'm afraid not," he said. "Any action on your end?"

"No, I think the word's out that she's got an armed guard. The tapestry's gone missing, and that may also be a factor."

But trying to think why someone might want her dead prompted Betsy to other morbid thoughts. She put the hot dish she'd just pulled out of the freezer into the microwave to thaw it and phoned John Penberthy at home. "I guess it's time to make out that will," she said, not very graciously.

"Do you want to come see me tomorrow?"

"I have to work tomorrow, so if you're free this evening, can you come over? Come to supper. We've got plenty to eat, if you like hot dish. Jill Cross is staying with me for a while, so there will be two of us to talk to."

"Yes, I heard about that arrangement, and I think it's a very good idea. All right, thank you, I'll be there. We've got that one asset to talk about as well. I'll bring the file."

Penberthy was prompt. He was about thirty, dark and good looking, with humorous, intelligent eyes. Under a short winter coat he wore khaki slacks, a white shirt open at the collar, and a sky-blue, V-necked sweater— his version of casual. He carried a shining old-fashioned briefcase that was probably older than he was.

Betsy had chosen a hot dish of potatoes, pork, onion, and cheese. After thawing it, she had put it in the oven to heat through. She made a salad of cucumber, tomato, endive, green onions, and herbs. That was the meal, plus seven-grain bread and milk, with coffee for dessert. Penberthy declined a slice of banana cream pie.

"Ah," he sighed at last, putting his second cup down empty. "That was delicious. My mother used to make that hot dish from leftover pork roast."

"Martha Winters made this one," said Betsy. "I only know how to mix peas and tuna with macaroni and cheese."

"Definitely not Lutheran, then," said Penberthy with a nod, and Jill laughed.

Betsy decided that was an obscure reference Minnesotans used as shortcuts to character. She also decided she didn't want to know what it said about her. She and Jill began clearing the table. "Is it a complicated thing, making a will?" Betsy asked over her shoulder.

Penberthy replied, "It can be. Depends on what you want to do. If you want to set up trusts, it definitely will be. Any idea who you want your executor to be?"

"No, but what I want is not very complicated. I want to leave Crewel World to Godwin du Lac, then split the money between Godwin and Jill Cross."

"Me?" said Jill, clattering plates into the sink. "Sorry."

"Well, I have to leave it to someone—"

Jill came to take the salad bowl from Betsy and said, "But Betsy, when he leaves, we'll be all alone and . . . well, I've got a gun."

Penberthy laughed hardest at that.

But when the two women came back from the kitchen, he had a thick file folder on the table. "Let's look at this first," he said.

"What is it?"

"Have you ever heard the term *silent partner?*"

"Sure. It means someone who buys shares in a company but doesn't help run it."

Penberthy said, "Yes, that's approximately correct. Your sister was a silent partner in a company called New York Motto." He opened the file folder and began handing over documents.

Betsy studied them for a couple of minutes, but then said, "I'm sorry, I don't understand what this is about.

In some places it looks as if Margot owned the company, but in others it seems like it was Vicki Prentice. Who's she?"

"At the start, she was a friend of mine. She owned a small property in Wisconsin, adjoining a lake cabin your sister used to own, so Margot knew her, too."

"It was a nice place," said Jill. "But Margot sold it when the developers moved in."

Penberthy nodded and continued, "But what I'm talking about happened a few years ago. Margot had been playing the market, but it made her nervous and it demanded a lot of her time, so she wanted someplace else to put the money. I had been fooling around with futures, and she came and asked me if I wanted to do some investing for her. It's unethical for a person's attorney to enter into a business connection with her, so I introduced her to Vicki.

"Vicki was taking law courses at night while she worked as a law clerk for a lawyer during the day. The lawyer specialized in bankruptcies and receiverships, and Vicki had come up with an idea involving bankruptcy estate assets. The auction of these assets is not advertised, and often valuable assets are sold for far less than they are worth."

Betsy began to smile. "And that's where Margot put her money, into buying these assets."

"In a way. Vicki was the one who wanted to do this, but she didn't have the start-up money. Margot didn't have the time it takes to find and attend the sales and then sell the assets. So what Margot did was start a shell company, called New York Motto. Did you know the state of New York's motto is 'Excelsior'?"

"I used to, but I'd forgotten."

Penberthy continued, "Excelsior was founded by immigrants from New York."

"Really? I didn't know that. I'm going to have to re-search the history of this place someday."

"You'll love it," said Jill. "We have a checkered history."

"We have a varied and interesting history," corrected Penberthy. Then he continued, "Margot kept ninety-five percent of the company, selling five percent to Vicki. Vicki quit her job and dropped out of law school when she was named operating officer. Vicki hired a highly talented CPA as comptroller and other staff, mostly scouts to research bankruptcy and sheriff's auctions. New York Motto has been doing quite well since its founding. But here," he said, handing Betsy another doc-ument, "this may be of special interest to you."

It was some kind of land contract. New York Motto agreed to sell a piece of land on which was a restaurant to Joseph P. Mickels. "Joe!" exclaimed Betsy, and Jill came out of the kitchen to look over her shoulder. The legal description of the location didn't mean much until Betsy got to "City of Pinewood, in the County of Hen-nepin, State of Minnesota." Pinewood was another of those Hennepin county "cities" that are really small towns. In Pinewood's case, practically a village. But it was just up the road from Excelsior, on the shore of Lake Minnetonka.

Jill drew air softly through her teeth. "I know that place," she said. "The manager was a crook."

"Was this restaurant bought at one of those auctions?" asked Betsy.

"Yes, at a bankruptcy estate sale in bankruptcy court."

"And Joe is buying it from New York Motto."

"He's buying it back."

"You mean it was his? Joe went *bankrupt?*"

"Not Joe, one of his companies." Penberthy explained, "Joe plays around with a lot of different kinds of real estate. When the deal seems particularly risky, he'll start a new company and put the holding in the new company's name. That way, if it doesn't work out, the loss doesn't put a drain on any of Joe's other holdings but is confined to the corporation that owns it."

Betsy nodded.

Penberthy continued, "Restaurants are chancy businesses at the best of times. Joe put his company and its restaurant into the hands of a cousin who, it turned out, really didn't know what he was doing. And when the cousin saw it was going bad, he ran it into the ground—it's called running a bust out—and absconded with most of the money. By the time Joe realized what was going on, it was too late. The company had to declare bankruptcy.

"In legal terms, what happens when a company goes bankrupt is that it disappears and a new entity, a bankruptcy estate, is created, and the court assigns a trustee to manage it. These trustees are often overextended, handling six hundred or more cases a year. When they don't investigate the background or search the estate thoroughly for assets, they may misapprehend its true value."

Betsy, holding onto comprehension with both hands, nodded again.

"In this case, after a halfhearted search for assets—the trustee knew this was a bust-out case—the trustee ordered the property sold to pay creditors. If he'd paid attention, he would have realized that while the restaurant was deep in debt, the lakefront property on which it stood was free of liens. New York Motto's scout wasn't as careless and recommended making a bid. Joe came to the auction with a cashier's check in an amount equal to about eight cents on the dollar of the value of the property. But Vicki came with a cashier's check for twelve cents on the dollar and, when Joe couldn't raise his bid—you must have cash in hand or a cashier's check—the judge dropped his gavel and New York Motto got it. Joe was very angry, of course.

"A week later, he contacted New York Motto and expressed an interest in the property. Vicki offered him a contract for deed, and, surprisingly, he took it. What I assume is that at the time, he was cash poor, but he was sure he would be in good financial condition at the end of the purchase contract. He planned to have The Mickels Building finished or nearly finished and figured he could handle a balloon payment at the time it came due."

"Oh, a balloon payment," said Betsy, nodding more easily. She'd known several people desperately worried about balloon payments.

Penberthy smiled. "This contract offered terms that amounted to paying interest on a loan of the purchase price, with the entire principal due as the last payment."

Betsy looked at the deed, found the amount, and whistled softly. "When was the balloon payment due?"

"It hasn't come due yet. The due date is January twelve." He pointed to a place on the document.

Jill came to the table, wiping her hands on a dish towel, to ask, "What happens if he can't make the payment?"

"He forfeits all he's put into the deal, and the property reverts to New York Motto."

Jill said, "No wonder Joe was so angry at Margot! She not only kept him from putting up The Mickels Building but stood in the way of his getting a valuable property back."

"No," said Penberthy, "Joe didn't know Margot was also New York Motto."

Betsy said, "He didn't? Are you sure?"

"He never said anything to me about it."

Jill asked Betsy, "Has Joe said anything to you, anything at all, that might indicate he knows that New York Motto is now yours?"

Betsy stared at her. "You mean Joe owes *me* all this money?"

"You're inheriting the company, aren't you? I'm asking how sure you are he doesn't know about this."

Penberthy said, "I never told him. Margot and Vicki wouldn't tell him. Betsy is obviously surprised to discover this, so I don't know how Joe would have found out."

Betsy said, "If Joe knew Margot owned New York Motto, he might very well think she was holding on to her lease just so he'd lose that land." Betsy smiled wryly. "In fact, it sounds like the kind of squeeze he'd love to put on someone else, doesn't it?"

Penberthy, smiling, nodded.

But Jill persisted, "Surely when he set out to contact New York Motto about buying the land back, he would have found out who the owner was."

Penberthy said, "On the contrary. New York Motto is incorporated in the State of Wisconsin, so there is no listing of it in Minnesota at all. And in Wisconsin, the only names that appear are Vicki's and the CPA's." He was still smiling, as if Betsy surely must now see the point of a complex joke.

"What?" she asked, feeling stupid.

"You are in a position of tremendous power over Joe Mickels. You can release this information to the press and if he's stretched thin—which I think he is right now—ruin him financially. Or, under a threat to tell, make him agree to a new contract at very high interest rate. Even add some other terms. Make him agree to rename The Mickels Building The Margot Berglund Building. He may be facing financial ruin if he doesn't agree to whatever terms you dictate." Penberthy shrugged. "Or you can be kind and renew the contract under its present terms. You can even keep silent and let Vicki decide what to do—which is, after all, what a silent partner does."

"What do you think Vicki would do?"

"Let him fail to make that final payment, lose everything he's already paid into the deal plus the property, then sell the property to someone else. It's already unusual for New York Motto to hang onto a piece of property this long. Normally, they turn around almost at once and sell at a profit. Joe must have done some fast talking to get her to agree to this."

"What fast talking? Look at the mess he's in!"

Penberthy said, "But look at it from his position back then. He was all ready to put up that building. There was only this one silly, helpless widow in his way." He lifted a sardonic eyebrow at Joe's ignorance.

Jill added, "And even if he thought it was risky, this deal with New York Motto involves land that was once his. Joe operates under Will Rogers's advice: 'Buy land, they ain't makin' any more of it.' It probably caused him a lot of pain to lose that lakefront site, and he was feeling very motivated to get it back."

"I think that's an accurate assessment," said Penberthy.

Betsy said, "What do you think, Jill? If he knew, this might give him a motive to murder me?"

Jill said, "Oh, yes."

Penberthy said, "But if he knew, he would have accused Margot of deliberately trying to damage him. Margot never said anything like that. And she would have told me, because I needed to stay one step ahead of whatever he was up to."

"Still . . ." Jill said.

"Yes," Betsy said. "And it's important we find out. I want to be the one who tells him."

Penberthy said, "There is no legal responsibility to tell

him anything. If it was me, and I felt he should know, I'd want to tell him long distance. From, say, Hong Kong."

Betsy snorted. Then she asked, "What's the total value of the company today?"

"You'll have to contact Vicki and ask for an accounting. I know it's been making money, but I don't think Margot was letting equity build up, she was using the money for some project or other, something charitable, I think. Here's Vicki's address." Penberthy gave her a business card.

"Thanks." Betsy asked, "When is this probate matter going to be wrapped up?"

"If you can get the information on New York Motto to me before the new year, I'd say we can finalize this by mid-January. Which is why I think we should now turn our attention to the matter for which you summoned me: your will."

He glanced up at her. She was gaping at him. "Really?"

"Really what?"

"Mid-January? That's about three weeks from now."

"I thought you'd be pleased."

"I am pleased. I'm also surprised. The way there's always one more thing to do, I thought it would be months before we got it all resolved."

"No, things have progressed very smoothly. No other heirs have stepped forward to make a claim, all the assets are found and will soon be accounted for, and there's no reason we can't make a final court appearance within that time."

Betsy sat back. "Wonderful," she murmured. And then she smiled.

Penberthy got out a yellow legal pad and prepared to take notes. "You said you want to divide your estate between Mr. Godwin and Ms. Cross," he said, writing. "Any charities?"

"Oh . . ." Betsy hesitated. Her head was spinning, and she was suddenly tired. "I—I can't think. Let's just get something on paper for now. We can revise it later, can't we? If I live." She meant that as a joke, but it came out through gritted teeth.

Through a slip in Penberthy's composure he gave her a look of such compassion she nearly threw herself on his shoulder to relieve her feelings in tears. But he was an even cooler head than Jill, and the look vanished as swiftly as it had appeared. Betsy, already leaning forward, feigned an interest in what he was writing on the notepad.

"For something as simple as what you describe," he said, "especially since it's very likely an interim will, you can just write it out in your own words."

"And then you'll turn it into legal language?"

"There's no need to do that. Holographic wills are perfectly legal. That means handwritten, not just signed. Written entirely by hand. You don't even need witnesses to a holographic will."

Betsy made a doubtful face.

"There is a case where a tractor rolled over on a farmer out in his field, and he wrote 'All to Mother' in his own blood on the tractor's fender, and it was admitted to probate. But be clear; don't attempt fancy language. A will is not subject to interpretation; it means exactly what it says." He tore off the top sheet of his legal pad, turned the pad around, and pushed it toward her. He handed her his heavy gold pen and said, "Use your full legal name."

I, Elizabeth Frances Devonshire, wrote Betsy—"I took my maiden name back after each divorce," she said—*hereby make this my last will.*

"Have you ever made a will before?" he asked.

She started to say no, then remembered. "You know, I *did* make a will, back when Hal and I got married. We each made one. You know the kind, where you leave everything you die possessed of—that sounds like you're leaving a flock of demons, doesn't it?—to your spouse." She put a hand over her mouth and stared at Penberthy.

"What?" he asked.

"I never revoked that will."

"So?"

"So *that's* what's going on here! Don't you get it? I never revoked that will! So if I die without making a new one, Hal gets everything—*everything!* That's why he's trying to kill me! Oh, my God, I've got to call Malloy this second!"

She ran into the kitchen, but before she could pick up the receiver, Penberthy called, "Wait! It doesn't work that way!"

She looked at him, hand on the phone. "What doesn't work that way?"

"The will you made probably said something like, 'to my beloved spouse, Harold What's-his-name—"

"Norman. Harold Norman."

" 'To my spouse, Harold Norman, I leave all of which I die possessed,' right?"

"Yes, just like that."

"Well, he's not your spouse anymore. That will isn't valid."

Betsy let go the receiver. "Oh. Well, I didn't know that."

Jill said quietly, "I bet Hal doesn't know it, either."

Betsy stared at her. "You're right! Of course! What a jerk, trying to kill me to get something he couldn't get even if I died naturally!" She picked up the receiver, looked on the refrigerator for a business card with a badge, and dialed the number inked on it. "Mike," she said when he answered, "We've got it. When Hal and I first married, we made out those mutual wills leaving everything to one another. And I never revoked that will. Now, my attorney just told me that will became void when we divorced—which I didn't know. And probably Hal doesn't know it, either. I'll bet you ten dollars he thinks that if I die, he gets my inheritance." She paused long enough for him to ask a question. "Last I heard, three million."

She hung up and turned a harshly satisfied face to the pair in the dining nook. "There, that solves that! He'll go arrest that bastard, and I can get back to living in peace!"

14

Betsy was sleeping the sleep of the just when a bumblebee flew into her dream, disordering it by trying to send a message to her in Morse code. It droned zzdah, zzdah, zit-zit-zit, zzdah, zdaaaaaaaah, and then she was awake and someone was ringing her doorbell very urgently.

She flung the blankets back, and Sophie thumped onto the floor. She grabbed for her striped flannel robe and heard Jill out in the living room grumbling, "I'm coming, I'm coming!"

Betsy followed, but Jill gestured at her to move so the visitor wouldn't see her when Jill opened the door. Betsy was shocked to notice that Jill had a gun in her hand. As Jill reached for the button that released the downstairs door, Betsy hustled sideways and heard the apartment door open.

There was a thumping of hasty feet on the stairs. "Patricia!" Jill exclaimed. "What are you—?"

"You've got to get out, quick!" Patricia Fairland said. "You're on fire!"

Betsy looked around swiftly. There were no flames, and she couldn't smell smoke. She hurried to the door. "What fire? Where is it?" she asked, standing on bare tiptoes to peer over Jill's shoulder.

Patricia was nearly to their threshold. "It's around back!" She gestured widely. "I was driving by, and I saw flames reflected off the snow. Come on, come on, you've got to hurry!" Patricia looked distraught, her hair was mussed, and her swing coat was gathered strangely around her, as if she had put it on over her head, or been hugging herself inside it.

Jill reached for the door of the microscopic hall closet and Betsy backed out of her way. Jill grabbed her heavy police jacket and began shoving her feet into her boots as she pushed the gun into a pocket. "Get something on your feet!" she ordered Betsy.

But Betsy ran instead to the window at the back of the dining nook. She couldn't see straight down, but there was a bright flicker on the icy coating of the parking lot and the banks of snow that surrounded it. The flicker appeared to be coming from somewhere near the back door to the building. "Oh my God, she's right, I can see it, we're on fire!"

She turned toward the kitchen, but Jill was already on the phone, her voice urgent as she told the emergency operator about the fire.

"Come on, come on!" called Patricia from out in the hall.

"Sophie!" exclaimed Betsy, and dashed for the bedroom. The cat was standing just inside the doorway, tail up in greeting, but not wanting to join the fuss until she knew what it was about. Betsy scooped her up.

"Rowwww!" objected the cat. Then Betsy's fear infected her, and she began a serious struggle to get away.

Sophie was not declawed, so Betsy ran to the bed and grabbed a pillow by the closed end of its case and shook hard. The pillow fell out, tumbling across the bed. Betsy dropped the case, grabbed it by its open end, and put the struggling animal in by pulling the pillowcase over her cat-laden arm.

Jill called, "Betsy! Let's go!"

Betsy shoved her feet into her corduroy slippers and ran into the living room, the heavy pillowcase thumping her leg. "Have you warned the others?"

"Oh, gosh!" Jill ran out, but Betsy paused long enough to yank her purse off the hook inside the closet door.

Out in the hall, Patricia was standing at the top of the stairs. "Hurry, oh hurry!" she begged, and started down.

But Jill ran across to thump with a fist on the door to one of the other two apartments. "Out, out, out!" she yelled. "Fire! Fire!"

Betsy ran to bang on the other apartment door. "Fire! Fire!" she shouted. "Get out! Get out! Fire!"

It seemed to take a long time to get a response, though it was likely only seconds. The door was yanked open, and an old man wearing only pajama bottoms stared at Betsy, his white hair standing up all around his head. "Where is it?" he asked, looking past her into the hall. "I don't see anything."

Jill was still banging on the other door, and he stared at her. "Who's she?"

"A police officer. Quick, quick, get a coat and come on!"

"Where's the fire?" the old man insisted.

"Downstairs, back door. I saw flames. Come on!"

Betsy ran to the stairs and hustled down. She stopped at the bottom. Patricia was gone, the front door left standing open. The dim night light revealed no sign of smoke, but Betsy could smell it now. Upstairs, the pair who lived in the other apartment were questioning Jill's insistence they leave right now. Betsy looked toward the

back of the hall, where an obscure door let into a narrow
hallway to the back door and the back entrance to
Crewel World.

I shouldn't, she thought, remembering all the warn-
ings that said get out, get out, get out. But she ran to
the back door and put her palm on it. It was cool. She
felt in the side pocket of her purse and found her keys.
She unlocked the door and opened it cautiously. The
smell of smoke was much stronger in the narrow back
hall, and when she snapped on the light, there was a
haze in the air. The door to the rear parking lot had a
small glass insert, and Betsy could see the shifting yellow and orange of flames outside, but none in the hall
itself.

The cat in the pillowcase was struggling and yelling
to be set free. Outside, she could hear Patricia calling,
"Help, help! Fire, fire!" Someone was coming down the
stairs.

Betsy closed the back hall door. She ran out the front
behind the old man, now wrapped in a purple chenille
bathrobe—the siren that summons the volunteer fire department began bawling—past him and around to the
front door to Crewel World. No flames in there. She
unlocked the door and went in.

Patricia was suddenly beside her, grabbing her arm.
"What are you doing?" she demanded.

"Fire extinguisher!" said Betsy, and handed the pillowcase to Patricia. She raced to the back storage area
where a small foam extinguisher hung on the wall. She
grabbed it, dodged around Patricia on her way back out.
She ran to the driveway to the rear of the building.

"Stop her!" shrieked Patricia.

"Wait, wait, wait!" called Jill, coming in hot pursuit,
but Betsy kept running. The ice-rutted surface of the
driveway hurt through the slippers. The grit and salt-
pitted surface of the parking area kept her from sliding

as she stopped short. The fire was bigger than she'd
thought it would be, as high or higher than the back
door. It was made of log chunks—fireplace wood!—and
smelled like a charcoal grill. She approached until she
felt the heat of the flames, pointed the fire extinguisher,
and squeezed the handle. It was stuck; it wouldn't move.

Jill grabbed it away from her. "Back!" she ordered,
and Betsy retreated, but not far. Jill pulled out the little
pin in the extinguisher's handle and squeezed as she
stepped toward the fire.

The fire ducked under the onslaught of the extinguisher, but rebounded. It was too big for the little extinguisher to harm it. Jill moved around to a different
angle, spraying white foam at the base of the flames.

Betsy became aware of approaching sirens and slith-
ered back down the rutted driveway to the street. Cars
pulled up to both curbs were disgorging men carrying
yellow firemen coats. As the pumper approached, its
huge engine roaring, she stepped out into the street to
raise an arm and point. The men from the cars ran past
her. The truck slowed, its siren cut off, then it obeyed
her urgent signing, turned into the driveway and
stopped. Two men bailed out.

Betsy went to check the entryway to the apartment
building. There huddled the other three tenants, a young
couple in winter coats and slippers hugging one another
against the chill and the elderly man hiding behind them
in his chenille robe and wingtip shoes on sockless feet.
"Everyone all right?" asked Betsy.

"Where's the fire?" asked the man of the couple.

"Outside the back door. I don't think it's gotten inside
the building yet."

Patricia hurried up, still holding the pillowcase. "Are
you all right? Where's Jill?" Patricia's voice sounded
harsh, unlike her normal quiet tone. Her makeup looked
strange because her natural color was gone. Her hairband

was a twist of black velvet and metallic gold, her earrings looked like real diamonds.

"Back with the firefighters. I'm all right." Betsy took the pillowcase from her. Sophie, hearing Betsy's voice, began complaining again about her strange confinement.

"How did it start?" asked the old man.

"I don't know."

A large blond policeman—Betsy suddenly realized it was Lars, Jill's boyfriend—came up and offered them a seat in his nice, warm squad car. But Sophie was beginning to experiment with burrowing, so Betsy went into her shop instead and closed the door. There was a faint light coming in the front window from a streetlight. She put the pillowcase on the floor. Sophie rolled it over a few times, then pushed her way to the mouth of the pillowcase. "Ree-ooooow!" she complained.

"Yes, your highness, I apologize for the rude treatment," said Betsy. "But we couldn't leave you up there to die, could we?" She was trembling all over, from cold and shock. Her voice sounded funny to her ears, so she shut up.

Sophie sat to make a single stab at putting her thick, long fur back in order. Then she looked around. Finding the surroundings familiar, if wanting in light, she did the familiar thing. She went to her chair, the one with the cushion on it, jumped up, and lay down. "Reeeew," she complained again. Betsy turned a chair at the library table around and sat down to comfort the cat. It took only a minute to have Sophie purring as Betsy tickled her under her chin, and soothing the animal soothed her own nerves. Still, Betsy kept an eye toward the back of the shop, expecting either flames or a fireman to come shooting through at any second.

But neither happened. In forty minutes Jill joined her, looking smudged, and said, "It's gonna be a real skating rink back there in a while, water all over everything.

Say, can the other tenants come in here? Lars wants to get back on patrol."

"Of course. Shall I turn on the lights and start the teakettle?"

"Better wait till we see if the wiring is okay."

The three tenants thanked Betsy, then wandered around the dim shop, strangers in a strange world.

After what seemed a very long while, an enormous fireman came in to declare the fire out, and the tenants followed him out, asking if they could go upstairs. Betsy turned on the lights.

They'd no more than left when Patricia came in to take Betsy by the hands. "I just heard a fireman say this fire was *set!* Betsy, this is impossible! You have to *do* something!"

"Oh, yeah?" said Betsy inelegantly, pulling back to release herself. "What do you suggest I do?"

"Run away. Get out of town. Get dressed and pack your bags right now. I'll drive you to the airport. You can buy a ticket on the first plane to—to anywhere. You can't stay here, you're going to get *killed!*" She'd straightened her coat and recovered most of her color, but her eyes were frightened.

"I can't run," said Betsy. "For one thing, I don't have anywhere to go. For another, I can't afford to go anywhere."

"I'll loan you the money—or we'll all get together and loan you the money, the Monday Bunch will. And what about what's-his-name, your ex-husband? He'd be glad to take you back. When I talked with him last week, he sounded so anxious for you to forgive him. He'd do anything for you, Betsy, truly he would."

Betsy shook her head. "What Hal's been doing is attempting to murder me. Mike Malloy is going to arrest him for it, if he hasn't already."

Patricia stared at her. "He is? Arrest Hal? How do you know?"

"Because I told him to. Hal and I wrote mutual wills when we first married and never revoked them. He thinks he'll get all that lovely money I'm heir to."

"But he won't," said Patricia, a woman whose husband had a law degree. "He can't."

"That's right," said Jill tiredly. "But Betsy didn't know that until her attorney told her, and it's unlikely Hal Norman consulted with an attorney before deciding to murder Betsy."

"Oh." Patricia had gone from scared and excited to anxious and regretful. Betsy felt a stab of compassion for her. Hal was so very handsome and charming, the pig.

"Here, come and sit down. Can you smell smoke in here?"

Patricia could not have been more surprised at Betsy if she had turned into an orange. "I'm sure you can smell the smoke blocks from here," she said, and sat down on Sophie's chair, the cat barely escaping in time.

Jill said, "How did you come to see the fire?"

"I told you, I was driving by and saw the flames reflected on the ice and snow. It just happened to catch my eye."

"What were you doing in town this time of night?" asked Jill.

Patricia stared at her, and Betsy could all but see the raising of the drawbridge the rich and powerful live across. "First of all, it wasn't 'this time of night' when I came by," she said calmly. "It was only a little past midnight. I was in the Cities attending 'The Messiah.' Peter couldn't come," she added, forestalling that question. "He had a political meeting to go to, and I just couldn't face another one of those things. So I said I already had tickets—which was a lie—and went by myself." She unbent a little and said, "And I drove through town because I grew up in Excelsior, and I wanted to look at it by night, see the Christmas lights on the houses, and on the house Peter and I used to own. So I was driving slowly, and I was looking around."

Jill's cop facade melted into a smile. "Pretty in town this time of year. All right. Thank you, Patricia."

The drawbridge came back down. "You're welcome, Jill. May I go now?"

"Have you talked to the fire marshal?"

"Yes, a few minutes ago. He said I should talk to the police before I left. Will you do?"

"Yes. Did he ask you if you saw anyone leaving the scene?"

"Yes, and I told him I didn't."

"That's too bad. All right, go on home."

Patricia stood with such weariness that Betsy said, "I don't think I've thanked you for ringing our doorbell. Thank you very much. You probably saved our lives. I'm sorry they made you wait."

"Well, as they say, no good deed goes unpunished. Good night."

After she had gone, Betsy said, "What do you think?"

"I think she was driving around town because she misses living here and because she didn't want to go home to an empty bed. Her husband is starting to be seriously noticed by the political kingmakers in this state. But it's taking up a lot of his time, spending the required hours at his law office, doing the legislative thing in Saint Paul, and keeping his political mentors happy. She's attractive and correct and smart, a good political wife. But I don't think she likes the attention nearly as much as he does, and she's becoming protective of the children."

"She doesn't talk about them, does she? That's sad.

That boy is handsome, and the girls are pretty. Are they very bright?"

"I hear the oldest is in a gifted program and the star pitcher on his baseball team. His parents didn't like Patricia, you know. Their son married very young and he chose a woman whose father worked in a factory and whose mother cooked in a café. And Patricia got pregnant. They stopped paying their son's college expenses, and Peter nearly had to drop out of his last year in law school. But she worked two jobs, and Peter graduated near the top of his class. He joined a prestigious law firm and became a state senator. Patricia began talking and dressing like she'd been to finishing school and insisted their first daughter be named after her husband's mother. And now there's talk about Peter making a run for Congress. His father died a couple of years ago, and his mother has decided it was all the old man's fault, that she herself has long suspected that her daughter-in-law is charming and perfectly acceptable."

Firemen brought big fans into the hall and the shop to began blowing the last of the smoke out. Betsy made an urn of coffee for them.

Joe Mickels turned up, ruffled and angry. "What's going on here?" he demanded.

"Someone tried to set fire to the building by stacking cordwood at the back door and squirting charcoal starter on it," said Jill.

"Is this another attempt to get at you?" Joe asked Betsy.

Betsy nodded, unaccountably embarrassed.

"Well, goddam it, why don't you leave town?"

"Because they might follow her," said Jill. "Here she has friends to help watch out for her, and she's on familiar ground. I don't think you want her to be put at more risk just so you don't have to fill out a few insurance forms."

"Hmph," snorted Mickels and borrowed the phone to summon someone to board up the back door.

After Mickels left, Betsy, too tired to lift her arm, asked, "What time is it?" and Jill looked at her own watch.

"Quarter to four."

The fire chief came in and said they could go up and gather a change of clothes and, if the apartment smelled too strongly of smoke and they had no place to go, a Red Cross representative would be called to find them a place to stay for a day.

Betsy went up with Jill. She stood inside it a long minute, sniffing, then said to Jill, "I can't tell if it stinks of smoke or not."

Jill said, "I think it does, but not too badly. I'm sorry about this, Betsy."

"Why? There wasn't anything you could do. I'm just glad Patricia was feeling homesick. If she hadn't seen that fire, it might've gotten into the stairwell. But I'm mad at Malloy. I thought he would have Hal under arrest by now!"

Jill said, "Maybe he does. He was probably waiting outside Hal's motel room for him to come home, and caught him with bits of firewood bark all down the front of his coat and a can of charcoal starter in his trunk."

The doorbell rang. "Now who—" began Betsy.

"Malloy, I'll bet."

It was. "Bad news, Ms. Devonshire," he said, once inside the apartment.

"What?" demanded Betsy. "Couldn't find Hal? Don't tell me you're here to take me to jail till you do?"

"No, Hal is down at the police station," Malloy said.

"Well, that's one good thing!"

"No, you don't understand. He was sitting down there telling me he loves you, he wants you to forgive him, yadda, yadda, yadda, when the fire siren went off."

That did it. Betsy was overcome by fury. She stomped across the living room and flung herself onto the love seat. "I can't stand this, I'm sick of this whole thing! It *has* to be Hal! It all made sense that it was Hal!"

Malloy said, "You had me convinced. But Hal Norman has one of the best possible alibis: he was sitting in our interrogation room telling me he had no reason to want to kill you at the very moment someone else was trying to do it."

There was a long, depressed silence. Then Jill asked, "So what do we do now?"

Mike shrugged like one who has had this happen before. "Start over. Look at everyone else. Obviously, we're missing something."

"No," said Betsy. "We've been trying to solve this by trying to see what we're missing, and that's not working. Let's look at what we do know. It can't be Hal, all right, that's one thing we know. We don't know why this is happening to me, okay, to hell with why. What else do we know? It has to be someone who knows what a brake line is. It's someone who knows where to get arsenic, and—well, I don't suppose there's any special knowledge to starting fires, is there?"

"There is, but not in this case. Pros use toilet paper, gasoline, and candles, not firewood and charcoal starter."

Betsy said, "I thought it smelled like a barbecue back there."

Jill said, "The fire marshal said he never saw an arson fire started with firewood before."

"And starting it by that back door was dumb, right?" said Betsy. "Why not start it by the front? If it had burned through the back door, it still would have had another door to burn through before it could climb up the stairs. Dumb."

"Because the back door was out of sight of passersby," said Jill. "Not so dumb."

"If it had been me," said Betsy, "I would have broken that back window, squirted the charcoal starter on the floor, and thrown a lit match in after it."

"That's what the fire marshal said," said Malloy. "Another reason he thinks it was an amateur."

"But I'm not an arsonist and I thought of it," Betsy pointed out.

"That is odd," said Jill. "What do you think, he isn't seriously trying to kill her?"

"Then what the hell is he doing?" asked Malloy.

"Maybe he's trying to scare her. Or keep her from doing something." Jill looked at Betsy. "What haven't you gotten done because of all this?"

Betsy scowled. "I haven't finished my Christmas shopping. I haven't picked up my dry cleaning. I haven't balanced my checkbook—well, I usually put that off anyway, so that's no big deal." She saw Jill was serious, so she started to think more deeply. "I need to be lining up people to help with year-end inventory. I need to figure out what goes on sale after Christmas. I'm supposed to be working more hours in the shop to cut expenses. I'm supposed to be thinking of other ways to cut expenses. What, you think this has something to do with the shop? Someone trying to make me close up?"

"Who besides Joe and Irene wants that to happen?" asked Jill.

"I don't know. Nobody."

Mike said, "So maybe he's trying to keep you from doing something else important."

Betsy said, "I'm not doing anything else important." She started to think more about that, then with a gesture sliced that thought off. "Now hold it, we're supposed to be looking at what we know. Why do people kill other people?"

Malloy said, "The usual motives are sex, money, and revenge."

Betsy smiled wryly. "Well, it's sure not sex. And since Hal has a perfect alibi, it's not money."

"Hold up on that conclusion," said Mike. "You're going to be a wealthy woman in a few weeks. If you die, who gets your money?"

Betsy looked embarrassed. "Well . . . right now it's Godwin and Jill." She had finished the hasty holographic will last night.

Blushing, Jill said, "That was all her idea, I don't want any part of it."

Malloy, grinning, said, "You can leave it to me instead, Ms. Devonshire."

Betsy lit up. "Mike, tell everyone that joke. And you, Jill, blush all over the place. Both of you, talk about my new will. If this is about the money, that should stop it."

Jill said, "But if it isn't—"

Betsy scowled but said, "Then back to what else we know. Where did Dr. McQueen say the arsenic mines were? That's the only weapon used so far that can't be found in any house in town."

Jill said, "New Jersey."

Mike said, "Arsenic *mines?*"

Jill said, "It comes out of the ground, like gold or silver."

"No kidding. Well, I don't know of anyone recently back from New Jersey. So I'll have to find out where else you could get hold of some." He pulled out his notebook and wrote that down. "Now, Ms. Devonshire, what I want to do is go over with you again everything you've done in the past few weeks. I know you already told me there were no quarrels, except with your ex-husband. But think over that period again. Anything at all strange, any new demands made on you? Any disagreements or quarrels, however minor? Have you overheard any odd conversation? Found anything that struck you as odd? Any feeling of being watched? Has anyone stolen anything from you?"

"Only something really trivial."

"What is it?" asked Mike, pen poised to write.

"I volunteered to supply the material to restore an old tapestry from Trinity Episcopal Church. I went over to look at it, and I saw some tiny pictures stitched onto it. The rector said they were attributes of saints. I recognized some of them, but a lot I didn't, so I copied most of them down, typed up notes about them, and Father John loaned me a book about Christian symbology. And the notes vanished."

"And you think someone could have taken them?"

"Well, I've looked and looked, and I can't find them. And the book I was using to look them up is still in my apartment. And now the tapestry is gone, too."

Malloy's interest sharpened. "What do you mean, gone?"

"I called over there yesterday, and the secretary said she didn't know where the tapestry was. She said it hasn't been seen since it got moved out of the church hall when they were clearing it out for the renovation."

Mike closed his notebook. "I guess I'd better go over to the church and see about this missing tapestry." He looked at his watch. "Well, in about five hours."

After he left, Jill said, "Why didn't you tell him about Joe Mickels and New York Motto?"

"Because if Joe doesn't know, then his money problems are nobody's business. You and I will go see him as soon as he gets to his office. In about five hours."

15

J ill and Betsy slept for two hours after Malloy left,
then washed and dressed. Jill toasted a frozen breakfast pastry. "Sure you don't want one?" she asked Betsy.
"We've got time."

"No," replied Betsy. "The shots are easier to take on
an empty stomach."

"How long does this go on?"

"When they can't get any more arsenic from a urine
test, that will be it. Today could be the last, or it might
go on into January." The thought of weeks of the painful
and sick-making Dimercaprol shots depressed Betsy,
and she fell silent as they got into Jill's big old car.

Jill picked her moment and pulled out of the driveway
onto Lake Street. Then, sensing Betsy didn't want to
talk, she snapped on the radio.

KSJN's morning show was mostly Christmas music.
Odd and eccentric, but definitely Christmas music.
Betsy's frown of discontent turned to dismay when an-
nouncer Dale Connelly casually noted that day after tomorrow was Christmas eve.

Where had the time gone? Betsy sighed, because she knew the answer to that. Gone to car accidents, the hospital, the doctor's office to pee into ridiculously tiny plastic cups leading to more painful injections.

Who'd be a medical technician?

Who, for that matter, would own a small business? She didn't want to go from the doctor's office to Crewel World. She didn't want to be reminded by some customer's question of how little she knew or endure the tireless chitchat of her help or Godwin's comments. She didn't want to see the stack of bills the postman would bring or argue with suppliers sold out of everything but what she didn't want. And tonight was another late closing night; she had a normal eight-hour day to get through, then another three hours of evening work. Same with tomorrow.

Most of all, she was sick of being the target of someone murderous, an unknown someone, angry for an unknown reason. Half frozen, poisoned, choking on smoke—not dead yet. Not yet.

Betsy snorted softly.

"What?" said Jill.

"Oh, I've been sitting here working myself into a foul mood, and I just thought that would be a terrible way to spend my last few hours on earth, grouchy and complaining."

"Last few hours?"

"If the assassin succeeds."

"He won't," growled Jill and set her jaw.

Betsy, looking at that grim profile, was suddenly reminded of a beer ad, hugely popular in Britain during World War II. It was just two words, a verb and the name of the brewer: *Take Courage*. She smiled and then set her own jaw.

A little after ten, Jill and Betsy were back in Excelsior, parking behind Crewel World. The back door was covered with a big sheet of plywood, so they went around front. Shelly was waiting there with a man Betsy thought she'd met before, though she couldn't place him. "This is Mr. Reynolds," said Shelly casually, sure Betsy would know him.

Jill unlocked the front door and they came in. "Whew!" said Shelly, wrinkling her nose. "Gee, you'd think there was a fire in here last night or something." Mr. Reynolds laughed.

Betsy turned on the lights. The smell wasn't strong, but it was there, like yesterday's campfire. But there was no visible smoke damage. She walked to the rear storage area, limping on the left just a little. The smell was stronger back here, and the door into the hallway had a dark gray edge. Betsy plugged in the teakettle, then reached and pulled a forefinger down the white-painted surface of the bathroom door. The finger came away dusty but not sooty.

When she came back out, Mr. Reynolds was taking off his overcoat, and Betsy, seeing the loud houndstooth sport coat he wore under it, recognized him as her insurance agent. "This keeps up," he said to her, "your rates will go through the roof." He had last been in the shop when it had been trashed by Margot's murderer.

"What can you do for us?" asked Betsy.

He looked around. "How long ago was the fire?"

"It was reported around midnight," said Jill. "It was out within an hour, pretty much."

He checked his watch. "And there's hardly any smell right now. But there were what, three closed doors between the fire and here? That's what really helped. I think you lucked out. If there had been smoke in here, you'd've lost your entire stock. Smoke gets into fibers something frightening, and it never comes out. So I tell you how we'll handle this. I'll call ServiceMaster and have them come by for a look-see. Likely they'll put in an ozone maker for a day, and that will be that. Any damage anywhere else?"

"The fire was set outside, against the back door," said Jill. "We caught it before the back door burned through. But the back door is charred, and the back hall is definitely smoky."

"Yeah, well, that's the landlord's responsibility," said the agent. "Mickels doesn't have coverage through us. What we cover for Ms. Devonshire is the contents of this store." He strode through, made some notes on a pad, and said he would call ServiceMaster. "We may be able to get them here yet today. Meanwhile, don't try any cleanup yourself; you'll only make things worse. And don't sell anything out of here until we deodorize the place." He appeared to really look at Betsy for the first time. She drew herself up straight and tried on a smile, but she didn't fool him. "You live upstairs, don't you? I think you should close the place, go upstairs, and sack out for about ten hours."

"No, I have things to do," said Betsy.

"Well, don't go far; I need to let you know about ServiceMaster. Can you give me a phone number?"

Betsy said, "You can leave a message on one of my machines. I'll keep checking."

"Oh-kay," he said, and left.

Shelly said, "Well, I guess that means I don't get any hours today, right?"

"That's right."

The phone rang, and Betsy picked it up. Godwin's cheerful voice said, "Do I get to go shopping the rest of the month?"

"My insurance agent says he may be able to get it cleaned up today. Can you come in tomorrow?"

"That's another reason I called. A case was settled out of court, so John is taking tomorrow off and wants me to go skiing with him. Can you get Shelly to come in?"

Betsy looked at Shelly, who had her hand up in a *Call on me!* gesture. "I'm sure she will. So consider yourself covered tomorrow."

"Thanks. I'll see you Friday. Oh, and Betsy . . ." There was a lengthy silence. "I guess I don't know what to say."

"That's okay, I wouldn't know what to say back, either. 'Bye, Godwin."

"So what do we do first?" asked Jill, when Shelly and the insurance man had gone.

"Let's go beard the lion."

A few minutes later, the two were climbing the old wooden stairs to the second floor of the Water Street building. At the far end of the hall they found a glass office door painted with plain black letters: Mickels Corporation. Jill went in first. They found themselves in a small room in front of a gray metal desk. A row of gray metal filing cabinets took up most of a wall. The young woman at the desk was working on a very modern computer. She glanced up and said, "May I help you?"

Betsy said, "I'm Betsy Devonshire. Is Mr. Mickels in?"

She glanced at Jill in her uniform and said, "Just a moment, please." The woman went through a back door, shutting it behind her. The door must have been a good one; they couldn't hear a sound through it. She came back, leaving the door open, to say, "Go on in."

Mickels's inner office was barely more opulent. It did have a big wooden desk with carved corners that was probably a hundred years old, but the chair behind it was an old wooden thing on casters with a back that curved into the arms. The single window overlooking the street was uncurtained. There was a wooden filing cabinet against one wall, and a low bookcase contained law books and three-ring binders. The floor was bare, and there were no pictures on the walls. A thick metal door probably led to a strong room.

Mickels sat behind the desk, his back to the window. "Ms. Devonshire, Officer Cross," he said. His white sideburns lined a very good poker face.

"Mr. Mickels," said Betsy, who had thought hard about how to approach Mickels on this, "you own the building that contains Crewel World, am I right?"

Mickels nodded, frowning a little. "You know that."

"And you know I am the sister of the founder of the company, the late Margot Berglund?"

Again Mickels nodded, his frown deepening.

In exactly the same tone, Betsy asked, "And you know that Mrs. Berglund was the founder and silent partner in New York Motto, right?"

Mickels blinked, then jumped to his feet. *"What?"* he shouted.

"I said, my sister was the owner of New York Motto."

"By God, I might have known!" roared Mickels, flinging his arms in the air. "That *bitch!* That sweet-talking, milk-faced, embroidering, conniving *bitch!*" His anger fed on itself, and the madder he got, the stronger his language became. Betsy, backing away, was further startled when the door to the outer office opened and the secretary stood in the doorway, her eyes wide.

"What's wrong?" she asked. "Shall I call—" She stopped, confused, because Jill Cross *was* the police.

"Get out!" shouted Mickels. "Just get out!"

"Yessir," she•said, and went, closing the door behind her.

"I think you'd better sit down, Mr. Mickels," said Betsy, a little alarmed at the color of his face.

But Mickels was too upset to sit down. "And she told you this, so you could just keep on grinding me down!" he growled.

"No, I didn't know about it until Mr. Penberthy came to see me last night—"

Mickels exploded again, describing the attorney in atrocious language. "It was probably all his goddamned idea!" he concluded, leaning on his desk, his breathing alarmingly loud and uneven.

"Mr. Mickels, if you'll just calm down—" said Jill in her smoothest voice.

"Calm down? I ought to go and shoot him down!" shouted Mickels. "Cheat me, will she?" And he spoke again about Margot Berglund in language that exasperated Betsy as much as it embarrassed her. Jill took her by the arm and signaled with nod and lifted eyebrows that they should just stand back and let Mickels get it out of his system.

When Mickels was reduced to merely walking around and around his desk, clenching and unclenching his fingers and grinding his teeth, Betsy tried again.

"It appears you didn't know anything about this until I told you," she said. "And a good thing, too."

"What?" Mickels seemed surprised to find them still in his office.

"Mr. Mickels, someone has made three attempts on my life."

"Yes, I know." Mickels's wide, thin, mouth pulled suddenly into an ugly smile. "I wish him luck."

"You don't mean that, Mr. Mickels," said Jill.

"Don't I? Do you know what this New York Motto has done to me? Ruined me, that's what! My whole life is going to slide into the toilet in less than a month! It's not just the goddam waterfront property, it's my credit rating! My reputation as a man of business! I may have to give up on The Mickels Building, the dream of my life! All because some dotty woman wanted to sell the means to make a piddling *doily!* She's *ruined* me, d'ya hear? She—and now you, *Ms.* Devonshire, who haven't the littlest clue how to run a business! And all over what? A piddling *doily!* I hope whoever's after you squashes you like a *bug!* I hope when he finishes with you, he takes after Penberthy! Now get out of my office!" Mickels stopped to do more of that effortful breathing, his fingers working. He threw a sudden glance at his strong room, then glared at Jill. "You, take her out of here, now!"

But that glance roused Betsy's sleuthing instincts, and when Jill stepped forward, she could tell that Jill had noticed it, too. With a crack of authority in her voice, Jill said, "We're not finished talking with you, Mr. Mickels. Why don't you sit down and answer a few questions?"

Mickels stopped pacing and actually went to his chair and sat down. But it was with an effort, and he sat so rigidly that Betsy felt if she were to tap him on the shoulder he'd shatter like cheap pottery. Mickels's hands were in white-knuckled fists, and again he glanced at the strong room.

"Something in there, sir?" asked Jill.

"In where?"

"In that room behind the steel door."

"Just some records."

Betsy asked, "Records of that deal with New York Motto?"

Mickels's shrug seemed sincerely confused. "Yes."

"What else?" asked Jill.

"You can't search that room without a warrant, you know."

"I could with your permission."

"There's nothing in there."

Betsy said, "Show us."

Mickels hesitated a long while. Then, with a too-elaborate shrug, he stood and fished in his pocket for a big, old-fashioned key.

The strong room was the size of a walk-in closet. There was a small, long-legged table beside a gray filing cabinet with a combination dial on its top drawer. A huge old green safe bulked large at the back. The light came from a naked bulb hanging on a wire from the high ceiling. The cabinet and safe were open. Betsy, remembering the old game of hot and cold, watched Joe closely as Jill looked first into the filing cabinet, pulling open one drawer then the next, fingers walking quickly along the file folders. Mickels didn't show much, so Betsy said, "Maybe it's in the safe."

Jill pulled the safe door wide. Mickels tensed, and Jill, aware of what Betsy was doing, touched various papers, while Betsy played hot and hotter. When Jill touched an old metal box with a padlock on it, Mickels actually trembled.

"What's in the box?" asked Betsy.

"My coin collection," grated Mickels.

The box was extremely heavy, and Jill couldn't lift it alone. Betsy hurried to help. It made a metallic noise when it tilted, and Mickels became a white-hot statue in order not to rush to their aid.

"Open it for me?" asked Jill, after they succeeded in sliding it onto the tall table.

Mickels came to unlock the padlock with a mild show of reluctance—or was feeling so much reluctance some leaked out around the edges of his attempt to disguise it. He put the padlock on the table beside the box and stepped back.

Jill opened the box. It was nearly filled with bright silver coins, mostly half dollars, but with dimes, quarters, and dollars mixed in. The coins were loose, not in the little cardboard holders collectors use.

Betsy, puzzled, picked up a few. They were badly worn and a trifle greasy, as if from much fondling. She turned and looked at Mickels, who looked back, grim-faced.

"I don't get it," said Jill, scooping up a handful of coins. She turned and held them out to Joe.

"They're all real silver, not those cheap alloys the government issues nowadays," said Mickels, staring at them, fingers working. "They're badly worn, and of no interest to real collectors, so I bought 'em at face value. I don't know why I keep them." He shrugged stiffly, and tore his eyes away. "Anything else I can show you in here?"

Betsy, feeling she'd come to the heart of a mystery without solving it, glanced at Jill, then said, "No."

Jill closed the box and would have snapped the pad-lock shut, but Mickels said, "Just leave it." He turned and walked stiffly out of the strong room, and they followed. "Anything else you want to look at?" he asked, going to his chair. He put his hands on the back of it, a seemingly casual gesture, except that his grip was so tight his fingernails were pressed white.

Jill said, "Are you the one trying to murder Betsy Devonshire?"

"No."

"She really didn't know about New York Motto until Penberthy told her, you know."

Mickels nodded once, sharply. "Yes, that's probably the case." The nostrils of his big nose flared suddenly. "If I'd found out she owned New York Motto on my own, I might be asserting my right to silence and phon-ing my lawyer right now. But before God, I didn't know." The anger suddenly left him, and he said, with an air that seemed close to despair, "I suppose this'll be all over the business pages tomorrow morning?"

"I have no intention of sharing this with anyone, Mr. Mickels," said Betsy. "And neither does Officer Cross."

"That's something, at least."

They left him still standing behind the chair.

Out on the street, Betsy said, "What was that about the coins?"

"Beats me. But I'd say it was pretty clear he didn't know about New York Motto. Whew!"

Betsy giggled suddenly. "I haven't heard language like that since I dated a first class bosun's mate." She sobered. "But damn. All right, let's go to Trinity and talk to everyone. Find out when the tapestry was last seen, or if maybe someone walked out of the church hall with a suspicious bulge under his coat."

Things were bustling in the church office. Jill and Betsy stood a moment inside the door, taking it in. A delivery man was standing beside a stack of boxes with a local printer's logo on them, waiting for someone to sign his clipboard. A plump, sad-faced woman in a head scarf waited on a hard wooden bench, and next to her a thin, nervous man in a light jacket, far too light for the weather. Betsy was surprised to see Patricia Fairland next to him. She was staring at the floor in front of her, looking ill with worry. Betsy thought, *Maybe she's going to ask Father John to ask me to leave town.*

Two chatting women were sorting green pledge cards on a table, and the secretary was at her desk and on the phone, saying in a calm voice that no, Christmas day being on a Saturday did not mean that Sunday services were canceled. She had the receiver tucked under her chin and continued typing some text onto her computer screen as she talked. *Probably Father John's Christmas sermon,* thought Betsy.

A noise came through the floor, as of a timber being torn in half the long way, and everyone paused to look down, waiting to see if the floor was going to collapse. In the silence, Betsy realized there were other sounds of destruction from the same source.

When the floor didn't open, the secretary said to the

room, "Renovation," and everyone nodded and went back to whatever they were doing.

The door to Father John Rettger's office opened, and a woman was heard saying, "But her sister was Mary two years ago, and Jessica is even prettier than Tiffany!"

Father John's mild voice replied, "But rehearsals for the Christmas pageant have been going on for weeks. We can't possibly make a last-minute substitution."

"Can she at least be the understudy?"

"We already have two understudies, and—" something like laughter appeared in Father John's voice "—I'm afraid every one of them is in very good health."

A tight-faced woman came marching past Father John into the outer office. She had a gorgeous blond-haired child about seven years old in tow. "But Mother, I don't want to be Mary," said the child in a reasonable voice.

"Of course you do, darling," replied her mother, weaving her expertly through the people and objects between them and the door to the outside hall. "We'll call the bishop."

Betsy wondered if it was in the bishop's power to make Jessica Mary. It might be worth a try; she remembered how the girls who played Mary in her childhood pageants were forever marked as special.

Father John stood in the doorway. He already looked tired, though it was still morning. His secretary hung up and started to sign to Patricia, who rose, but Betsy spoke up quickly.

"Can I just ask something first? Father, can you tell me anything about the disappearance of the tapestry?"

Father John looked blankly at her. "Did it disappear? All I know is, I brought it up to the sacristy that day I loaned you the book, wrapped it in a white sheet, and put it in one of the drawers." He looked at the secretary. "Crystal, did you take it out of there?"

"I didn't know it was in there, Father. I don't think anyone did. We've been looking for it."

Betsy said, relieved, "I was hoping you'd let me have another look at it."

"Of course. Crystal—"

But Patricia, already moving, said, "I'll get it for you, Betsy. I want to talk to you about the project anyway." She gestured at the thin man on the seat. "You may have my turn."

The man looked at the secretary, then at Father John, who nodded and said, "Hello, Hadley. Come on in."

Patricia had vanished down a short hall. She was gone barely a minute, then came back, to walk past Jill and Betsy to the secretary's desk. "Crystal, I can't find the tapestry in any of the drawers," Patricia said. "I wonder if Father John is mistaken." Her voice was a trifle thick, and she coughed. So it was a cold, not worry, that had Patricia looking ill.

"I wouldn't think so," said the secretary. "I mean, he said he wrapped it in a sheet and put it in a drawer in the sacristy, right? That's kind of specific for even him to be mistaken about, you know what I mean?"

"May I look?" asked Betsy.

"I can help, too," said Jill.

Patricia glanced at the secretary, who shrugged, then said, "Go ahead, if you like."

"Come on, Betsy," said Jill.

Jill led her down the short hall to a small room lined with wooden cabinets. There were two sets of wide, shallow drawers. One of the top drawers was pulled out, showing a green chasuble, the vestment that covers the arms and torso of a priest during the communion service.

Betsy bent and looked to the back of the drawer without seeing anything but chasuble. She closed it and pulled the next one out. It was empty. The one below that had a red chasuble.

Jill opened a vertical door and began gently pushing aside the rows of albs, the white gowns worn under vestments.

Finished with the drawers, Betsy opened a tall cabinet full of long candle holders designed to be carried in a procession. Another cabinet contained shelves with censers and other paraphernalia. A tall, narrow hanging space held stoles, the long, narrow bands hung from the neck. Next to the cabinet was a door, in the wall opposite to the one they came in by. Betsy opened it and saw it led into the chapel, which was as innocent of white sheets as the cabinets she had searched. She closed it again and opened the cabinet of albs, and checked each one to make sure Jill hadn't mistaken a white sheet for an alb. She hadn't.

Even with total overlap, it took less than five minutes to complete the search.

"What do you think?" asked Betsy.

"I think it's not in here," said Jill. "I don't know why."

"Where else could it be?"

"Beats me. It's not in the outer office, and I doubt if it's in Father John's office, You looked in the chapel and didn't see it."

They went out of the sacristy. Betsy saw another door on her right that had a small metal sign: Rest Room. It was slightly ajar, and she opened it to find the world's smallest bathroom. It had a toilet and a tiny sink. If the sink had been full size, there wouldn't have been room for the toilet.

"Find it?" said Patricia from outside the room.

Betsy turned around and said, "No."

Jill said, "Maybe someone saw it in the sacristy, realized it didn't belong, and put it somewhere else."

Patricia said, "Now that sounds very likely. I'm afraid Father John does put things down instead of away, so the staff is pretty used to picking up after him." Her voice was more indulgent than annoyed, and Betsy remembered Patricia was on the vestry.

Betsy said, "I bet Father John was kind of a letdown after the fabulous Father Keane."

Patricia frowned a little at Betsy. "Not at all. He's different, but every man is different from every other. John's kind and wise and has an amazing sense of humor."

Betsy laughed. "Good to hear someone finally say that."

"Say what?"

"Most of us women complain that men are all alike!"

Patricia started to laugh, but sneezed instead. "You're right, you're right!" she said, pulling a handkerchief from her coat pocket and blowing. "But don't tell anyone I said it, or I'm liable to be drummed out of the gender corps!"

Betsy said, "But what are we going to do? This will hold up the restoration."

"Well, nothing's going to get done during the holiday season anyway; you know that. Even I'm going out of town—but I think I told you that. We're leaving this afternoon for Phoenix. The tapestry will very likely turn up a day or two after Christmas, when it's less of a madhouse around here."

Jill said, "So you think it will be found."

"Of course! After all, it's not exactly something someone would steal. And everyone knows about it, so they aren't likely to throw it away by mistake. It's around here somewhere."

Betsy said, "Yes, I suppose you're right. Okay, I'll just wait for it to turn up. If I don't hear between now and New Year's, I'll call Father John or you."

"Thank you, Betsy."

16

When they got back to the apartment, the phone message light was blinking.

Betsy pushed the Play button, and the happy voice of her insurance agent said, "Hello, Ms. Devonshire! ServiceMaster says they want to stop by with a pair of their ozone generators. Call me as soon as you hear this and let me know where you'll leave the key so I can let them in."

Jill reminded her, "Don't leave your key with anyone. Ask him when they want to come, and we'll be here to let them in."

Betsy did so, and found they would be over within the hour. Then she went into the kitchen to open a can of tuna and heat some tomato soup for lunch. "Do you think Patricia could have taken that tapestry?" she asked, handing Jill's plate to her.

"I don't know where to. You looked in the chapel, didn't you?"

"I looked through the door. But she didn't have time to go in there to tuck it back behind something, did she?

She was only gone a minute, barely long enough to open a couple of drawers."

Jill nodded. "You're right. And in that short coat and slacks, she wasn't wearing it. So assume someone else got there ahead of her. We'll have to ask Father John who he told about putting the tapestry into the sacristy."

"Yes," said Betsy, "because I agree with Crystal: He was too specific about where he put it to be mistaken."

Since she'd skipped breakfast, she finished her sandwich quickly and drank her mug of soup before calling Trinity. Father John had gone out but she was told he would be back soon. Betsy left a message, asking him to call back.

The ServiceMaster man was tall and young and wore a forest-green jacket and shirt. The ozone generators were small black boxes that made a faint humming sound. "It's like concentrated oxygen," he explained. "It just eats smell."

Soon the box on the checkout desk was emitting a sharp, unpleasant odor. "Do we have to rent another box to get rid of this stink?" asked Betsy.

"No, ma'am," said the man. "An hour after you shut it off, there's no smell at all."

After he left, Jill and Betsy went upstairs, Betsy carrying a bundle of sales slips to enter them in her computer.

But she'd barely started before she was overwhelmed by a nap attack. She managed to stagger to the beautiful four-poster bed before collapsing across it and falling almost instantly asleep.

When the silence in the back bedroom had gone on for a while, Jill peeped in and saw Betsy sound asleep. Jill went into the closet, pulled a soft blanket off a shelf, and laid it over Betsy, who didn't stir.

Jill went back to the living room and sat down on the love seat with her needlework, but in half an hour her needle slipped from her fingers, and she dozed off.

The phone's ring yanked her awake, and she hurried to the kitchen to answer it.

"Hello, this is Father John at Trinity. May I speak with Betsy, please?"

"Oh, hello, Father. This is Jill Cross. Betsy's asleep. What she wanted to ask you was, how sure are you that you put the tapestry in that drawer?"

"Very sure. I wanted it in a safe place, but also where it wouldn't come in contact with anything else—that mildew, you know. I don't know how it got out of the drawer; I certainly didn't remove it."

"Did you tell anyone it was there?"

The priest thought for a bit. "Phil Galvin," he said. "Phil said something to me about it, and I told him where I put it."

"Anyone else?"

"I don't think so. I should have told Crystal, of course, but I didn't. Now, when I talked with Phil, it was after the Wednesday Advent service, and we weren't alone. There might have been a dozen eavesdroppers. And of course, Phil himself might have told others."

Jill nearly groaned aloud. "All right, thank you, Father. I'll pass this information along." So long as she was in the kitchen, Jill made a pot of coffee—and added coffee to the grocery list on the refrigerator—drank a cup, then went back to her needlework refreshed.

Betsy slept for three hours. She came out of the back bedroom with a grumpy face. "Why'd you let me sleep so long?" she complained.

"You looked as if you needed it."

Betsy stood still, blinking, then nodded. "I guess I did. But now I won't sleep tonight."

Jill smiled. "Wanna bet?"

Betsy yawned suddenly. "No." She lifted her head, inhaling gently. "Is that coffee I smell?"

"Yes, I'm afraid I drink it all day long."

"Well, how about I get a cup and then we'll go Christmas shopping."

"Mall of America?"

"No, that place is too big. What's near here?"

"Well, there's Ridgedale in Minnetonka."

Soon Betsy found herself standing on a mezzanine overlooking a tiled square whose center was taken up by what looked like an in-construction snow-country lodge with a big stone fireplace and plank floor. In front of the fireplace was a big wing chair, and sitting in the chair, entertaining one child at a time, was Santa Claus—the really good kind, who hangs his red coat on a hook and whose beard and stomach are real.

In a little less than two hours, her credit card still smoking, Betsy piled her purchases into the backseat of Jill's big Roadmaster for the drive home.

There is something relaxing about spending a lot of money in a short time. Betsy, still tired from last night's adventure, felt she could melt into the comfortable passenger seat. The short winter day was nearly over, and Betsy was recalled to her childhood, being driven home in the purple dusk. How comforted and at peace she had felt then—and now, with warm light from house windows making safe the coming night, and Christmas lights gleaming and twinkling—those new icicle lights were like lace edging on the eaves of houses, very pretty.

Jill had to wake her when they pulled into the parking lot.

Betsy had planned to look again at the saints' attributes after supper, but she didn't even stay awake long enough to eat.

Around eight the next morning, driving Betsy in light traffic to get her daily shot of Dimercaprol, Jill asked, "Which Christmas service are you going to?"

Betsy hadn't planned on going to church for Christmas. She didn't think much of people who went twice a year, at Christmas and Easter. Well, maybe that wasn't true any longer. It was more that she was uncomfortable with what had been her unchristian opinion of them, back when she was a regular churchgoer. On the other hand, since Jill was assigned to Betsy, if Betsy didn't go, neither could Jill, and it would be unkind to make Jill miss church. Besides, Father John had saved Betsy's life with a prayer, and Betsy felt a debt of gratitude. It wouldn't hurt to go. Maybe it would jump-start her back into going regularly.

So she said, "Which one do you go to?"

"I always liked the first service Christmas morning."

"All right," said Betsy. After a few minutes, she asked, "What were your other plans for Christmas before you volunteered for this?"

"Nothing much." And Jill could not be moved in any direction from that statement.

They got back quicker than usual from Dr. McQueen's office, and Betsy went to lie down until her stomach stopped doing flip-flops. But she was smiling; Dr. McQueen pronounced this the last shot.

A few minutes after they got back, the ServiceMaster man rang the doorbell and asked to be let into the shop to take away his ozone makers. By the time the shop opened at ten, the smell of ozone had in fact melted away, leaving nothing in its wake.

Shelly came at five after, exclaiming over the sunshine and relatively high temperature—thirty-four degrees, actually above freezing, in late *December!*—though an Alberta Clipper was predicted to blow through in the afternoon. She helped dust and vacuum and rearrange displays as the shop opened for business. It being Christmas eve, there was an urgent press of customers.

One young woman, with blond hair and a brisk air, went to the bookshelves to see what they had on blackwork. Another, a middle-aged woman in a pale gray coat, came to the desk with a Crewel World bag in her hand and a pleased smile on her face.

"Good morning, Mrs. Hamilton," said Betsy, smiling back.

"I finished it," said Mrs. Hamilton, holding up the bag, whose contents were small. Betsy rose and went behind the checkout desk.

"How did it come out?" she asked.

In reply, Mrs. Hamilton brought out a belt made of needlepoint canvas with a pattern of cats in various poses, each with a different design of coat. Made to be worked in silk or cotton floss, Mrs. Hamilton had decided to do it in beads. The canvas and beads, plus thread and the hair-fine needles, which broke or bent often, had cost over a hundred dollars. The work had taken months. And now the belt needed to be finished: washed, blocked, attached to a strip of leather, and given a good brass buckle, which was going to cost another eighty dollars. And the result would be a "fun" belt.

But to a needleworker's sophisticated eye, the beadwork was flawless. The texture pleasured the fingers. Betsy looked up at Mrs. Hamilton and saw she didn't need to say a word in praise; Mrs. Hamilton understood.

The woman at the bookshelves came over with her selection. "Ooooh," she said. "That's very nice. Did you make it?"

Mrs. Hamilton nodded. "Do you do beadwork?" she asked.

The woman laughed. "I can barely sew a button on. I came in to buy this for a friend who does blackwork, whatever that is. I've never been in here before. I usually buy her Christmas gift on eBay or Amazon dot com, but time got away from me, and I can't wait for shipment now."

Mrs. Hamilton said, "My daughter shops on the Internet, but I'm afraid I don't trust it. I mean, who are those people?"

"Well, there's all kinds, just like in real life. I like it because I can shop from home, plus you find things there you won't find anywhere else. Especially on the auction sites. I can search for exotic gifts and I don't get tired feet or lose my car in the parking lot. And by exercising a little care, I haven't been burnt yet."

Betsy said, "I know someone else who loves eBay. She buys antiques."

The woman nodded. "I've done that, too. I got into the glass bottles the other day and bid on two items. One was a medicine bottle from the 1800s with the pills still inside it! Of course, it came with a warning not to take the medicine." The woman laughed. "I'm Christine Schleuter, by the way."

"Betsy Devonshire," said Betsy, "and this is Mrs. Hamilton."

"How do you do?" the women said to one another.

"You aren't really going to give this to your daughter, are you?" asked Betsy, getting the conversation back on topic.

"Yes, I am. She's going to specialize in small-animal medicine, and she's always loved cats. She'll enjoy wearing this."

Shelly and Jill came to admire the belt while Betsy wrote up the order.

"You'll call when this comes back?" asked Mrs. Hamilton.

"Of course. Merry Christmas," Betsy added, as Mrs. Hamilton went out the door.

"Oops," said Jill behind her.

Betsy turned. "What?"

"Didn't you know? Mrs. Hamilton is Wiccan."

"She is?"

Shelly giggled and nodded. "She belongs to a coven in Minneapolis."

Betsy and Ms. Schleuter looked at the closed door. "Funny," said Ms. Schleuter, "she doesn't look like a witch."

"Yes, but who does, nowadays?" said Betsy. "Next time I'll wish her a happy solstice."

Toward noon, Betsy was just finishing with another customer when Joe Mickels came in. He glared at Shelly when she approached, and she retreated to a spinner rack, rearranging the floss a shopper had disordered. He looked with equal anger at Jill, who only looked back.

He should play the lead in A Christmas Carol, thought Betsy when she was finished, noting his long coat with the lamb collar, the big silver sideburns that framed his shaggy eyebrows, the arrogant nose and angry mouth. She said, "May I help you, Mr. Mickels?"

"I need to talk to you," he said, glancing again at Jill and adding, "Alone."

Jill said at once, "I'm sorry, Mr. Mickels, but she's under police protection and is not allowed to be alone with anyone."

Mickels turned as if to leave, but Betsy said, "Jill knows everything, Mr. Mickels. You know that."

Mickels looked at Jill, and for the briefest instant there was again despair. Betsy started, "Look, I'm really sorry about—"

"Sorry don't cut it," he growled.

Jill said, "I think we should send Shelly out to buy us all some lunch."

Shelly, who had been trying to eavesdrop from behind the spinner rack, came shamefacedly out.

"I can't afford to buy lunch today," she said.

"Me, either," said Betsy.

There was a pregnant pause. Jill held her tongue until Mickels with a soft groan said, "All right, I'll buy us all a McDonald's hamburger!" He took an ancient coin purse from his pocket. It was all Betsy could do to keep from laughing when she saw it. He twisted the catch open and removed with regret a ten-dollar bill. "You've got coffee here," he said, "so no drinks. Get two big orders of fries, and we'll share. And bring me my change."

"Yessir," said Shelly, not bothering to hide her grin. She grabbed her coat and hurried out.

"Do you know why the rich have money?" Mickels said to Betsy.

"Why?"

"Because they don't spend it."

"I'll take that as the good advice it probably is. Won't you sit down?" Betsy went to the library table and pulled out a chair for him.

As he came to sit down, Betsy was struck, as she had been once before, by his slightness. His wealth and arrogance made him seem large; from behind he was a scant two inches taller than she was.

Jill sat across from him, hands on the table and chair not pulled in close. Betsy sat at the head of the table, facing the door so she could see anyone approaching.

Mickels said, "I had no idea your sister was such an expert on bankruptcy estates."

"She wasn't," replied Betsy. "It was Vicki Prentice who knew how to do it. What Margot did was give her the money to start the company. Margot was a silent partner; she didn't take any part in running it. Vicki found the assets and bid on them, so even if she knew you were the actual owner of that restaurant property, she didn't know of your relationship with Margot."

"Huh," said Mickels, doubting that.

"Well, if she did, she didn't tell Margot. Because Margot didn't tell me, and I think she would have."

"Fat lot of good your ignorance did me."

"Look here," said Betsy, "acting like a sulky little boy isn't going to help. You signed that contract of your own free will, so the consequences of not making the balloon payment are your own. You're going to lose that property, along with all the money you put into making those payments."

"And I'm supposed to smile and take that?"

"There isn't anything *you* can do about it," she snapped.

He brought keen gray eyes to bear on her from under those eyebrows. "And you're going to dance on the ruins of my prosperity, right?"

"I could, if I liked. While I agree Margot was responsible for you losing that property, it wasn't on purpose. And your behavior toward her was disgraceful. I could consider the two of you even. But perhaps we can work something out."

When Shelly came back with the hamburgers, she was surprised to find the three of them talking almost cordially. But even after Mickels left, neither Jill nor Betsy would disclose what brought about Mickels's change of attitude.

Soon after lunch, Betsy sold a huge order of needlepoint, counted cross stitch, and knitting materials to a woman who was leaving for Texas in the morning, where she would spend the winter. Her loyalty to Crewel World was touching, and Betsy said as much to her while Shelly carefully added up the bill.

"You always have everything I need," the woman said, writing out a check, "and you allow me to return unused materials. And I just love your staff." She looked around the shop as if for a particular one.

Betsy said, "Godwin has the day off. I know he'll be sorry to have missed you."

"You'll wish him a happy holiday from me, won't you?"

"Yes, of course. And we wish you a happy holiday, too."

Shelly helped the woman carry her order out to her car. Betsy said, "That order should put us in the black."

Jill said, surprised, "Are you operating at a loss?"

"We might have, if she hadn't come in. In fact, we may still. I'm supposed to be working more so I can cut back on employee hours, but with all that's happened . . ."

Shelly came back in, dusting snow off her shoulders.

"Again?" groaned Betsy. It had clouded over without her noticing.

Shelly said, "The radio says it's only supposed to be an inch or two."

Jill said, "Be glad you live in Minnesota. If they got snow like this in, say, Atlanta, the city would be paralyzed."

"If they were getting snow like this in Atlanta," retorted Betsy, *"we'd* be fighting off glaciers."

Laughing, they looked around and saw no customers. They sat at the table to continue some projects. Shelly was knitting a minuscule cap on tiny needles to be donated to a preemie program for local hospitals. Betsy was trying out some DMC rayon floss. She liked the shimmer it gave to the snowflake she was working in counted cross stitch on maroon evenweave.

Bing went that annoying door alarm, and as she did often, Betsy promised herself a new, more dulcet-sounding one.

Jill was moving to get between Betsy and the person coming in: Hal Norman, hat in hand.

Hal said, "Betsy, I'm leaving Sunday for California. I'd like to talk to you before I go."

"We're busy here. I can't talk to you now."

"Then how about supper? Do you still like Chinese? There's a decent Chinese place here in town, the Ming Wok. I can meet you there after closing." He saw her about to refuse and said, "Or I can bring Chinese to you."

Betsy hesitated, then gestured surrender and said, "Bring carry-out for three to my apartment tonight."

"All right. Thank you." He hesitated, obviously hoping his sweet reasonableness would make her say something more, something nice, even just "You're welcome." But she didn't.

He remembered her favorite, chicken with pea pods and straw mushrooms. He also brought Mongolian beef and moo shu pork, and everyone took a little of everything.

He was attentive and humble. He had a little box of loose jasmine tea, another favorite, and brewed it for her, making funny jokes about not being able to find the tea strainer in the strange kitchen. He used chopsticks with grace, and put a series of tasty tidbits on her plate. He remarked on the tree, apparently not realizing it was the one he'd bought—or too clever to say so.

Jill sat quietly, watching and listening.

When the meal was over, he said, "There, was that so bad? Was that so difficult? Please, please, darlin'—yes, here in front of a witness—can't we work something out? It's Christmas eve, and this would be a great present, just knowing you're willing to try once more."

"There's nothing to work out."

"Are you sure? You don't act like you're still mad at me."

"I'm not mad."

"Then what's the problem?"

"I don't care."

Hal's look of charming contrition slid off his face, leaving a confused expression behind. "What?"

"I used to think up ways to get back to you, to humiliate you like you humiliated me. I was so mad at you, I got physically sick. But you know something? I got well again. It could be learning that I can stand on my own feet, run my own business. Or maybe it's the chelating agent, taking you out of my system along with the arsenic. All I know is, when I poke around for my feelings about you, I can't find any. I don't care about you anymore."

"You've found somebody else, haven't you? Don't tell me it's that little pansy down in the store!"

"Okay, I won't."

"Oh, Betsy, how could you fall for someone like that?"

Betsy giggled. "I haven't fallen for him."

"But you just said—"

"You said not to tell you, so I said I wouldn't. Now go away."

"Won't you at least accept my apology?"

"No."

"But you don't know how sorry I am!"

"I don't think you're sorry enough. I don't think you're able to be sorry for anything except yourself. Now go."

And he went. Betsy cried when he'd gone, but it was tears of relief. Jill said nothing, only handed over tissues until the storm ended.

17

The first Christmas service, at 8:30, was for the children of the parish. Children formed the choir, they took the collection, the sermon was aimed at their level. Betsy found it all passable, though she had trouble with the hymns. She'd gotten too used to "O Come, All Ye Faithful" in secular settings to think of it as a hymn anymore. Father John's sermon, on looking inward rather than outward for the true meaning of Christmas, was good but hardly original. *What was I hoping for?* she asked herself, as the Eucharist came to its end. *Did I think God was going to arrange a particularly brilliant service just to tempt me into coming back again?* And then she realized that was exactly the sort of question the sermon had addressed.

After the service, the congregation scattered, rather than staying for coffee. By the eager manner of the children as they rushed for the exits, they were going home to open presents.

Betsy lingered a while in the silent nave, saying a personal prayer or two. Jill stood watch in the aisle.

The moment Betsy stood, a man's voice behind her said, "I'm glad to find you here, Betsy." She turned and saw Father John. He continued, "I hope you find here a further support for the admirable courage you've already shown in your troubles, and perhaps some comfort. It must be terrifying to have someone trying to take your life and not know why. I've been saying a prayer for your protection, a very militant prayer to Saint Michael the Archangel that has stiffened my nerve in difficult situations. 'Defend us in battle' it says, against 'evil spirits, who prowl about the the world seeking the destruction of souls.' "

"Amen," said Jill.

"I must say, however," continued the priest in his mild voice, "that I can't imagine what a ten-year-old tapestry might have to do with a current attempt on your life. After all, the woman who designed it is dead, and her husband is beyond saying anything about it."

"I assume Mike Malloy talked with you?" said Betsy.

"Yes, that's right, a few days ago. He's an interesting fellow. Catholic, of course, but not fervently so. He . . . his questions seemed rather vague."

"I'm afraid he's as baffled as we are, Father," said Betsy. "None of us understands where these attacks are coming from."

They got back to Betsy's apartment in time to listen to the Festival of Nine Lessons and Carols from King's College, Cambridge, rebroadcast by KSJN, a local public radio station. Betsy heated water for tea and the oven for some of Excelo Bakery's holiday bread, Shelly's gift to her. As usual, Betsy had to stop what she was doing when the lovely boy soprano's voice wafted up all alone, "Once in Royal David's city . . ."

Over tea and sweet, fragrant bread, Betsy said, "It's been twenty-four hours since someone tried to kill me."

Jill nodded. "And it's not like you've been sitting at home."

Betsy said, "I wonder if maybe Patricia saw something or someone, and doesn't realize it. Like in that Agatha Christie mystery, where the murderer dressed up like a postman or milkman, I forget which, and so the eyewitness said she didn't see anyone on the street, because she was looking for a chance pedestrian, not someone making his regular rounds. But the person Patricia saw realized he'd been spotted, and so he's gone into hiding."

"All right, who is supposed to be walking on our street on a winter midnight?"

"Okay, maybe not walking but driving. Someone in a police car, or a snowplow."

Jill thought about that. "I'm the only person you know who drives a squad car. And I don't think you know anyone who drives a snowplow."

"There's Vern Miller, of Miller's Motors."

"But he's the one who reported your brake line had been cut. And he hasn't shown any sign of being unhappy that you suspected him of murdering poor Trudie. In fact, I think he's proud of it. It adds to his reputation as a tough guy, having been a murder suspect."

Betsy said, "Speaking of Vern Miller: Do you think Malloy would let him get started on my car repairs? One of these days I'll be able to drive again, and I'd like to have a car."

"We can ask Malloy on Monday. What do you want to do today?"

"Can we go somewhere? I'm feeling really good, completely well, and I'd like some exercise. How about that cattle roundup you promised you'd look into back in September?"

Jill laughed. "It's a cattle drive, not a roundup. And I don't think they're doing any of that this time of year.

But I did look into it. There's one in June. It goes on
for a week and costs a hundred and ten dollars a night."

"A hundred and ten dollars—to eat beans and burnt
beef and sleep on the ground?"

"Well, nowadays I guess it's more comfortable than
that."

"I don't want a comfortable cattle drive. I want a real
one."

"All right, I'll look again."

Then they opened presents. Jill expressed gratitude for
the book, and was surprised to find tucked inside it a
gift certificate for framing her next project. She watched
with a face she could not quite keep smooth while Betsy
opened Godwin's gift: a needlepoint horse in T'ang Dy-
nasty style, done in blues, buffs, and a muted orange,
matted and framed. It was very like one that had once
belonged to Betsy's sister Margot.

Betsy stared at it, then at Jill. "I don't understand,"
she said.

"Godwin found a photo of the horse and copied it
onto graph paper, then onto sixteen-count canvas."

"But Godwin can't design patterns! He told me so
himself."

"I know. He struggled hard with this, and he's afraid
it didn't come out as well as the one your sister designed. But he wanted to do something special for you,
especially when he realized the scarf you were working
so hard on was for him."

"That was supposed to be a surprise!"

"If you want to knit something as a surprise, don't
ask the recipient what his favorite colors are, then knit
in those colors where he can see them."

Betsy giggled. "I forgot I asked him." She reached
under the tree for another gift, a long, narrow one, and
showed it to Sophie, who sniffed the bow politely. Inside
the wrapping was a toy fishing rod with a cluster of

feathers at the end of its line. Sophie chased and leaped for the feathers and at last caught them and wouldn't let go.

There were other gifts to be given over the next week or so as chance allowed. "One thing my first husband's family taught me, to celebrate the twelve days of Christmas. All that preparation and pleasure can't be exhausted in just one day."

Jill said, "Yes, I'm going to have another celebration with Lars when this assignment is over." That nearly spoiled Christmas for Betsy, until Jill added, "I think the last Christmas I had on Christmas Day was in 1995. I'm always involved in something over the holidays. But none of them have been as pleasant as this one."

"Thank you, Jill. I don't know if that's true, but it sure makes me feel better."

Jill said, "When we get back, let's get on the Net and see if we can find a cattle drive that's more like the real ones were."

"Get back from where?"

"The arboretum. You said you wanted some exercise? There's a very pretty cross-country skiing trail I want to show you."

They weren't gone long. Betsy had seen cross-country skiers on television any number of times, and they appeared to float over the snow with smooth, dancelike movements of arms and legs. Not so in reality. Cross-country skiing is a total body workout, and Betsy, while no longer sick, was not remotely in shape for a total body workout. She lasted less than half an hour.

The two came through the door to the apartment, Jill partly supporting Betsy, for whom the stairs reawakened the ache in her back and legs. Jill helped her off with her coat and then to the chair with the footrest. "So," she said, "which part did you like best?"

Betsy started to laugh; she couldn't help it. "And I

have asked you to take me on a serious cattle drive? I am out of my mind."

"Tea or cocoa?" asked Jill.

"Cocoa," said Betsy, and Jill went into the kitchen.

Betsy sighed and leaned back in the chair. "You know, though," she said, "when we found that big fallen log and sat down, and it got really quiet, that was nice. And then that fox the same shade of gray as the bushes he came out of stopped and looked toward us for the longest time. Do you know, I've never seen a fox in the wild before? Are the red ones only in England?"

"No, we have both gray and red. They're getting braver, our foxes, and moving into the cities. There's one that lives down by Lake Calhoun, only a few blocks from Uptown."

"Only one? Poor fellow, he must be lonesome. Maybe we should introduce our fox to him."

"No, the one by Lake Calhoun is a red fox. I don't think foxes believe in mixed marriages." Jill brought a mug of cocoa to Betsy. "I couldn't find the marshmallows, sorry."

"I don't have any, sorry."

They sipped in companionable silence for a while. "Jill," said Betsy, "were you hoping the person who's after me would turn up out on that trail?"

"I was hoping he wouldn't."

"Would you have shot him if he did?"

"Only if I had to."

It was Jill's turn to get dinner. While she worked, Betsy went in to check her E-mail. She sent some replies to the mail, including one to an excited Abbey in San Diego, who had once been her best friend and now at last had her very own E-mail address. Then, dinner not being ready yet, she surfed for a while. She went to eBay and found a gorgeous bronze of a Scottish terrier puppy currently going for thirty dollars. She started to register, then changed her mind. Just because she would soon be able to afford it didn't mean she should start buying things she didn't absolutely need.

Dinner was yet another hot dish, this one made with turkey. But the salad had candied pecans and bits of tangerine in it, and the dessert was lemon meringue pie. Over dinner, Jill said, "So, since you are going to buy this building, I take it you're staying in Excelsior?"

Betsy said, "I guess I am. Funny, I don't remember consciously making that decision."

"Even funnier was Joe's face when he realized you were serious," laughed Jill.

After dinner, Sophie politely played again with her new toy. That night, while the women were asleep, she dragged it far under Jill's bed and showed a blank face when Betsy wondered the next morning where it had gone.

Sunday, Boxing Day, December 26, Jill and Betsy were in the shop by eight. Signs proclaiming an after-Christmas sale were brought out of the storeroom and put into the windows. Inventory was repriced and rearranged to display the extra-special merchandise. When Godwin arrived at 9:30, they put him to work redoing the window. Shelly came in fifteen minutes later and started taking down Christmas decorations. Betsy turned on the radio and discovered the Christmas music station had gone to something extremely experimental. She retuned it to KSJN and heard the merry clarinet of Purcell's Third Symphony. Though Epiphany was eleven days away, the three kings had already come and gone.

With them all working hard, the place was ready for the sale—and set up for inventory—by noon.

"All right, that's it, I'll see you both back here Monday morning," said Betsy.

Back upstairs, Jill said, over leftover hot dish, "I don't suppose you want to try cross-country skiing again."

"I thought I'd get caught up on my computer records. We sold quite a bit Christmas eve, and I've still got sales slips from before that."

She went to the computer, finished entering sales, and returned to the living room. Jill was trying a crochet pattern, marking her progress in the book with a straight pin. Betsy walked over and plugged in the Christmas tree and stood admiring it for awhile. She wandered restlessly to the upholstered chair and opened the needlework bag that stood beside it on its little crossed legs, but she didn't take anything out.

"Something the matter?" Jill asked.

"Kind of," said Betsy. She went into her bedroom and came out with the Christian symbology book and her notes. "I keep thinking that if I look at it long enough, it'll make sense."

Jill got her notebook out, found the page on which Betsy had copied the list of attributes and, handing it to her, said, "Abraham Lincoln said that persistence is the key to success."

"He should know; he failed at a lot of things before he got to be president." She sat down at the dining table like a reluctant child preparing to do homework in a difficult subject. Like the child, she just sat for a few minutes, tapping the table with her pencil, glooming over the notes. As before, she began reordering them, trying to spell a word. Frustrated in that, she opened the book at random and found one of the pages with three pairs of line drawings. She found herself again trying to make a word from the symbols, without success, went back to her notes.

Since each attribute could represent several saints, she began ordering saints represented in columns. That she done looked the list over selecting saints, jumping from one column to another: Kentigern, Eligius, Nicholas,

Eleutherius—"Well, I'll be darned, there it is!" she exclaimed.

"There what is?" said Jill.

"It's the saints they stand for! Look at this." Jill came to look over Betsy's shoulder. "The boar can stand for Saint Kentigern, the horseshoe for Eligius, the anchor for Nicholas, and another E you can get from the whip, for Saint Eleutherius."

"Keane is spelled with an A," Jill pointed out.

"Yes, but I told you I didn't write them all down. You just wait; when that tapestry shows up, there will be a symbol right there." Betsy tapped the sheet of paper. She was no longer bored and resentful.

"Then the hangman's noose *was* for Father Keane."

"I'd've used it for Hal, and she had even more reason to be furious. He betrayed his calling and his church." Betsy looked at the paper. "Just like Judas."

Behind Saint Kentigern were Saint Elizabeth's crowns, then an anvil, which could be Saint Natalia, then who was the bird? From the shape of it, perhaps a dove? Then a wolf or a dog. Was there more than just a name?

The dove was symbolic of the Holy Spirit, of John the Baptist, of Noah, of Saint Clovis and a flock of other saints, including Oswald. "This will be an O here, if this is money," muttered Betsy.

"Then the letter before it should be M," said Jill. "And where's the Y?"

"The cat, for Saint Yvo, was on here twice, so let's assume the second time was right here." Because sure enough, if the animal was a dog, it could stand for Saint Margaret of Cortona.

"I think you've done it," said Jill. "That's what this is, an accusation. I bet the word before that is 'stolen.' "

But it wasn't. "I'm missing some of them; I don't know how many," said Betsy. "There's a lit candle, and rowboat, which I think is Saint MacCald, and a chain, which is probably Ignatius, if the candle is Genevieve— *if* the word Lucy was spelling is *missing,* as in *missing money.* And above them is a cross, which can stand for Jesus, Saint Bartholomew, Saint Peter, Saint Jude, Saint Philip, Saint Andrew—no, Andrew is more like an X than a plus sign. Then Yvo's cat, then a double-bladed ax for Saint Olaf, then the Star of David, which can stand for Caspar, Melchior, or Balthazar."

Jill frowned. "Why do those last three names sound familiar?"

"They're the three kings who of Orient were. But I don't know which one this star represents."

"Maybe we're getting into random attributes here. We've got the message: Missing Money equals Keane the Traitor."

Betsy's eyes widened. "That's brilliant, Jill!"

"What'd I say?"

"Equals. That's what this thing I thought I'd only started to draw is. Two horizontal lines, that's an equals sign! Missing Money equals Keane!"

"So you've solved it, then," said Jill. "Lucy Abrams left both a name and a message on the tapestry: Her husband Keane was a thief."

The phone rang and Betsy got up to answer it.

"Hello, Betsy, this is Mandy Oliver. I hate to break into your holiday, but talking to you made me remember something, and I wanted to tell you that your problems matching the tapestry colors may be over."

"Really? What did you remember?"

"My mother had a little wooden box she kept leftover floss and yarn in. It's such a pretty box that I didn't sell it with her other things. I found it way in the back of a closet today, and in it are tan and gray and orange lengths of yarn. I think they're from the tapestry you volunteered to help restore. I'll bring them to you, if you like."

"Oh, Mandy, that would be wonderful! Can you come to the shop tomorrow? We'll be open from ten to five."

"Yes, I can come in the afternoon. See you then."

18

Father John sat behind his desk, something he rarely did; but he felt this was a situation in which he needed all the authority he could command. On the other side of the desk were Betsy Devonshire, Jill Cross, Ned MacIntosh, and Howland Royce—the last two his verger and a man who had been on the vestry when the Reverend Keane Abrams was forced to retire.

"This is terrible, just terrible," said Royce. He was a frail-looking eighty and was wringing his hands, which with his arthritis looked a painful thing to do. "But when Keane offered to repay the money and resign immediately, we thought that would be the best way to handle it. He was of an age to retire and was vested in a small pension fund, which he had no access to and so couldn't use its moneys to repay what he'd taken.

"When it turned out he didn't have enough in savings to make total restitution, his wife came to us and begged us to forgive him the rest, not make a public spectacle of him in front of the parish and especially his daughter, who was just starting high school. She looked danger-ously sick, and my wife, who was a nurse, had told me Lucy had a heart condition. Lucy was dead a week after we accepted Keane's resignation, and we were so scared the forced resignation triggered her heart attack that we voted unanimously to forgive the rest of the debt."

"I don't understand," said Betsy. "Had he stolen an enormous amount of money? Or were his savings that small?"

"Six of one, half a dozen of the other," said Royce. "The reason he had no savings was because he'd been paying hush money to a string of women, starting two churches back."

Father John said, "Why wasn't I told about this?"

"What good would it have done?" said Royce. "It was a private thing, and he was good as dead. No need to keep talking about what's over and done with. Or so we thought."

Ned MacIntosh said, "He should have been arrested. It's bad enough he failed to discern between his discretionary fund and the ordinary funds of the church. It's even more disturbing that he converted at least some of the church's money to his personal use. But using church funds to pay blackmail is beyond my forgiveness!"

"I'm afraid this isn't a situation in which your personal forgiveness matters much," said Father John gravely.

Royce said in his old man's voice, "I agree, this is a situation in which the church failed both him and its members. And now, because we hid the truth, we may have put Ms. Devonshire in a position of great danger. But I'm afraid that if we reveal the facts now, Trinity's reputation will be harmed, maybe the reputation of the Episcopal church. We have to decide whether we're going to tell everything, or nothing—or do something in between."

"What do you recommend, Ned?" asked Father John.

MacIntosh replied, "I say we announce that a review of Father Keane's term as rector of Trinity has revealed some irregularities in—well. Shall we just say 'irregularities,' or should we go further and say 'bookkeeping irregularities'? I don't think we should get more specific than that."

Royce said, "We'd better at least say 'bookkeeping irregularities,' or people will start to ask questions. And remember, I'm not the only person who knows the answers. There are probably eight others who have at least an inkling of why Father Keane resigned so abruptly. That's not counting the women he was paying money to, including one who was a member of this parish."

"Do you know who the local woman was?" asked Jill.

"No. Keane wouldn't name names."

"Gentleman to the end," snorted Betsy.

Royce said, "His wife knew. He told me he had to tell her when all this started to break. He used to lie about how much he was making, but the verger, that was Smith Milhaus, found a checkbook and called her, asking questions. That started things moving. I was a comptroller for Sweetwater Technologies back then, so I volunteered to audit his books. It wasn't hard to find what he'd been up to, and I confronted him. He seemed almost relieved to tell someone, poor devil."

"Who did you tell?" asked Betsy.

Royce twisted his head in a kind of shrug. "I reported to the vestry that he hadn't been faithful and was paying money—church money—to some women."

"Do you know anything about a tapestry Mrs. Abrams was working on?" asked Betsy.

Royce frowned at her. "I remember someone found it after they left and said he'd take care of it. I assume that's the one that turned up and started all this mess up again."

"Is that person still around?" asked Jill.

"No. That was old Milhouse again, and he's dead. On the other hand, three of those vestry members are still living in the area, and so are their wives. I'd like to believe nobody told anyone else, but that would be going against what I know of human behavior."

"You may be wrong," said Jill. "My parents were members of Trinity, and I was baptized here, but I never heard anything about why he quit."

MacIntosh said, "And I never heard anything, either. Come on, Royce, you must have an inkling—"

"No," said Father John. "We're not here to speculate. We're here to decide what we are going to do about our plan to name the expanded library after Father Keane. We haven't formally announced it yet, but I know Patricia Fairland has been talking about it for weeks."

"She got a real bee in her bonnet about this, didn't she?" complained MacIntosh. "She didn't used to be such a big noise in the church. Is it because her husband's gonna be the senator from Minnesota?"

"No, it's because she's not working like a dog anymore," said Royce. "She liked coming to Sunday school. It was only while she was putting her husband through law school that she quit coming to the adult education classes. She taught a class on medieval church art just a year ago. So don't blame her. It could've come from any direction. But what do we do about it? Can we say there's a rule against naming things after someone who's still alive?"

"No," said MacIntosh. "There are too many of us who know about the auditorium named for Dean Fontaine of Saint Mark's. Last I heard, he's still spending his pension money on fishing gear."

A thoughtful silence fell. At last Father John said, "Okay, there are enough people in the parish to ensure trouble if we continue with our present plan. My advice is, we announce the financial irregularities and name the chapel after someone else."

"I think we should name it after the first Native American Episcopal priest in Minnesota," said MacIntosh. "The Reverend Enmetahbowh."

"You're probably the only member of this parish who ever heard of him," said Royce. "I think we should name it after Bishop Whipple, first bishop of Minnesota."

They looked at Father John who said, "I think we should consult the membership. At least these two nominees have the saving grace of being long dead, along with everyone who knew them."

Betsy and Jill lingered after Royce and McIntosh left. "Thank you for arranging that, Father," said Betsy. "I think we've confirmed what I suspected. Mike Malloy will be in touch about tonight."

Even sitting in total darkness, there was no mistaking where they were. "The odor of sanctity," Betsy's father had called it, that mix of beeswax, incense, stone and mortar, and furniture polish. Also present was a strong scent of Christmas tree.

Betsy was sitting on a stone bench near the entrance to the new church in the wide hall, partly hidden behind the tall and beautiful fir. Beside her was Jill in an alert and patient waiting mode Betsy could only aspire to. There were other police officers hidden around the hall. One, she knew, was partly down the stairs to the basement. Mike Malloy was near the door to the hall; Betsy fancied she could see a faint light from the street glinting off his shoe. Another was inside the new church, which is why the doors to it were open—and why the odor of sanctity was carried to Betsy's nostrils. Two were inside the chapel. Elsewhere in the hall was Lars, Jill's boyfriend, and he'd brought another officer with him.

They'd been there for two hours. Betsy knew what a

stakeout was, of course. But she had no idea how difficult it was to sit still for a very long time.

And what if after all she was wrong?

No, she wasn't wrong. It was sad, but she wasn't wrong.

She felt herself beginning to stiffen on the bench and began stealthily to tense and release various muscles, in her arms, her back, her stomach, her legs, her shoulders, her neck. Jill breathed, "Sit still."

Betsy started to reply, then realized it wasn't because Jill had noticed her squirming but because someone was approaching the outside door.

There was the sound of a key in the lock, then the door opened with a very faint squeak. Booted feet padded softly into the hall, paused, and then the lights went on.

Patricia whirled, but Malloy was guarding the door, his hand coming down from the light switches. "Who are you?" demanded Patricia. Her voice was thick, as if her cold lingered.

"I'm Detective Sergeant Mike Malloy, with the Excelsior Police Department. May I ask what you're doing here?"

"I'm a member of the vestry."

"And there's a meeting of the vestry at two o'clock in the morning?"

"Now look here—" she began.

"It's over, Patricia," said Betsy, and Patricia whirled again. Too bad she wasn't wearing the swing coat; it flared so prettily. "We know what was on the tapestry. I'm sure you rearranged the appliqué while you were in Phoenix so it no longer spells your name. That's it hanging over your arm. Where were you going to put it, in the rest room? That's where you hid it the first time, isn't it, on the hook on the back of the door?"

"I don't know what you're talking about," said Patricia with a faint show of puzzlement. "I found it after you left and decided to take it along and treat the mildew. I'm allergic, you know, and I couldn't work on it like it was." She started toward Betsy, her arm with the white-wrapped drape moving outward as if to hand it over, but Malloy took her by the other arm. She gave him a look that might have withered an ordinary mortal, but he only gazed back until her eyes dropped and her arm came back against her coat.

Betsy said, "You hadn't looked closely at the tapestry at first because you're allergic to mildew, but when I showed you those little symbols in the halo, you saw right away that the first three were a shamrock, a lamb, and a flaming heart, the attributes of Saints Patrick, Agnes, and Theresa, whose initials spell Pat, and you realized you were in big, big trouble."

Patricia replied, still very calmly, "What makes you think I saw at a glance what nobody else saw?"

"Because you knew Lucy liked to hide words in her stitchery, *and* you taught a course about medieval Christian art, which is all about symbology and attributes."

"And even if I recognized them, so what?"

"Because there was a message in those attributes: *Pat's boy + missing money = Keane.* Father Keane did what he could, even stealing money to help you with the cuckoo's egg you laid in Peter's nest. The boy Peter is so proud of, the grandson his mother finally approves of, isn't theirs, is he?"

"You're wrong, the attributes spell only Keane's name, that's all. Look at it, if you like." Again she held out the folded white sheet draped over her arm.

Betsy persisted, "Do you know you were not his first affair? There might even be other children."

Patricia's face reddened. "You don't know what you're saying," she said in a flat voice.

"Howland Royce, a member of the old vestry, found

evidence that Father Keane had been misappropriating funds for a long time, going back years, and that he admitted he'd been paying off a string of women."

"I don't believe you," said Patricia.

"It's true, Patricia," said Jill. "I was there, too, and I heard him say Father Keane admitted it."

Patricia coughed harshly. "Well, I still don't see how that involves me. I was a young married woman trying to put my husband through law school when Father Keane quit. I don't remember hearing why. But of course, back then I barely had time to come to Sunday service, much less stay after to hear the latest gossip around the coffee urn."

"I'm sure you've noticed Brent has Keane's hazel eyes," said Betsy relentlessly. "Just like his daughter Mandy."

"Do you know what would happen to my husband if you—" She raked the hall with her eyes. "If *any* of you repeat any of this in public? Do you have any idea what my husband would do if he thought that was true?"

"What he'd do to us?" said Betsy. "Or to you? That's what this is all about, isn't it? Your son. Your marriage. Your place in this community. You were young and risked your future for what you thought was a glorious love affair. Was it because your lover swept you away with his ardor, his charm, his—what? His assurances that you were his first and only extramarital affair? But then you got pregnant. And Keane wouldn't leave his wife for you. If he did that, he would have had to give up his calling, wouldn't he? He couldn't continue being a priest after such a scandal. And at his age, it wouldn't be easy to build a new career, one that would support a wife and child. Plus his former wife and daughter. With the gauzy curtain of love ripped apart, you could see this wasn't going to work. So what to do? Your husband was still in law school and you'd agreed not to start a family until he finished. His wealthy parents disapproved of his early marriage to a woman beneath him and had cut off all aid. If any hint of the truth reached them, your bright future as wife of a wealthy attorney was dead. What a mess to find yourself in! And how sad that you're right back in it."

It was as if the whole room held its breath. "You don't know," sighed Patricia, her shoulders slumping. "It was so hard. Keane said he loved me. He said his marriage was a sham, that he had never loved anyone like he loved me in my whole life. I thought we had a special kind of love, one that excused anything. Like Abelard and Heloise, like Hepburn and Tracy. To sit in his office and hear him plan to steal—*steal!*—money to help me with the baby, was a kind of death. I wanted to say no, but Peter's part-time job paid so little, and babies are more expensive than I dreamed . . ." Patricia's voice trailed off.

"It was just easier to pretend the birth control failed between Peter and me, rather than with Keane. And it worked. Then Keane had that stroke, I thought it was the stress of the theft, and I felt so guilty. But I didn't break, I just kept going, and at last things smoothed out for us. Peter's father died, and his mother came around. She bought our new house for us—it has *three* fire-places!—and invited us to Phoenix for Christmas.

"And then, after all this time, after all I'd gone through, all the sacrifices, all the secrets—that *wretched* tapestry! And worse, there you were, writing down the little symbols, taking that book home to look them up . . .

"I *had* to do those terrible, horrible things to you, Betsy. It was harder than you'll ever know. You're a very nice woman, working so hard and bravely to pick up the pieces of your life, I felt just awful about it. I really didn't want to, and I kept hoping you'd leave

town, but you wouldn't go. But then Father John said
he had the tapestry, and told us where it was, and I ran
and got it and hung it on the hook on the back of the
door of that little rest room. And I took it with me to
Phoenix in a big plastic bag, and though I treated it for
mildew it still made my eyes water and my nose run and
I had to pretend I had a cold. But that was fine, I was
so relieved, everything was going to be all right, I'd
destroyed the proof. And even though now it's all coming out, oh my God, Betsy, I'm so *glad* I didn't kill
you!"

"I know you took that car course and knew about
brake lines, and I suppose you must have plenty of firewood for those three fireplaces, but how did you get the
arsenic without giving your name? When I went to eBay,
they wanted my name and address."

"I started a new AOL account under a new name. And
there are places that will forward your mail. And when
you buy a money order, you can put any name you like
on it. I did that some while ago when Peter thought I
was spending too much on antiques. I just did it for fun,
buying those old medicine bottles. I suppose they had a
different definition of medicine back then, because some
of those old bottles have arsenic, mercury sulfate, even
strychnine in them. Some come in little bottles shaped
like coffins, isn't that amusing? I keep them in a locked
cabinet, of course. Then when this happened, I read a
book that said the thing murderers do is put just a little
bit in the food to start a medical record of gastritis. I
put it in the order of chicken salad and brought it up
with the hot dish, and I couldn't believe how sick it
made you. I was just horrified. I am truly sorry, Betsy."

Betsy fought a rising sickness by getting angry. She
said tightly, "It's possible you did these things with great
reluctance. I think you would have come to my funeral
and wept genuine tears. But I also think you would have

gone home from the funeral sighing with relief."

Patricia's smile came with sad eyebrows. "Well, yes, I suppose I would have." She turned to Malloy. "I suppose you're going to arrest me now?"

"Oh, yes, you are definitely under arrest," said Malloy. "You have a right to remain silent. If you give up the right to remain silent, anything you say can and will be taken down and used against you in a court of law. You have the right to consult with an attorney and to have an attorney present during questioning. If you wish an attorney, but can't afford one, one will be supplied to you at no cost. Do you understand these rights as I have explained them to you?"

"Yes, I do."

Malloy took the tapestry and handed it to one of the uniformed officers, saying, "Tag this and bring it to the station." Then he cuffed Patricia's hands behind her back. She took it with grace and walked out ahead of him, her head high, her face settled into a withdrawn calm.

Betsy turned away, covering her face with her hands. She said through her fingers, "Can I go home now?"

Jill replied, "I'm sorry, but you have to come with me to the station. You would not believe the paperwork we have to fill out."

"My God," said Godwin the next morning. "That is . . . *terrible!* Who would have thought Patricia was doing this? Betsy, that is just *terrible!*"

"I know, I know," said Betsy, turning her chair away from the library table to face Sophie. She stroked the cat, who lifted her head to accept the caress, exhaling a pleased purr.

Godwin continued, "How did you figure it out?"

"A collection of little things. First, she was the one who had a source for arsenic. She's an antiquer, and she uses eBay. I was amazed when I looked in the collectibles section of eBay and saw what was in some of those old bottles.

"Also, this whole thing was about the notes I made on the attributes. She stole the notes I typed but couldn't get at the originals—and only Patricia knew about them; she saw me making them on the back of my checkbook. She visited me in the hospital after the poisoning, and there I was with the original notes and the book on Christian symbology. She must have been sick with fear that I'd figure it out.

"It was the day she came to confess to Father John that Keane was the father of her oldest child that she got hold of the tapestry."

"Father John *knew?*" exclaimed Godwin.

"No, she didn't tell him. I saw her waiting to see him, looking very miserable, which I imagine she was. I thought perhaps she was worried about me, and in a way I was right. She'd tried three times to kill me, without success. She was afraid that tapestry would turn up while she was in Phoenix and that I'd see the whole set of attributes in its correct order and figure out how they spelled out an accusation against her. Her comfortable life was going to pop like a messy bubble. But then Father John came out of his office and said the tapestry was wrapped in a sheet and laid safely away in the sacristy. So she ran ahead to remove it from its drawer and hide it in the rest room, and then say she couldn't find it. She even encouraged me to take Jill along to help search for it, a very risky thing to do. But she had to convince me it hadn't been there when she went to look for it."

"Cool head."

"Oh, yes, that's why I really don't think she was trying hard enough to kill me. She's far too organized not to have gotten it right in three attempts. She really didn't want to kill me, she wanted me to stop fooling with those attributes so she could go on being the cool and competent wife of a rising politician, the respectable mother of his three children. But her boy isn't her husband's, he's the result of a passionate love affair. It's a shame it was only true love on her part; Keane was an experienced adulterer. Not that it mattered; what was important was that the secret be kept, both so her husband wouldn't find out and because Brent is the only remnant of that affair she could openly brag about and show off. I suspect Peter Fairland is not happy to learn his wonderful son is in fact not his. It may change the boy's life profoundly. Patricia did all this to prevent that happening. Having to choose between Brent or Betsy—well, out goes me."

"Bitch," remarked Godwin.

"No, she's not a bitch. She may be what my mother called a toom tabbard, an empty shell. She came from a very different background from the one she married into, and she had to rebuild herself from the ground up, casting off attitudes, behavior, and opinions that revealed her real self. Possibly there is no real self anymore, only that remade surface. So she was willing to go farther than most to retain that surface, which is all she has."

"You really do feel sorry for her!"

"Yes, I do."

"What are you, a saint?"

"No, of course not. But I can't feel as pleased over this one as the others, Godwin. I just feel a little sick." She stroked Sophie some more. "I hope Mandy is right, that there is some awareness in her father, that those tears he keeps shedding in that nursing home are not for himself but for his victims."

The door made its annoying *bing* sound and Joe Mickels came in. He marched up to the table. "Ms. Devonshire," he said in a clear but very quiet voice, "when this mess you are in is over, may I take you to dinner?"

Betsy, surprised, very nearly replied, "Whatever for?" but bit her tongue in time. "Why don't you wait until this mess is over and ask me again?" she said instead.

"Very well, I will," he declared and walked out again.

Godwin gaped after him, then at Betsy. *You* are going on a *date* with *Joe Mickels?*"

"I may," replied Betsy. "Though it's more in the way of a business meeting."

"What kind of business are you in with Joe?"

"Well, I'm buying this building from him—"

"Strewth!" exclaimed Godwin, grasping the front of his beautiful sweater with a splayed hand. "How did you get him to agree to that?"

"Let's just say I made him an offer he couldn't refuse." And she would say no more, which is possibly why there was a rumor flying all over Excelsior the next day that Joe Mickels had gone out of his mind.

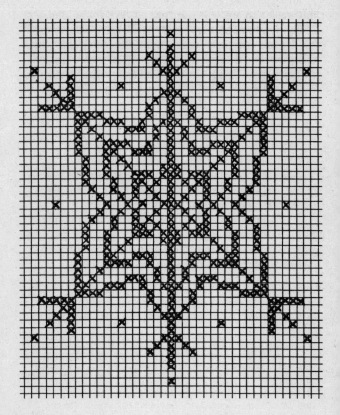

This counted cross stitch snowflake can be worked on any dark-colored evenweave fabric or canvas in white or metallic. The designer, Denise Williams, worked it on 14-count navy blue canvas with Balger #8 floss, for an interesting, sparkly effect. On that count, the snowflake is 3.5 inches across.

Directions: Find the center of the pattern and mark it. Find the center of the fabric and begin there, making Xs as the pattern indicates. It may be helpful to grid the pattern by drawing a line with see-through marker every five or ten squares. A corresponding line may be stitched with a single thread on the fabric. (Beginners like Betsy find this very helpful!) Then pull the marker threads out when the pattern is finished.